PRAISE FOR MAX BYRD

"Max Byrd is an expert at mingling real historical figures with his invented characters."
—*THE NEW YORK TIMES*

"Lock Byrd's cage and throw away the key—until he slips out a few more thrillers." —*THE PHILADELPHIA ENQUIRER*

"Max Byrd's plots, like his wit, are sinister and charming."
—DIANE JOHNSON,
bestselling author of *The Shadow Knows*

"Max Byrd is a fine and forceful writer."
—LAWRENCE BLOCK, bestselling author of
Eight Million Ways to Die

"Max Byrd is in the first division of American crime writing."
—*THE NEW YORK TIMES*

"Sharp writing . . . exciting . . . fulfills the promise of its title."
—*PUBLISHERS WEEKLY,* for *California Thriller*

"Solid entertainment with warmth and wit."
—*KIRKUS REVIEWS,* for *Finders Weepers*

"A literate, sensitive story with plenty of action."
—*THE NEW YORK TIMES BOOK REVIEW,* for
Target of Opportunity

"Wow! This is storytelling at its very best. Max Byrd uses the whole deck of cards—character, place, history, humor, and intrigue—to weave his magical story. You want a good ride? *The Paris Deadline* is your ticket!"
—MICHAEL CONNELLY, for *The Paris Deadline*

"*The Paris Deadline* is the best 'code and cipher' novel I've ever read, a wonderful historical thriller, combining terrific characters with wit, erudition, more cool facts than your average encyclopedia, and a blistering narrative drive that makes the pages fly. Do not deny yourself the pleasure of reading this book!"
—JOHN LESCROART, for *The Paris Deadline*

CALIFORNIA THRILLER

ALSO BY MAX BYRD

CALIFORNIA THRILLER

A MIKE HALLER MYSTERY

MAX BYRD

TURNER
PUBLISHING COMPANY

Turner Publishing Company
200 4th Avenue North • Suite 950 Nashville, Tennessee 37219
445 Park Avenue • 9th Floor New York, NY 10022

www.turnerpublishing.com

California Thriller

Cover design: Glen Edelstein
Book design: Kym Whitley

Cover image: Masterfile

Library of Congress Cataloging-in-Publication Data

Byrd, Max.
California thriller / Max Byrd.
    p. cm.
"A Mike Haller mystery."
 ISBN 978-1-61858-026-9
1. Private investigators—California—San Francisco—Fiction. I. Title.
 PS3552.Y675C35 2012
 813'.54—dc23
                                        2012022542
Printed in the United States of America
12 13 14 15 16 17 18—0 9 8 7 6 5 4 3 2 1

HE WHO BITES GETS BITTEN

I sat up straight and showed the cuffs, keeping my elbows close to my sides, palms up. He put the light on them.

"You left these way too high, Kenny. I've already snapped two links in the chain."

"You're full of it," he said, bending over to look. "I left these things——"

I never found out where he left them, because I rammed the cuffs straight up, hands stretched as far apart as I could hold them, the chain taut as an axle. The chain caught him at the base of the nose and drove the bone up with a sound like snapping your fingers, and blood cascaded down my arms.

I hadn't killed him. Bruce Lee could drive the nasal bone straight back into the brain with the heel of his hand, but Kenny was still gushing blood and trying to sit up.

This one is for
Brookes and Kate and David

CHAPTER 1

"THESE THINGS ALWAYS BEGIN IN A BAR, I SUPPOSE," MY HOST said. The cardboard coaster stuck to the bottom of his glass and he blinked at it in an unfocused way while he swallowed. A waiter cruised off into the darkness for refills. I put an olive between my teeth and pulled a little pink sword out of it, like a plastic Excalibur.

"Evidently it wasn't normal social drinking at all," he went on. "Some days he came into work about 11, just blotto. Other days not even a drink at lunch. And of course he always got the column out, no matter what. Once, before this, he skipped a whole day, never showed up. He told people he had gone off to the place in Napa to be by himself and think."

The waiter brought us another round and I started right away with the olive, lining the sword up beside the two others Mr. Shoults had bought me. The table was beginning to look like an armory for elves.

"Did he go up to this Napa place alone?"

"Cabin. A small cabin up in the Sonoma Mountains, west of Oakville. Past the Mondavi vineyards about 20 minutes."

I nodded twice, because I knew the area and because I like the northern California habit of giving distances according to vineyards. Metric is coming.

"Alone, you think?"

Shoults inspected the ice in his drink. He was not really evading the question. He was just uncomfortable about the whole interview, the loyal family friend helping out the panicked wife, not a voluntary witness. A lot of lawyers are like that. Then again, maybe he was only deciding how truthful to be. A lot of lawyers are like that too. The ice cracked loudly.

"Well, he said so. Anne asked me to talk with him about it, so we got together for lunch and we talked. I asked him the same question. I got a funny answer." He took a swallow. "A very high-strung guy, you understand. Very intense on occasion. He said he had gone there as a kind of retreat."

"Retreat?"

"He said he could hear time rushing by him and he had to come to terms with it." Shoults looked down at his drink. "He said when he stood on the mountain he could hear the passage of time howling like wind in a tunnel. I remember that exactly, like a quote, because, after all, that's not usually how people talk in a law office, is it? I thought it was pretty poetic."

"He probably read it in the Sunday papers," I said, and regretted it. There was no reason to get Shoults annoyed just because I had put in a long, weary, useless day in Santa Barbara talking to a runaway 19-year-old and still had a file in the back seat of the car to get through and a report to dictate. Besides. I thought it was poetic too. In my business, it usually comes out, "Honey, I'm going down to the corner for a pack of cigarettes."

"What did you think?" I asked. "Did you believe that?"

"I guess so. I actually chalked it up to a sort of mid-life crisis thing. I've seen it before. A guy gets close to 50, starts to look around at his life and wonder what's the point. He begins to feel he has to change something—anything—about the way he lives." Shoults sipped his martini. "Usually he just changes the wife."

"Is that a problem here?"

Shoults shrugged and continued as if I hadn't spoken. "Sometimes these guys don't change anything at all, and then they go a little sour inside and shrivel up. That's a shortcut to old age." He paused. "George is given to imagining scenes of his own success, if you know what I mean. The big story, the big break, the rich life somewhere else. He's the kind of guy that might half bust loose and go live on an island." Shoults looked past my shoulder. "For a week or two. Not many people ever really do more than that."

I nodded and Shoults sucked a piece of ice. If he had gone through a mid-life crisis thing himself, it hadn't taken. He was wearing a black pin-striped suit like I used to see in the City of London, dark blue triangle of silk handkerchief in his pocket, Brooks light blue button-down shirt, and a dark blue tie with little red foxes stitched here and there; if he had more hair you would have said he was wearing a crewcut. He looked like the kind of guy who could cause a riot in parts of Berkeley just by walking down the street.

"You sound like you've been there," I said, to keep him talking.

"Just a paperback psychologist." He was a big man, bigger than me, but he had a pointed, slightly overhanging upper lip that, together with his fleshy cheeks, made him look like a three-year-old who shaved.

"You're one of the trial men for your firm?"

"That's right. We have three or four people who argue the cases in court that other people draw up. I'm the senior litigation specialist." An automatic smile. "Most of the time I talk about debentures to an empty room."

"And how is it you know George Webber?"

"He covered the Frank Brazil trial, when he was just a spare hand at the Oakland *Trib*. I was working for the U.S. Attorney's office then. We used to talk about the case. Brazil got off, you know."

I snapped the plastic swords with my thumb and put the jagged edges on my napkin. "He usually does," I said. "I remember the case. Webber's not mixed up with Frank Brazil, is he?"

Shoults swung his cheeks back and forth. "Oh, hell no, that was years ago."

I nodded and stabbed the white fluff of the napkin a few times. Frank Brazil was a prominent para-legal thug in Oakland, owner and operator of a uniformed guard service called Bridgestone Security, which doubled as a protection racket or a vigilante outfit, depending on your point of view. From time to time, every muckraker in the Bay Area had taken a shot at Brazil, and one or two of them had come back looking as if they'd made a running tackle on a cement truck.

"But George wrote a hell of a series of stories," Shoults told me, "and the *Constitution* hired him on the strength of that. From there on, it was all glory."

I remembered that too. Webber had worked on the city desk briefly, until he had persuaded the paper to let him try a weekly gossip column that would rival Herb Caen's at the *Chronicle*. It had been a roaring success, going to five times a week almost at once, a clever, funny little San Francisco institution now, with quirky word games and an occasional idealistic crusade on behalf of good causes. Once or twice a year, Webber resumed the city beat for a few weeks to write a piece about politicians on the take and try to get somebody indicted. I liked his column better than Caen's.

"I gave him a little advice then," Shoults was saying, "did

a little legal work for him, and we've just kept in close touch since my firm does a good deal of work for the *Constitution*." His face was a little flushed with alcohol now, coarsening his features. Or maybe it was the cavelight of the Polynesian bar he had chosen. I studied the foxes on his tie and wondered why businessmen decorate themselves with so many animals—alligators, foxes, penguins. The warpaint of the boardroom, I suppose. Says something about yourself. My own tie was a bright red item that had been unfashionably wide even when I bought it. It was like having a giant tongue hanging down my shirt.

"He's a good-looking man," Shoults said after an uncomfortable pause. "Keeps himself in shape."

"But you don't know the names of any girlfriends?"

He shook his head firmly. I dug a cigarette out of my pocket and stuck it in my mouth. Shoults flicked an elegant Cartier lighter under my nose while I fumbled for a matchbook, and I took in a lungful of cottony smoke. The bar was growing crowded. Customers were circling in and out of the tropical foliage like strange fish in a bowl.

"I told the police pretty much what I've told you," he said. "They were no help at all, except for keeping the thing quiet. Their position is, it's not a crime to disappear, so while they were willing to open a file and put his name on a list, that was about the extent of it."

"No, it's not a crime to disappear unless you're a minor or you do it to evade justice or the payment of lawful debts." The phrases just rattled on by, and I wondered for a moment if he liked hearing a lecture on the law. Martini power. "Wife support doesn't rate too high as a lawful debt, and minors go on the same list as stolen cars. Without any evidence of foul play, they'll let it go."

"There's certainly none of that." The ice cracked again in

his glass and he swirled it gently. "I really think he'll turn up in a few days with nothing worse than a hangover and a guilty conscience," he said.

"Did anybody check with Napa again?"

"I drove up with Anne two days ago. No sign of anything."

"And it's been a week?" I was writing dates in my pocket notebook.

"A week yesterday. That's when she asked me to see about private help." He made a vague gesture of irritation. "I don't think she's buying my mid-life crisis theory any longer. The paper's just run a notice saying he's on vacation." He took a big swallow of his drink and looked across his shoulder toward the bar. "The other thing is that they found his car on Thursday," Shoults said after a pause. "On Eddy Street, with three sets of parking tickets on the windshield."

I stopped writing in the notebook and sat back in the booth. Eddy Street is a main artery, so to speak, of the Tenderloin district. And if the name suggests a meat market to you, that's the idea the founding fathers intended. In the past few years the whores and dealers have started to move farther south, as the welfare department has gotten to like the idea of using Tenderloin hotels and apartments for their overflow. But you still see a lot of action there, a lot of tough black guys in floppy hats and big Frye boots leaning against fenders and listening to their radios; and you can find pasty faces and hot-pants backed into any doorway. You also see a lot of old men in cardigan sweaters and thin suits sitting in hotel lobbies, feeling their teeth and watching the johns walk by. Around the Hilton and Union Square is all the San Francisco glamour they like to put in travel folders, the smug limousines, the long-legged debutantes, the boutiques stuffed full of shiny Scandinavian chrome and designer geegaws, the expense-account restaurants done up as mosques or brothels. Alongside them the massage parlors and topless bars bounce and glitter like bubbles rising to the surface. But Eddy Street drains the city like a sewer.

"Any explanation for the car turning up there?" I asked quietly. I didn't like Eddy Street at all.

"None at all. George usually parks in the office garage on Powell. He drives all over town, of course. The police said it had probably been stolen and left there."

"But they don't know where it was stolen?"

He shook his head.

Or if. "Why me?" I had to ask.

"I'm sorry?"

"Why me, Mr. Shoults? You're a senior partner in a big law firm; you must deal with a lot of private investigation agencies. You didn't just look me up in the yellow pages."

"The agencies we deal with are mainly uniformed services, guards, escort types, and so on. George is an unusual man. I thought somebody with a little more imagination was needed. Actually, I called Carlton Hand and he recommended you."

That surprised me. Carlton Hand was the editor-in-chief of the *Constitution,* a big, important figure in the newspaper world. About a generation ago he and I had started out on the *Times* together in LA, but Carlton had stuck it out when I left. Stuck it out and struck it rich. I didn't think he remembered me. I was sure he wouldn't recommend me.

"He said that you make missing persons a specialty."

"I'd want $500 retainer, Mr. Shoults, and $200 a day plus expenses."

"That seems like a lot." He pursed the overhanging lip into a frown, thinking it over. Lawyers like Shoults charge $120 an hour for their services, a little less than a brain surgeon, a little more than the pilot of a 747. They worry about anybody fleecing their clients.

"You can get somebody from Bridgestone Security for half that, Mr. Shoults, if that's what you want."

The lip came slowly unpursed, and he bobbed his head once briskly, the gesture toward economy finished. "My office will mail you a check." That made me part of the inventory, naturally. Note pads, paper clips, peeper. "Can you start right away?"

I shuffled the papers he had given me into a neat stack and put them in my jacket pocket. "Tomorrow afternoon."

"I'll tell Anne you'll call," he said. "She's quite upset, really."

I nodded and started for the door.

"Haller?" he called me back.

He was still sitting in the booth. "Hand also said that you were pretty rough-and-tumble." I waited. The lines around his eyes were crinkled deep and he turned a little smile on and off, like someone testing a light. "I guess that can't hurt," he said finally.

CHAPTER 2

SPOUSE EQUIVALENT?" I LOOKED ACROSS THE desk AT MY PART-time personal assistant, gadfly, and grandfather figure.

"It's a new form. Computer service made it up."

"I don't know, Fred. This hurts more than the money."

"You want to call Edwin Newman?"

Fred reminds some people of a California sea lion, thanks to a big Irish nose, no forehead, a thin chest that balloons around the beltline and short legs that taper abruptly to a halt. That and his habit of wearing his gray suits too shiny and too tight. Since his wife died, I've seen him at home in madras shorts and a Hawaiian sport shirt that his married daughter had picked out, but he wasn't working then and didn't care how he looked. Right now he was explaining, with his usual invention, the items on his expense sheet.

"What's $23.65 for lunch with colleague?"

"I ran into Betty Jo Rule and took her to lunch."

"Did you have to take her to the Sheraton?"

"You got a reputation to maintain, Haller."

"I have now. What's she working on?"

"Same as us. Missing kid. Girl from Detroit, 17. Ran away from school, hopped a bus as far as Salt Lake City, apparently hitched a ride here. Her father flew out and hired Betty Jo to bring her back. He thought a feminist detective bureau might do a better job."

"Don't Betty Jo and her partners think that's parentist or something?"

"Yeah, they do. But they gotta eat."

There wasn't much to say to that, so I chewed my franchise hamburger and hosed it down with black coffee. "Is she having any luck?" I asked. The hamburger tasted like a charcoal briquette.

"She'll find her. Betty Jo knows every pimp in the Bay Area. Sooner or later the lost little girls meet the pimps. Sooner or later the boys do too, I guess. But honest to God, Mike, it's depressing work, going up and down Telegraph trying to talk to them. Or the Haight. These kids are practically inert, you know? Betty Jo and I just sat there swapping zombie stories."

"Do you think we should give Hoffman back his retainer?"

Fred sighed and ran fingers through his thin hair. He worried a lot about the kids I spent more and more time chasing, and lately I was afraid that he was going to quit part-timing for me and go back to collecting retirement from the SFPD.

"Let's give it till Monday," he said wearily. Leonard Hoffman's youngest son had gone out the patio door three weeks ago, robbed a Motel Six with his father's .22 target pistol, and disappeared in the direction of Oakland. The police lost interest when he didn't rob anybody else, but Hoffman, who ran a clothing store in the Sunset, was on the telephone to me twice a day, crying. The kid was 15.

Fred stood up to leave. "Anything there for me?" he asked, pointing at the manila folders on my desk.

"Just a bigger kid. George Webber's gone around the corner."

"Him?" Fred tucked himself into a raincoat and patted it smooth. I wanted to throw him a fish. "The writer, the funny guy?"

"The one."

"He's supposed to be a chaser."

"You know that?"

"Animal, vegetable, or mineral. Tell Hoffman till Monday." He closed the door and I heard the elevator bump a minute later. I finished sorting old folders in about half an hour more, closed the office and followed him down into Friday afternoon.

The ancient blue Mercedes was just where I had left it, one block down by a broken meter. I inspected a fender that had begun to peel in the summer sun. A 1958 model, the 190SL, 172,000 miles to the good, still the color of fine old silk. It had the dignity of a Social Register matron, though it had been through more hands than an Eddy Street floozy. I patted its haunch in admiration. Then I stood for a moment to watch a sailboat come out from the shadow of the Bay Bridge and luff, flapping its sails like an excited gull. The offshore breeze was fresh and cool. Across the bay you could still see the ridge of Tilden Park and farther south the wide stern of a navy cruiser heading for dock in Oakland.

I shook a cigarette out of the pack and lit it. The sailboat came around, and the sails gradually calmed themselves, puffing and smoothing their chests with a final indignant shake. I had been in San Francisco for eight years now, accustoming myself to the view of the bay, the hillsides, the bridge, and perversely the view still reminded me of Boston. I took a long drag from the cigarette. Boston, of all places, a gray city nibbling on a greasy sea, the very opposite of everybody's favorite—little

cable cars and Babylon-by-the-Bay. Boston, the goddam Puri-
tans' cradle, where not so upright citizens prowl the Combat
Zone instead of the Tenderloin. New Englanders like me have
a lot of trouble yet with San Francisco. Even if I did leave New
England at the tender age of 19, two decades ago. The sailboat
curled out to the center of the bay, glossy and bright. Not quite
two decades ago, to tell the truth. I was 37 years old. Thirty-
seven and no doubt coming up soon enough on a mid-life crisis just like George Webber's, except I had no wife to change,
no house to abandon, no boss to worry. My idea of a crisis
would be moving to the suburbs.

I threw away the cigarette. They had told Shoults I make
missing persons a specialty. A truant officer for the now society.
I hunched up my shoulders against a gust of wind and squinted. The sailboat had vanished into the sunshine, dissolved like
a cube of sugar. I waited for a black-and-white to pass—my
office is across the street from a police station, which doesn't
seem to hurt business as much as it should—and then pointed
the car up Market and north on Van Ness.

When he wasn't disappearing, George Webber lived in a pale
white Victorian townhouse between Pacific Heights and the Presidio, an elegant upper-middle-class neighborhood with views
of the water on one side and of the rolling Presidio greenery
on the other. Clumps of eucalyptus trees rose out of the center
dividers in the street, overshadowing little beds of red and white
anemones. I found a parking place on the right block, slanted
the wheels to keep from rolling into the distant bay, and walked
back uphill to his house. A tiny teenage girl with braces on her
teeth answered the bell and went to call her mother.

The house was cool and dark inside, furnished with heavily upholstered chairs and expensive Spanish cabinets. It had

books the way other houses have ants, shelves of them running over doorways, up the staircase, around the window frames. Everything from worn leather sets of nineteenth-century novelists to paperback westerns and science fiction. A big, handsome glassed-in cabinet held books that seemed to be mostly about California, an open case of polished walnut had more sets of novels. Some things I recognized from my distant, interrupted student days. The Beards' *American History* stood on an end table, along with five or six books by Samuel Eliot Morison. A set of Boswell's Johnson sat on the window ledge imperially, just as it did on my shelves at home. Old bookworm that I am, I handled one volume tenderly, resisted the temptation to browse further. Behind me the coffee table was buried under three roughly equal stacks of magazines. Over the couch, on one of the few stretches of open wall, hung an undistinguished painting of a sailing ship at sea, and close to the front door, in a hallway nook with a rolltop desk, hung what appeared to be a Stubbs horse. I went over and looked at the way the four white legs stood on the bare path, tense, like nails ready to be driven into the ground, while a groom pulled at the bridle.

"That's my favorite painting," Mrs. Webber said. In another part of the house two girls' voices were quarreling. She came down the stain and stood beside me. "George hates it. I bought it years ago at an auction in London, before they became so hard to get."

She was English, a small, trim woman in her late 40s, black hair cut short in the style of a helmet. She moved past me toward the living room.

"Would you like something to drink? Sherry? Vodka?"

I said vodka and tonic would be fine, and she went to the glassed-in cabinet, opened the bottom and pulled out glasses and bottles. I watched her while she made the drinks in slow, careful movements. On top of the coffee-table magazines lay a Carlos Casteneda book of recent vintage and a fat, badly printed paperback entitled *Peace at Hand,* which could have been about Neville Chamberlain but turned out to be a manual of massage. Mrs. Webber came back with the drinks. She was tanned a rich, permanent brown, the color of good caramel, and it looked even better against the simple white belted dress she was wearing. You see tans like that all over California, usually on people who have beat their way here from somewhere else, somewhere wet and cold, and who just park themselves in the sun until they wrinkle up like old leather. The English are the worst of all, still bloody Druids at heart.

"Tommy Shoults thought you could help," she said after we had taken polite sips. "Things are really . . . I'm rather at a loss." She was remarkably poised, even cool, as if I were an underling or new employee at her husband's paper. The anxiousness was in her voice, climbing up the register a little at the end of sentences. Her face had stiffened into formality, but her eyes kept moving from me to the window to the books.

"I'll do everything I can, Mrs. Webber," I said. "It hasn't been as long as it must seem. Did you put together the papers we talked about?" She told me they were in the study, all the gasoline, telephone, and credit card receipts from the past six months. But she had noticed nothing out of the ordinary, no sudden expenses, unexplained charges. Friends, routines, work were the same. No suitcases or personal items were missing. He had just gone out one morning and never come back.

She finished her vodka and tonic, glanced at mine, and went to make fresh drinks. I picked up Carlos Castenada and found Joyce Carol Oates underneath. In another room a radio started to blare pop music.

"Do you know of any reason for your husband to go away?" I asked when she came back.

"Tommy has a theory."

"He told me you didn't like it."

"No. I don't like trendy California explanations for what we do. People's lives aren't predictable, like trains pulling out of a station on the way to the same old stops." She twisted her head to reach for her drink. In the soft light of the room her tan looked brittle and unnatural, ready to fall off in chips. "George isn't at stage five or whatever it is. He's no more afraid of growing old than I am." She didn't like something about that and started over. "George gets tired of the column. And sometimes I know he thinks writing jokes about socialites and television stars—excuse me, personalities—is a trivial way to make a living. He may be bored once in a while. But at heart he's a big, enthusiastic boy." She took a swallow and looked a little startled at the empty glass. "He has to be, to do his work."

"There's always the chance he's gone for some other reason."

"You're rather tactful, aren't you?" She smiled sadly at some private thought. "I suppose I expected something blunter from a detective. You mean another woman. You're wondering if he's run off with some chippie for two weeks at Tahoe and shouldn't I just wait patiently until she wears him out or he spends all his traveler's checks and comes home to mum. I don't think so. George has had affairs before. I know his reputation. He gets all the fluff he wants."

"I see." Always ready with the snappy comeback, Haller.

"I'm not exactly the warmest person in the world," she said. She was watching a car outside the window. "In bed. British reserve and all that, you know."

"Mrs. Webber, there's no reason for you to feel guilty. This happens all the time. I see it every day. Your friend Shoults is probably right. It probably doesn't have a thing to do with you."

There were tears in her eyes. She ignored them and kept looking out the window.

"People get scared," I said. "Men get scared."

"As a matter of fact, George has been seeing a young girl in the city regularly. Connie Larkin. She lives in a flat off Union Street, near the Marina. I've known about her for more than a year." The tears stood in her eyes, but she was keeping her voice briskly under control, and we could have still been talking about paintings and auctions, except there was an uneven rising quality to it, like a rock skipped hard over water. "I called her two days ago. She hasn't seen George in almost a month. That's why I began to be worried and asked Tommy Shoults to find someone like you. Something's gone badly wrong."

I looked away, through the window toward the eucalyptus trees, now no more than tall shadows in the soft twilight. Beyond them city lights winked. Between two houses I could just see the black ribbon of the bay. It's not a peaceful landscape, California, despite the unending beauty. You don't look at it and stretch your toes out in satisfaction. It seems to invite people to project their discontent. You want to move around it, get over it, take it down to size. Maybe Shoults was right and George Webber had just had a fit of the restless blues after all and would come back in a little while to find his mistress moderately anxious and his wife a little drunker and not much more unhappy than before. But he had left his car on Eddy Street. I finished my drink and asked to see the study where he kept his papers.

CHAPTER 3

THE TIDE OF BOOKS HAD RECEDED FAR ENOUGH IN THE STUDY to leave one wall free for photographs. Three neat rows, framed and glassed, showed chiefly vacation scenes— wife, two daughters, an elderly cocker spaniel around various pools and picnic tables. A group picture of the *Constitution* city staff dated 1969 had Webber third from the end in the back, a thinnish young man with big teeth and hornrims. There were two recent color photographs. One, a stiff studio portrait, looked like the original for his column masthead. In the other Webber stood attentively beside a tall gray-haired woman wearing a long, gloomy dress that matched the expression on her face. Both of them held drinks. A waiter's white jacket disappeared from the left side of the picture. Carlton Hand grinned at the camera a few paces behind them. Roses sprang up in front of them in pink and yellow puffs. I recognized the old woman. Mrs. Edison Browning, owner of the *Constitution,* a grande dame of San Francisco society, widow, and heiress to a breakfast-food empire as well. Treating the employees to a glimpse of the garden, I assumed. I bent closer. Webber had put on weight since 1969, thickened in the jowls, thinned in the hair; hornrims had given way to contacts. But his face still gave the impression of intelligent good humor that came through his column, the face of someone who has just remembered a joke to tell you.

Anne Webber had laid out the papers on the desk, clipped together in groups and stacked under a paperweight, miniature gold scales like the ones Justice holds in statues. I dropped a paper clip in one tray and sat down to work.

The telephone bills went quickly enough. Most of the long distance calls were in the Bay Area, to Oakland, Berkeley, Marin. Recurring numbers were probably friends or relatives, called at night or on weekends. I wrote down numbers and dates to ask Mrs. Webber about and picked up the credit slips. He owed Breuner's furniture store $640 for a bedroom bureau; he owed L & A Liquors $190, two months late. That didn't bother me: most newspapermen owe most liquor stores something. You can't drink ink. He owed the local Toyota dealer $177 for fender work, more money to an electrician, a florist, and the Book-of-the-Month. His American Express was a month overdue. I found a pocket calculator in a drawer and turned it on, feeling middle-aged guilt that I didn't do the sums by hand, as I had been laboriously taught by good women in another era, or in my head, as Japanese housewives do. He owed $2,600 altogether. Not bad for 1978. Not bad enough to squeeze him into hiding. And he had $7,300 in a savings-and-loan account marked "girls' college" in pencil.

The gasoline cards were harder to fit into a pattern. Most people go to one or two stations regularly, at three- or four-day intervals. Anne Webber did that, according to her signature. But George Webber roamed almost at random all over the Bay Area, chasing stories, I assumed.

They had two cards, Shell and Exxon. The current Exxon bill had arrived on the 24th, three days ago, and had stopped its cycle on the 15th. There were charges from Sausalito that month, from scattered areas of San Francisco—none from Eddy Street. There was one from a station on University Avenue, Berkeley on the 12th, another from the same station on the 15th. On the 16th there was a charge for a full tank from a Shell station in Walnut Creek, north of the Bay, and on the 17th from a freeway station near Yuba City, in the heart of the Sacramento Valley. Webber had disappeared on the 19th.

I scratched a few numbers in my notebook. The Shell billing cycle stopped on the 21st; the bill itself should arrive on the 29th, if the post office and the computer got together. I swiveled and stared at the black window to my left, which opened onto the back of a neighboring house. Lights were on in it, and I saw a man's shadow stalk past twice, then a woman's shadow, her hands waving above her head as if she were warding off a swarm of bees. The man hurried past the other way. I swiveled back to the desk and rooted out the telephone book. Ten rings, no answer. Connie Larkin had found something else to do on a Friday night. I looked at my watch and then dialed another number, one I didn't have to look up, and grinned when Dinah Farrell answered.

"It's me," I said. "I'm afraid I'm going to be late."

"I thought two weekends in a row would overtax you," she said. "I just got off work ten minutes ago anyway. The hospital was a madhouse."

I grinned again. Dinah is a psychoanalyst at Washington General Hospital.

"Where are you hiding?" she asked.

"Would it be too far for you to drive out by the Presidio?" She groaned.

"At least you wouldn't have to cook. We could go to Guido's." I decided to try my famous tact. "And I hear there's a motel on Sutter that has mirrors on all the floors, ceilings, and walls."

"I know the place," she said. "You'd get dizzy. Come back here when you're through."

"It might be a while. Are you sure nothing will burn or freeze over?"

"Bring a can opener," she said and hung up.

Almost an hour later, with a makeshift calendar of Webber's charge slips and travels folded in my jacket pocket I began to rummage in the desk. The usual strata of envelopes, paper, business cards, pens had accumulated, dust balls, eleven-cent stamps, unidentifiable bits of plastic. I poked to the end of the center drawer and found two fifty-dollar bills tucked into a notebook, along with a picture postcard of Carmel signed Connie and postmarked last summer. In the deep drawer on the left were dozens of manila folders, most of them labeled with a, blue ballpoint and stuffed with clippings, jokes, scraps of paper, drafts of columns, all the detritus of the working writer. Useful? I opened the first folder, "Column Ideas June & July." Inside were sheets of five-by-eight memo pads with handwritten titles in the left corner and notes in the middle. I read the first few.

Palindrome—July
    He goddam mad dog, eh?
Famous Names
    Rudolf Diesel (?)—biography—gas crisis
    Thomas Crapper—invented flush toilet
Etymologies
    jargon—twitter of birds, Old French

paradise—space enclosed with a wall
Persian thug—British Army slang
India desire—Latin, de-sidere, be away from stars (?)

> "He whose face gives no light shall never
> become a star"—William Blake

I tapped a pencil against my teeth. Whatever happened to the old-fashioned clues—fingerprints, smoking pistols, blood-stained egg cozies? Then I sighed and lifted out all the folders and put them on top of the desk. You never know what is enough until you know what is too much. William Blake. Shoved behind the folders in the drawer, bought and forgotten who knows when, was a secondhand copy of *Organic Chemistry* by T. W. G. Solomons. Underneath that were six xeroxed pictures of mutilated cats.

I sat back carefully and pulled a cigarette from my pack with the tips of my fingers. The photographs had come from a book, but the captions had been cut off by the copying machine. The back of each one was blank. I lit my cigarette and looked at the fronts again. The first one showed a cat whose head had been shaved completely bald. A knife had sliced diagonally from the left ear almost to the right, and a wide triangle of bloody skin was being lifted and held by tweezers. The second photograph showed the same cat, more skin and bone peeled away, more blood running into its neck fur. The cat's eyes were closed and its neck was turned at an unnatural angle. The third picture showed needles attached to wires and inserted in different parts of the cat's brain, with tiny capital letters superimposed on the gelatinous mass inside the skull. The other pictures showed different cats shaved and wired. Two were staring at the camera with expressions of insane rage, teeth bared, paws raised to swipe, eyes as big as silver dollars. The last one was falling through space, on its side.

My cigarette tasted sour for some reason. I ground it out and sat for a long while, looking across the way at the empty window, thinking slowly about nothing in particular. Then I gathered up the folders and pictures and went to find Anne Webber.

She was in the kitchen alone, working on a new drink and watching a small color television. Her index finger stuck straight across her glass, as if she were marking her place. The governor was on the screen, four inches high and moving his right hand in a rhythmical, hypnotic manner.

"Any theories yet, Detective Haller?" She slurred the first three words together and gave my name a broad English pronunciation.

"I'm terrible at theories, Mrs. Webber." Early in the morning would be soon enough to show her the pictures, I decided, watching her grip the glass, before the coffee hour was over. If there was one. "There's a certain amount of routine in a business like this," I said. "I'd like you to write down the names of the people that go with these telephone numbers when you get a chance. I'm taking some papers from the desk to go over." I gave her a card. "If you want to reach me the answering service will take the message."

She read the card several times and put it down in a little puddle of vodka on the counter. A teenage girl peered in anxiously from the corridor. The governor said, "Only in an era of reduced materialism and less conventional law enforcement can the citizens of this state reach their full human potential." I excused myself and started back to Dinah Farrell.

At 6:30, I got up quietly and went to the window. A few

joggers were already out, pumping up and down the hills. I looked back at Dinah's red hair on the pillow and long curves under the blankets. She had taped the mirror from her purse to the ceiling, and I smiled at it as I went to the kitchen, wrote a note with lots of Xs on the tablet she keeps by the refrigerator, and went downstairs.

The Mercedes sounded loud and angry in the empty streets. After it had coughed for a minute or two like an early-morning smoker, I let out the clutch and started up Broadway, through the heart of North Beach, flicking the wipers once in a while at the gray air. The honky-tonk joints were shut tight, doors barred, lights off. No barkers lolled, no conventioneers cruised. I stopped at a light and a shaggy-haired wino lurched out of the fog like a ghost and stared; then the fog blew him away again. A cat skittered across the pavement after him, wireless. San Francisco, flat on her back, was sleeping off Friday night. And all that mighty heart was lying still. Webber wasn't the only reader in town. But on the other hand, I wasn't as poetic as Wordsworth. A still heart was a dead heart to me.

Nobody got up to greet me when I reached Green Street. Nobody took the croissants out of the pink sack and warmed them. I scrounged butter from the refrigerator's secret places, started water boiling; then I walked into the living room to open the windows.

I had been in the place five years, about four years longer than anywhere else, and you could see my mark, I suppose, in the walnut bookcases I had built last summer to go along one wall, in the massive stereo system I had put together bits at a time, in the anemic little fuchsia I kept trying to nurture. I gave it some Schweppes that was standing in a glass on the coffee table. Straightening, I caught a glimpse of my face in the mirror at the end of the bookcase. Long, flat, big eyes like a horse.

Once in a while there's still a Massachusetts twang in my voice, I reminded myself. But face it, Haller, you look like a Californian now, a beefsteak with a tan, medium bland. Except that underneath the California mask was a Puritan's face—I could see it—descended from ten generations of witch-hunting and not exactly clear of the family business yet. The face in the mirror stuck out its tongue. The red-rimmed eyes went nicely with the scattered premature gray hairs, I thought. A distinguished effect. I would wear my blue sweater. I left the fuchsia to its own devices and walked to the end of the room.

The living room and study open into one another, and both look north over flat pastel roofs toward the Golden Gate. As always, I peered out to see if the bay would surprise me with a new trick or mood, but a thick fog still hung over it, spongy, blowing aside here and there to reveal the bright orange of the bridge, then settling back again demurely. I have always preferred empty landscapes to peopled ones. Don't know why. On slow nights, when nobody was lost, nobody that I knew about, and Dinah wasn't on call, we could sit for hours by the big windows, swirling brandy and watching the cold ships come and go. But Dinah was due at work at ten today, Mrs. Webber was missing a husband, and the kettle was whistling.

I put a record on the turntable, the first act of *Don Giovanni,* which seemed the right choice for Webber, and went back into the kitchen. The croissants were eager for their jam, the cup for its coffee. I put it all on a tray and took it into the study, where Webber's manila folders covered the desk in a beige fan. Holding them down was the old Olympia portable typewriter I had carried up from Los Angeles eight years ago. I sat down and moved it to one side with a grunt. An old-fashioned machine, like the blue Mercedes, I guess. But I don't like the electric ones that just sit there and buzz accusingly while you stare at the keyboard and try to think of something to say. Right around the time I had quit the LA *Times,* in fact, the management had distributed bright new electric IBMs to the whole city room and put in something called a Word Processor for the rewrite desk. A Cuisinart for copy. Mash your nouns and verbs and dangling participles into soy sauce. I quit my job, packed the Olympia along with a spare suit and went off to San Francisco to find myself. And if not myself, then somebody else. Snoop by day, type by night. I wiped buttery fingers on a napkin and opened the top folder. *"Notte è giorno faticar,"* sang Leporello in a good-humored bass, complaining a little about his lot in life too. About a hundred measures later, his master would ram a bloody saber down an old man's throat and liven things up. After that I would be in the right mood to visit a spot I knew on Eddy Street.

Toward the south end, a few blocks before Van Ness, the welfare hotels trail off and the sidewalks bustle with a younger, rougher crowd. I parked beside a meter that had been bent into an S, locked everything I could find, and strolled half a block to the Marinella Deli. A group of blacks was standing at the door, drinking beer and watching the other side of the street; they gave me an inch on each side and I went through to the row of wooden booths beyond the deli counter. Grab was in the last booth. From the opposite bench, a black man about half my age and twice my height got up, looked me over, and walked to the front in slow motion, keeping his palms spread against his thighs with his shoulders swaying back and forth. John Wayne. A salami slicer began to hum. Grab looked at me with a huge grin. He was wearing a powder blue leisure suit and a yellow silk shirt with a collar so long and narrow that the points reached his armpits; two gold necklaces with various little medallions hung from his neck, and the hand I could see was studded with rings of various precious and semi-precious stones, about six in all. The other hand came up from the bench with a bottle of Chivas Regal.

"Who's your tailor, man?" Grab asked as he poured himself a drink and then me.

I looked down my front. I was wearing ordinary gray slacks, a tweed sport coat, no tie, and a Shetland sweater over a blue shirt.

"You want to look him up?"

"Naw, man. I want to let the boys know. He a born trouble-maker." And he laughed delightedly and handed me my glass. I was a long way from the beautiful people in Tommy Shoults's Polynesian bar, but at least I was still getting free drinks. "Up yours," Grab said and laughed again. "Hard on, hard on, hard on."

Grab was about 40, wiry, a little shorter than I am, with a beautiful brown complexion and a full set of nicely capped teeth. He was at present in the rackets. Anything that was bought, sold, or destroyed in the Tenderloin usually put a little something in Grab's pocket; if it didn't, he was likely to be interested and to have plans for leverage in the future. He had been to prison, naturally, putting in four years for a fatal episode with a knife in Hayward, and thought he had been unfairly treated. He was right, too. Four years is considerably over the average prison term for homicide in California, even for a ghetto black. I had met him not long after he got out, as he was being arrested for a burglary charge in Pacific Heights. Since I had been sitting in my car watching the house next door for a missing daughter and had seen Grab stroll by in-nocently enough, I had testified for him at court, and we had done a little business occasionally after that. His full name was Thomas Jefferson Randall, but he had been called Grab all his life. You only had to do business with him once to know why.

"So, man, you want a little chat about honkies on Eddy Street?" he said as we knocked back the Scotch.

"Just one in particular."

"Um. You know how it is, brother."

I sighed. "You still collecting, Grab."

"Just pictures, man. Just pictures of Grant."

"How many?"

"Two, baby. He freed my people."

"How about Lincoln? He was the great emancipator."

"Shit, man," he laughed, taking the two bills I handed him and tucking them into a very thick alligator-hide wallet. "You never serious."

I reached into my coat pocket for the pictures of Webber I had brought along. Grab took them without looking and held them up carefully at shoulder length. John Wayne materialized out of nowhere, got the photographs without a word and went outside.

"Come on upstairs, Sherlock," Grab said. "See the show."

We walked to the front of the deli and started up the stairs of the adjoining doorway, evidently the entrance to a second-floor auditorium. The stairway was lined with men of all ages, mostly black and Chicano, talking loudly and drinking out of beer cans and bottles in paper bags. We walked through double wooden doors and into a good-sized room that ran the length of the building and up another floor to a high, cross-beamed ceiling. There were tall windows at the street side, but they had been covered with brown wrapping paper. Somebody had scattered green sawdust over the floor and had set up a boxing ring in the center of the room, a raised platform maybe a foot high with dirty, frayed ropes drooping sadly, and around it a larger crowd of perhaps a hundred men shuffled their feet, drank, and talked. Sweat, garlic, and the smell of urine mingled in the close air. Nobody asked us for a ticket.

"This the Odd Fellows Hall, Grab?"

He snickered and led me up to ringside. Several people looked at me curiously, and they left a little space around us. "This the dogfight room, baby. Baddest dogs in California piss on those poles."

"Grab, I can skip the dogfights."

"Hey, Sherlock," he said, smoothing both hands in an umpire's safe sign. "This Saturday. This ladies' day." He uncovered a watch that looked like it had gone to the moon. Red digits announced that it was 2:58 and counting. "You gonna like these foxes. They meaner than the dogs by one hell of a lot."

While he spoke, a door in one dim corner pulled open and a rasping cheer went up from the crowd. People started coming in from the hallway. Loud disco music suddenly boomed from big portable speakers by the windows. Two women pushed forward through the crowd to the ring, followed by a burly gap-toothed black man, who knocked away groping arms with good-natured laughter. The women climbed through the ropes and began to parade around the ring, shaking their bodies to the deafening rhythm of the music. They were about equal in height and age, one black, one white, dressed in loose-fitting cotton blouses and medium-length skirts but no shoes. The white woman, a pockmarked brunette in her early 20s with the strapping shoulders of a man, had the clear advantage of weight. The black woman topped the lean build of a sprinter with a red Afro.

"You like the white girl?" Grab asked me over the growing shouts of the crowd. "If she win, maybe we can fix you up, baby!" And he doubled over with laughter. Around us, money changed hands rapidly as the betting heated up. "You wanna lay a Grant on the white girl?" Grab asked, still laughing a little. "Name Susan. I like the fox, Josie the fox."

I shook my head. Susan was now strolling in circles around the ring, snapping her skirt in grand style, while Josie stood with her hands on her hips and jeered. A guy near us said something unintelligible and taunting, and she bent over him, shaking her loose breasts in his face till the light blouse danced with the motion.

"Show us the knockers, Josie!" a deep voice bellowed, and the other woman, ludicrously flat by comparison, cupped her hands to her blouse and waddled in stiff-legged imitation. Susan flung her skirt high and farted, and the crowd whooped.

The burly man climbed over the ropes and waved the women to separate corners. The crowd grew briefly silent. The fighters crouched, their bare feet stirring the sawdust on the ring. He raised a tiny children's bell over his head and just as the disco speakers thumped into "Fly, Robin, Fly," he shook it hard and dodged backwards. Josie flew toward Susan with a yell, jabbing her fists in a flurry, face-high. The slower Susan stumbled backwards, then shoved her away. They circled each other warily, flicking light blows, feinting. The crowd started to mock them, and an apple whizzed through the air toward the back of the room. As if in answer, Susan lumbered forward into a rough clinch, using her massive chest as a cushion, so that Josie was forced to kick her way free, tripping and sprawling against the ropes. The referee danced out of the way, clapping his hands happily, and the two women collided, rebounded, hit again, and stepped back. Their hair was already matted and wet, and a trickle of blood rolled down the white woman's temple.

Josie wiped her hands through her Afro during the pause,

then closed in, slapping wildly and grunting obscenities, until they both went down in a clumsy fall, like mannequins toppling in slow motion. Another apple sailed up, and the referee made a nice backhanded stab to get it, grinned, and took a bite with the side of his mouth. A long arm from the crowd clawed at the women's clothes. They rolled apart and stood up. The white woman's blouse was in tatters, and in the hot overhead light you could see that her torso had been coated with thick, clear grease. Her big breasts quivered as she retreated, bright rivulets of blood and sweat curling toward her waist. The black woman faked a kick and laughed.

"Looks like you saved youself a dollah, Sherlock," Grab said, giving me a little punch in the arm.

"Tear that honky's ass!" somebody shouted in my ear.

The black woman lunged again and slashed with her nails at Susan, who beat them away, howling with effort. The crowd gave a yell and surged forward until I felt myself pressed against ringside. Both women were naked to the waist now, coated with blood, grease, and green sawdust, and the white woman's skirt gaped wide up one leg. They settled into an exhausted rhythm of shoving and slapping. Then the black woman, nipples distended like bullets, ducked and bobbed by mistake into a flailing uppercut, staggered, and dropped to her back. The white woman swayed over her unsteadily, legs spread.

"Get up, baby!" Grab said and punched both fists in the air.

She hesitated. Josie rolled and scrambled away and began once more to stalk the weary white woman, whose skirt fell away as she rubbed against the ropes and left her completely nude. Voices rose in a cheer. A man began to climb into the ring and disappeared in a shower of fists. Somebody spilled beer over the sawdust, and the referee leaned across for a talk.

I looked back toward the doors and saw that John Wayne

had joined us, arms crossed, shoulders braced against the wall, about as excited as a two-by-four.

Grab saw him too and looked back at the fight. Josie, moving in for the finish, had stopped to kick at a hand that tugged for her skirt. The white woman backed to a corner. Josie lunged and she dodged. Another hand from the crowd caught the skirt and ripped it free, exposing tight curls of black pubic hair and lean, sweaty thighs that trembled and kicked again. Josie wrestled the heavier woman sideways and down into the sawdust, where they churned, naked and bloody, back and forth. For some reason, I thought of the motel with all the mirrors. Susan grunted, rolled and pinned the redhead for a moment, mashing their breasts together before losing the grip and sliding away again. Even in the crowd's roar, I heard the smack of skullbone against wood. A white man with a bright flushed face crawled halfway onto the ring and flung his hands forward against slippery flesh and higher against bone and nipple. Josie's mouth twisted toward him in a snarl, and she spat, viciously, blinding him with saliva, her teeth bared and mouth working like one of the maddened cats in Webber's pictures. I turned and threaded my way through the crowd and went downstairs to Eddy Street.

The music was remarkably muted out on the sidewalk, and the sun shone pleasantly against the concrete. I lit a cigarette. The city had tried hard from time to time to close down fights like Grab's, reasoning that they stirred up feelings best left out of sight, encouraged violent behavior in the uneducated masses, as one city councilman delicately phrased it, just skirting the charge of racism, put undue stresses on the Peaceable Kingdom of San Francisco. But after a few weeks, down one mean street or another, the fights or something like them always reappeared. They'd have better luck stamping out the fog.

In five minutes or so, Grab sauntered out, took a cigarette leisurely from the pack in my jacket breast pocket and lit it himself with a flat gold lighter that would have interested Tommy Shoults.

"Dog fights tomorrow, baby," he told me. "Fucking Chicanos love it."

"What about the pictures, Grab?"

He let smoke drift out his nostrils. "Yeah. Some of the brothers seen them. The man want to talk about buying a gun."

"Don't bullshit me, Grab, You can buy a gun anywhere in this state. They sell them at the Lucky Market. What's he come to Eddy Street for?"

"Hey, man, take it easy. You too quick to jump."

"Grab."

"Somebody want a brother to kill the dude, that's all."

CHAPTER 4

"WHERE THE FUCK IS BERNIE HAUPTMAN?" CARLTON HAND glowered through the open door. "I need a goddam executive assistant to find my executive assistant." His secretary rubbed her palms on her skirt and glanced in my direction.

"Mike Haller?" he said, banging on through and pumping my hand with both of his. "Mike Haller! Jesus Christ, you don't look a day older—come in, come in—I'm just squirreling around trying to get the Sunday sheets clean—come in, come in." As one arm clamped my shoulder and pushed me toward his office, he turned and shouted again to the secretary. "Get Hauptman's butt up here before the print room goes on break. Come in, come in," to me. He pointed to a leather chair and punched my bicep hard. "Jesus, it's nice to see you. Wait right here while I talk to the girl."

I watched him bull a path back to reception, all shoulders and head, and I heard the start of more shouts before the door jumped shut. The last time I had been welcomed like that I had just bought $10,000 worth of insurance. The last time I had seen Carlton Hand was nine years ago, in an LA bar where *Times* reporters hang out, near La Brea. The Tar Pit. Carlton had been at the center of a party celebrating his appointment as managing editor of the *Constitution.* I had been sniffing out old haunts before moving north too, in a sentimental mood. But he hadn't seen me and I hadn't gone over.

He was one of San Francisco's famous characters now, a part of local media legend, a raunchy, fat-fisted brawler with a loose sense of libel and, most people thought, irrepressible political ambitions. He had come to the *Constitution* by an indirect route, to say the least. Reared in an orphanage in Baltimore—the same one Babe Ruth had lived in—he had put himself through an obscure Maryland college and plodded back to the orphanage to teach history and biology. Then the Korean War happened along, exploding that placid life and detonating some control center in the orphan kid's personality. He had been drafted and chucked into Inchon along with a few thousand other bewildered draftees, like calves herded up a gangway, and six months later he had come home again with enough metal up and down one leg to put in a zipper. They sent him to Long Beach for recuperation, by a screw-up he once told me—it was supposed to be Boston—and he never looked back: it was love at first sight, the promised land, *fucking California.* He had picked up a job stringing for the LA *Times* when he got out of Long Beach, squirmed his way onto the regular staff, took a deep breath, and stormed straight up the ladder, so good that his stuff was quickly syndicated over half the West and twice nominated for a Pulitzer.

I looked around his office, noting the wide oak desk, the signed photographs of celebrities, the tall, well-dusted bookshelf of reference material, plaques, circulation awards. He was ten years older than me and had it all. Power. Success. Style. I swallowed something sour. What did envy taste like? We had all watched in amusement then as the pudgy kid from the East, moonfaced, crude, outrageously self-confident, turned himself into a Hollywood parody of a reporter—the trenchcoat, the Dobbs hat with the drooping brim, the Dixie cup of cold coffee he held in one hand while he pecked out stories.

But the stories were good. The stories in fact were unbeatable. He had the instincts of a muckraker and the good hands of a revival preacher. Every time he unearthed a civic scandal—and sometimes they were beauts, like the prostitution ring that ran out of the city morgue—he somehow left his readers with the reassurance that such things were really the exception out here in the promised land; once the outrage had been savored over breakfast, we could all go back to our righteous conviction that the Golden State referred chiefly to sunshine. The *Constitution* had known what San Francisco needed. In eight years, Hand had transformed the paper from a listless, second-place rag into a hammer, the state's crusader. He had gone after wayward cops and politicians with more zeal than ever and had pushed the *Constitution* over the *Chronicle* in sales and ads for six years running. Last month he had started a new series on police corruption, a San Francisco perennial and about as full of surprises as Dagwood. But somebody had slugged him in a restaurant over the first installment—his picture ran on page one—the series had taken off, and the press was now baying at full strength around City Hall, while talk of the governorship (mostly in the *Constitution*) was becoming as rhythmical as clapping hands. Don't ask me why I preferred to read the *Chronicle*. Dinah once said that Hand was locked into the missionary position.

"You want coffee, Mike?" he asked, returning.

"No thanks, Carl. I just came by to see about getting into George Webber's office, to scratch around."

"All you want." He leaned back against his desk. His stomach rolled over his belt like dough rising in a pan. "It's a crock, isn't it? I hope you're not wasting your time. Skirts," he said. "Skirts, skirts, skirts, am I right?"

"Everybody tells me." I stood up. "Your secretary can show me the way," I said. "And by the way, thanks for mentioning me to Shoults."

"The lawyer? Oh hell, listen, I always felt, you know . . ."

We both let the sentence trail off into the air. A buzzer sounded on his desktop phone. He grabbed for it and called as I opened the door, "Come back when you're through, we'll talk. What's it been—ten years, for Christ's sake? We'll put something in the coffee. The goddammed chapel's giving me fits right now."

I closed the door and set out for Webber's office.

Cubbyhole, actually, as it turned out to be. A drab little square in one corner of the newsroom with a desk, two chairs, two filing cabinets, and a window that opened north onto the city. I sat down at the desk and looked out at the rows of fragile glass stalks that make up the San Francisco skyline now. We were 15 floors up, but a few scraps of paper circled outside the window, coasting on the wind. Nobody else this side of Trafalgar Square still called a newspaper printing room a chapel. The sun threw long, sad shadows east. Grab wouldn't tell me who had wanted to hire a gun to kill Webber. A honky, he had said, pleased. But the brothers in question said that the buyer hadn't returned with the $1,000 deposit, and on Eddy Street, business was strictly cash and largely confidential. He could still come back. "On the other hand, they could be lying," Grab had said. "But if they are, they ain't goin' to tell me to tell you." I grunted obscurely and pulled open the drawer marked "Correspondence."

"So what's there?" Hand poured a stiff shot of malt Scotch into our coffee and came around the desk to hand me mine. "Anything to help?"

"Not much," I said and sipped tentatively, then swallowed. The coffee made the whiskey taste like creosote. "I looked mainly at what he was writing over the last few months."

"Just the column." He sat down beside me in another leather club chair.

"Recognize these, Carl?" I handed him the pictures from Webber's house. He thumbed through them rapidly without any comment and handed them back. "I don't like cats either," he said. "What is it, some anti-vivisection stuff?"

"I found them in his desk at home."

"People send all kinds of things to reporters. What the hell."

"I found this here, in his 'Current' file all by itself." It was a clipping from *The Chronicle of Higher Education* announcing that Dr. Martin Fells had left the National Institute of Mental Health and accepted a full professorship of biochemistry at UC, Berkeley. Hand glanced at it.

"Probably an interview. He does a lot of university hokum in the column. That clipping's two years old anyway."

"Yeah." I took a memo routing slip from the stack of papers I was carrying and handed it to him. "This was the other thing I didn't understand."

He read it, frowned, turned it over and looked at the back. Blank. "Goddam pain in the ass," he said. "Chapel won't set ads for Levi's, some anti-union thing. You got any idea how much revenue that is? What's this supposed to be?"

"Memo for a story conference with you?"

He looked at the "Sty Conf" in thick black ink with "CH

4 pm" in a whirl at the bottom. The date at the top was two weeks ago, Thursday, June 19.

"Christ, Mike, I don't remember what that is. I have 20 story conferences a day, you know that. He probably wanted to ask about using some name in the column. Whether he'd piss off an advertiser or not. That's policy." Hand pulled the Scotch bottle off the corner of the desk and replenished our cups. As an afterthought, he added a little more coffee.

"Was he covering anything for you that might get somebody mad at him, Carl?"

"Mad? You mean like in foul play? Oh hell no, last guy in the world. All anagrams, word games, palindromes. You read the column. He wasn't on the police series, if that's what you're thinking, maybe some cop with dirty fingers coming after him down an alley. Never." He wagged his head owlishly over his cup. "You know something I don't know, Mike?"

"Just checking all the routine angles, Carl, stirring the pot."

Hand pinched his nose gently. "He might have had something going on his own, I suppose." He spoke slowly. "The whole building wants to play like Woodward and Bernstein. Webber used to do that stuff, too. But I don't know. He would have checked with me. He's no kid."

"He didn't go out to the valley for you then?" I looked at my notes. "June 20 or 21?"

"Valley? Which valley—Mill Valley? Napa Valley?"

"The Central Valley, out by Sacramento."

"The Central Valley? Christ, no. What do you think this is, the Sacto *Bee?* My readers don't give a shit about anything east of the fucking port of Oakland. I wouldn't cover the Second Coming in the Central Valley. If he went larking out there, it was on his own time. Quiff." He leaned toward me and I saw the high spots of color on each cheek, smelled the whiskey as he tapped my knee. You could easily miss the expression of the eyes behind the thick-lensed, gold-rimmed glasses, eyes of arresting sensitivity, as if the rich food and drink that had swollen the rest of his body had not yet reached them. "I'll tell you just what I told the lawyer. He's gone off with some popsie for a lost weekend or two. The guy's like that. You want to find him, go knock on motel doors in Tahoe or down in Carmel. Have you seen his wife?"

I nodded.

"All right," he said. He didn't lean back but continued tapping my knee. "You know about the praying mantis?" he asked. "While they're fucking, the female praying mantis devours the male, starting with the head. And all the time she's devouring the head,å the rest of him keeps right on humping." Now he leaned back and sucked in coffee. "That's George Webber," he said. "Sometimes I think that's the whole goddam country," he added after a pause.

CHAPTER 5

WHEN I GOT BACK TO THE APARTMENT, THE ANSWERING service told me that Fred Wrigley had called. And Dinah Farrell. I looked at my watch. It didn't light up or guess my weight but it said 4:30. I dialed the Marin County number Tommy Shoults had given me.

A boy's voice answered, grunted a few times into the middle distance, and told me to wait. I listened to the ping of electrons jostling each other off the line for a little while. Then Shoults picked up an extension. He was by the pool, and the splashes and laughter in the background made it hard to hear him. He was also a little sloshed.

"This is Michael Haller, Mr. Shoults."

"Oh. Yes. What's up?"

"I've made some progress and I'd like to talk with you about it."

"Now?"

"If I can."

"Well, look, Haller—" I lost a few words to the party "— tonight. Can't it hold until tomorrow? You haven't found him or anything?"

"Shall I come by your office in the morning?"

"Sure. That's fine. No, wait a minute." There was a pause and somebody named Molly got loudly dunked. "I've got a conference in the morning. All morning. How about 2:00, after lunch?"

I took what I could get and hung up. A big tanker was coming under the Golden Gate Bridge and slapping its way fast by the window. I left the telephone and walked over to the table where I keep the binoculars, a beautiful wide-angle Tasco 6 x 50 that Dinah had given me for my birthday. On the catwalk that ran from the bow to the bridge at the stern, right down the center of half a million gallons of crude oil, a sailor was turning some sort of pressure wheel all by himself, a wheel about the size of an open umbrella with thick metal spokes. It was windy and the catwalk was wet with spray, so that he kept slipping to one side as he turned. A few gulls were circling overhead, offering advice. He looked like he didn't know what the hell he was doing.

I called the Berkeley number Fred had left. He picked it up on the first ring.

"Pay phone," he said. "I've been fighting off perpetrators for an hour. Where you been?"

"To the opera. What have you got?"

"Maybe I got Hoffman's boy. I don't know yet. You might want to come over and see. Bring a couple of bills."

"What for? You going to take Betty Jo Rule to supper this time?"

"As a matter of fact, she set this up. She's sitting at a table right here in the middle of a Baskin-Robbins with me."

He gave me directions and went back to Betty Jo. I called Dinah, and then I went over to the desk and took out the little green toolbox in the bottom drawer. There were ten fifty-dollar bills nestling in it, under a bent screwdriver and an unopened roll of electrician's tape. I took six of them, reminding myself never to do anything by halves. Three hundred dollars was pin money to somebody like Shoults, mad money to somebody like Webber, who also stashed 50s in his desk for Connie Larkin or whoever. To me it was just part of the medium I worked in, like oil and water to the sailor, neurosis and dream to the shrink. I folded the wrinkled green bills into my wallet. *Radix malorum cupiditas est,* as I had learned long ago in the days when Boston Latin still made you take Latin. The root of all evil is the love of money. And even the dimmest private eye could see that. I snapped the toolbox shut and put away my treasure. Aside from old Allan Pinkerton, William Burns, and maybe Frank Brazil, I didn't know of any rich free-lance detectives. Just rich lawyers.

As I started down the stairs I remembered that Dinah had once corrected my little translation. *Cupiditas* really means love of power, she had said. Love of power over other people.

The traffic was light all the way. Weekenders hadn't started back from Tahoe yet and nobody was stirring from San Francisco. I spread out in the center lane, lit a cigarette, and enjoyed the rare sensation of being practically alone on the Bay Bridge. They had drilled a spectacular tunnel in the center of Treasure Island when they built the bridge, under the naval base, to join the two spans, and I roared into it like a wounded Spitfire, belching cigarette smoke and climbing into third. One day last year a hopped-up navy pilot had said the hell with it, dropped his F-104 a thousand feet and flown right through, screaming straight up the blue curves of the suspension cables and scattering motorists from there to Fremont. Sublimation, Dinah tells me. I dropped sedately into fourth and trailed a highway patrol car to the East Bay.

Two rights at the toll plaza took me toward the narrow section where Berkeley and Oakland meet in a grim clinch. The weather was a little better, no fog yet, but that only meant you could see the bleak faces of the buildings more clearly. A few bleak human faces could be seen, too, mostly young and black, shuffling along in the litter or waiting impassively for a bus. The lowland factories struggled a little way up the hillside and then disintegrated into ramshackle warehouses and pale stucco apartments, with a scattering of Victorian houses on the bigger lots. The neighborhood stores had more steel mesh across their windows than San Quentin. In the late afternoon light they looked like enormous mouths with braces, glinting. I went around a traffic barrier the city of Berkeley had erected out of white styrofoam barrels on short wooden posts and parked in a shopping center not far from the BART station. After I had locked the car and buttoned all my pockets, I found Fred sitting in a brave little Baskin-Robbins ice cream store, working on a sundae called an Earthquake.

"Where's Betty Jo?" I asked him.

"She went to feed the meter. Lot of cops around here."

"I can see why. Have you got the Hoffman boy?"

He wiped his mouth with a paper napkin and offered me a bite of the sundae. It wasn't bad. "Watch the aftershock," Fred said. "Betty Jo was showing the Hoffman picture around, just like I was showing a couple for her, and she found a guy thinks maybe he'll see the kid this afternoon."

"What kind of guy?"

"Real nice fellow. Pusher. About 30. Bunks down over there." He pointed toward the window with his plastic spoon. Across the street was a three-story building with a 7-11 on the ground floor and doorways on either side. "The kid apparently likes angel dust. The pusher says he's sold it to him three or four times in the last week or so."

"What's the pusher's name?"

"Zeke."

"How much did he want?"

"Two hundred. For that he told the kid to meet him by the 7-11. Usually they meet at the BART." He pushed away the empty plate and put a hand in front of his mouth. "Betty Jo already paid him. You owe her."

Betty Jo came in the door just then, a brown-haired woman in her mid or late 30s, tall and starting to get heavy. Or maybe it was just the effect of her assortment of sweaters, jackets, and scarves. With her long straight hair and granny glasses, she looked like every man's dream of a sociology major. In fact, she was the daughter of a welder from Dallas, had run away and joined the WAVES when she was 17, and spent a tour of duty in the Shore Patrol at Oakland. There was a husband and child somewhere in the Midwest that you didn't hear much about. She had come back three years ago to open an agency with two other women, and they were supposed to be doing well now. They used to specialize in divorce cases, but after she had disarmed a berserk gunman in a Market Street bar with a blackjack and a can of Mace, other kinds of business had started to come along.

We said hello, and while the counterman was bringing us coffee I paid her back the four 50. The counterman looked bored.

People drifted in and out. We watched the sunlight give way to wisps of fog, gray floating puffs, like the ghosts of little shadows. Betty Jo began to pick her nails. Fred started to read the 31 flavors again. "It's past seven," she announced finally in her soft Texas drawl. "Zeke set it up for six."

"You want to go talk to him?" I asked.

She got up and walked across the street, pushed an outside button, and opened the door. Fred took his porkpie hat from the rack and we followed slowly.

It was cold on the street, the way only a San Francisco summer is cold. We stamped our feet and blew white breaths of smoke and circled a few yards from the 7-11 door. A set of steps led down to a basement flat, which seemed to be closed up tight. By bending I could just see the front door, where dozens of posters were curling in the damp air. The 7-11 sign flickered off a polished brass mezuzah to the right of the handle.

Fred blew his nose. "Don't turn your back," he said. "That's a gay synagogue."

Betty Jo stepped out. In the hallway, holding the door open, was a man in a gold and brown dashiki, carefully faded blue Levi's, and leather sandals. His hair fell down to his shoulders and covered his ears and parts of his beard; he wore a necklace of thin gold hammered into various-sized crosses. His face was unlined and his eyes were clear blue and rather beatific.

"I'm not giving back the money," he said.

Betty Jo looked at me.

"Is he usually late like this?" I asked.

The eyes looked me over, flicked to take in the rest of the street. A blue and gold Dodge sedan moved slowly past with a swish of tires against black tar. On the door was painted a silver badge that said "Bridgestone Security" in tight, angular letters, and above the door a white face, pale as marble, stared carefully at us.

"He's always been there waiting for me," Zeke said after a while.

"You don't have a number or an address for him?"

Zeke rotated his head very slowly as if turning a wheel.

"Where'd you first meet him?"

"I told her. Across from Moe's on Telegraph." Moe's is a big used-book store near the Cal campus.

"Was he OK?"

"Hey, I'm not going to stand around answering bullshit questions. He was OK. He's crashing around, that's all."

"Will you call me if he shows up, Zeke?" Betty Jo asked in her quiet way.

"Yeah. I got your card." He liked her. He frowned at me and started to close the door. "Second time this week, dammit."

"You mean the second time Hoffman hasn't shown up?" I asked.

He answered Betty Jo, not me. "No. Second time a regular buyer hasn't come around." He closed the door sharply and vanished in the gloom.

"You don't dress right for this kind of thing," Fred told me.

As I drove back across the bridge, from the upper deck I could still see north toward San Pablo and the Napa Valley; the bay itself was daubed with whitecaps, flickering on a black background. Twenty-seven workmen had been killed building this stretch of the bridge between 1927 and 1931. I thought about the three of them who had fallen into open pillars and were buried somewhere below in tons of concrete and steel. Permanently missing persons, of fixed address. I pressed the accelerator and left Zeke's world farther behind. Zeke's world and little Lennie Hoffman's. My brother would have been about Zeke's age if he had lived. If he and my mother had not got in the car together one rainy night almost 30 years ago. The great permanent missing persons, Dinah once said. The thought drifted through my head like one of the wisps of fog passing among the cables of the bridge. More fog blanketed the entrance to the Treasure Island tunnel. Inside it, the big fluorescent lights along the walls looked bright and cold. It was like driving through a bone.

"You're a nomad," Dinah Farrell said two hours later, when

I picked up our plates and carried them into the kitchen. Chunks of swordfish were steaming in a bowl on the stove. I put a lid on the bowl and turned off the gas. Wine glasses went in the dishwasher, spinach and Delmonico potatoes into separate plastic containers. Brandy into two snifters.

"Not," I said. "Haven't I returned to hearth and woman?" I kissed her and sat down beside her on the couch.

"The hearth has three burglar alarms," she said, picking up her brandy. "And the woman goes home early tonight. Shirley and I are running a seminar for visiting gurus on new forms of the family."

"The baleful Mendelsohn," I said with a grimace. We watched a lonely freighter steam west toward the Golden Gate. Shirley Mendelsohn is another psychoanalyst at the Washington General Hospital. She and Dinah run a seminar on the Family and Neurosis, like a medical tag team, which draws doctors from all over. "I wanted to show you my pictures of mutilated cats, but I left them at the office."

"Charming," she said. "Other men want to show me their etchings."

"What other men?"

"Do you want to know why you specialize in hunting missing persons?" Dinah rarely stops working.

"I thought it was because I admired Mr. Trace, keener than most persons."

"Because you're a romantic at heart."

"Where else?" I murmured.

"You want to take on different identities, discover your missing self, escape responsibilities. You envy the people you find, like George Webber and his open marriage."

"Open and shut. And that's Shirley talking, not you. Shirley specializes in envy. What do you think?"

She snuggled closer and started twisting a button on my coat.

"I think you're a self-righteous Massachusetts Puritan who likes to stop people from finding themselves when they get lost. Webber's just escaping an alcoholic wife, a trivial job, a dead-end life. And don't say they're all dead-end." Her hand slid lower. I turned my head to watch the freighter disappear into the fog.

"What do you think of the way I dress?" I asked. She laughed and turned out the last lamp in the room. Outside, there were ripples of moonlight on the water. You could see a few low lights winding toward Sausalito. "There's a difference between being lost and missing," I said a little later. Her fingers traced delicate filigrees on my skin.

"Would you look for me if I got lost?" she whispered.

"My silence is my love," I said, and she giggled and then there was only the rustle of clothing.

CHAPTER 6

"ANOTHER GODDAM BEAUTIFUL DAY."

Connie Larkin was sitting on a window bench drinking instant coffee and staring out at the Marina. The sun was hot, a breeze was up and about, some sailboats were putt-putting by on their way to the open bay. In the abstract there wasn't a lot to complain about, but she was a New Yorker.

"No wonder people drink so much out here," she said. "You wake up every morning and go to the window and look out and it's another goddam beautiful day. I'll start putting bourbon in the coffee soon."

I resisted saying it couldn't hurt the coffee. It was early for her, almost 11, and I hadn't brought any good news. Nobody seemed to have brought her good news lately. I sipped and watched her pull the silk bathrobe tighter. Late 20s, I guessed; thick black hair with a big, blowsy body that put a lot of strain on the bathrobe. She had come to California five years ago, trying LA first, then San Francisco. Mistress was a little grand as a word to describe her. She saw George Webber, but not exclusively, and sometimes did a little modeling. I looked at her pouty mouth and round, healthy face. Doxy, maybe.

"I had to dip into savings for the rent this month."

We both looked around the apartment. A clean, modern little place with lots of plants and pillows. A nice Tiffany lamp hung over the low white coffee table, which held ashtrays, a few copies of *Elle,* and a ragged issue of *People* with Diane Keaton on the cover. If there were any books, she kept them in the bedroom.

"And then his wife had to call up and ask if I knew where he was." Connie played with her hair.

"Was she unpleasant?"

"No. Very matter of fact. She asked if I needed anything."

"She did?"

Connie Larkin nodded and stared out the window again, past the boats. "Kind of motherly, actually," she said.

I finished my coffee and thought of Connie and Anne meeting for long lunches at Blum's and going shopping in Union Square for shoes and handbags and pillows and plants and having comfortable, unexcited talks over tea somewhere not too expensive.

She had noticed nothing unusual in George Webber's mood before he disappeared, except that he had spaced his visits longer and longer apart, then stopped altogether. She shrugged. It happens.

"Did he talk much about what he does, friends and so on, people he liked and didn't like?" Did he mention anybody who wanted to have him wasted?

"He talked about himself mostly, about striking it rich and getting out of newspapers. Other people, his wife sometimes, his editor, some types at his office."

"Did he ever get any mail here?"

"No."

"Make phone calls?"

"Sometimes."

"Local or long distance?"

"I didn't pay attention."

"Do you keep your old phone bills?"

"Yes, but I don't think I want you to look at them. Other people make calls too, you know."

"OK. You'd know which days he was here, wouldn't you, from an appointment book or something?" She made a sniffing sound. "Could you check to see if he made any calls?"

"You're taking a lot of my time," she said. "I don't know if you thought about that. I had to dip into savings for the rent."

"I remember." Practice makes perfect. I took a 50 from Shoults's retainer and spread it along the table edge. "All right?" She picked it up and went into the bedroom with her coffee. I studied *People* and poured myself another cup. Cold, it tasted like Quaker State. She had taken one look at my pictures of cats, made a horrified face that was mostly sincere, and told me to put them away. George Webber had never mentioned them.

After about ten minutes, she came back to the living room. The silk bathrobe made a swishing sound as she moved, and the door of the bedroom stayed open, so that I could see the corner of a large bed covered by a fluffy pink spread. She looked at me as if she were aware for the first time that we were alone in her apartment. I had kept it in mind all along.

"Did he make any calls?"

"I found one. This is the date and number." She handed me a piece of yellow paper with bold handwriting in felt-tip pen across the middle, and I inhaled a cloud of Shalimar. "I don't remember what it was, though. I usually go out of the room when somebody makes a call." She sat down on the couch and leaned one firm shoulder against me. "Do you recognize it? The area code is 916."

I scratched my chin with my ballpoint and said what I had been wanting to say ever since I had opened my office eight years ago. "I haven't a clue," I said.

But 916 was the whole goddam Sacramento Valley.

Shoults canceled out on me. Called to court suddenly, his sweet young secretary explained at 2:15, tied up all day. She shook her head sadly at this legal fiction. He was evidently not as worried Monday as he had been Friday. The secretary wrote down my number and stuck it in a wooden In tray. I left under orders to have a nice day, drove too fast across the financial district, and parked by the police station in a meterless space freshly painted "Official Business Only."

Fred was in my office when I arrived, standing at the window and looking at my car.

"That used to be a cathouse, next door to the precinct," he said when I came in. "Where you parked your car. Before it was a precinct, of course. Pretty well-known landmark."

"The sporting life." I sat down behind the desk and slapped my notebook on the blotter.

"A game of inches," Fred said solemnly. "Mrs. Webber called you. I was reminded by that sign they painted. I used to be a driver for a lieutenant when I first started out, lieutenant of detectives in the 19th. Monahan, Moynahan. Drove him everywhere, City Hall, the docks, the whole goddam city, sort of an apprentice thing, watch him, learn the ropes. Very fine lieutenant, dignified, aloof, businesslike, clout." Fred lit a match from a book with one hand and put it to a balloonlike cigar. "Once a month, he had me drive him there, in the afternoon right after lunch. I put up the little card on the dashboard, Official Business PD; he told me to go off and get a cup of coffee and come back in half an hour."

I started to thumb through the notebook. "Her number's on the pad," he said. I saw it and pulled the telephone over.

"Did you get your friend at the telephone company to check that other number?" I asked him. Fred knew people in every building in the city.

"Yeah. You gonna tell Hoffman no? This is Monday."

I picked up the receiver. "I don't think so yet."

"That's what I figured," Fred said. "That's why you're still driving that 20-year-old hog." He blew gray smoke against the window pane and then waved it away. "The lieutenant took me there when I got transferred to Burglary, my last afternoon. Amazing place—red plush on the walls, piano player, little bar with a German girl pouring champagne—this was Prohibition too. The madame was some Russian refugee, former countess. Very strict. No profanity, no drunks. Half an hour."

"You missing your lost youth, Fred?"

"Just wondering where it went."

I figured he meant the brothel. I started to dial. "They don't exactly advertise in the papers, do they?"

"Word of mouth," he said in a stage whisper and turned around and winked one big seal's eye.

I was still laughing when Anne Webber said, "Hello, hello."

"The Shell oil bill came today," she said after a few desultory remarks. "You asked me to let you know. There's nothing after the 19th"—the day he had disappeared—"but there are two charges on that day. One on the Shell station at Geary and Green. The other one from Stockton, a station on Interstate 5."

"Are you sure about the date?"

"It's in ink stamp on the upper left-hand side of the receipts," she said. Fred sat down in the straight chair opposite the desk. "Is it important?"

I read her the telephone number from Connie Larkin and asked if she knew it.

"No. I've never seen it. That's a different area code, isn't it?"

Fred pushed a notepad toward me and touched my sleeve. I read silently the name and address he had written under the number.

"Do you know an Estes Sullivan in Truro? That's the Sacramento Valley, not far from Stockton."

She thought a long minute. "No," she said finally. Her British accent sounded tinny over the telephone. I heard a glass bump against the mouthpiece. "Is that one of his—"

"I've got an idea I should drive out to the Valley, Mrs. Webber." And I asked her one or two questions as gently as I could. Fred walked over to the window and leaned against the sill with both hands while I talked. Thinking about the ancient cathouse. Thinking about the Hoffman kid. Thinking about what I was asking Mrs. Webber. The dirty old man, the wise old cop. I hung up and blew out a cheekful of air.

"You just got a ticket," Fred said from the window.

CHAPTER 7

THE SHELL SIGN FLASHED 97° AND THEN 5:15. THE green and white road sign said Truro, pop. 584, elevation 14'. I got out and a fat Chicano girl in maroon boxer shorts and a San Francisco Giants tee-shirt started to pump gas into the Mercedes. I walked across the glassy bright concrete and into the office, where a redwood tub sat in the middle of the floor filled with ice and cans of beer. I pulled the top off one of them without losing a finger and walked to the window. There's a Truro in Massachusetts, on Cape Cod. I had visited it one summer as a boy, when my grandfather had died and my grandmother had been understood to be lonely in her big, white clapboard house in the sand. Bradford's Mayflower pilgrims had marched through the high, sharp grass along that shore, across my grandmother's acre and a half of history, down Pamet Creek toward a freshwater pond; and before them copper-colored men had crept up through the shadowy scrub forest of Nausett to use the same water. I wondered what possible resemblance had inspired some nineteenth-century settler to think of the name again here in the Sacramento Valley.

The Sierra Nevada, maybe. I squinted at the gigantic shadows on the eastern horizon. Did they look like Atlantic waves when they were crested with snow? Only if you were homesick enough. Down here the ocean had long ago turned to burning dust. Across the flat valley floor to the west, the low coastal range of mountains looked like sharks' fins breaking a still surface.

The girl in the tee-shirt looked at my picture of George Webber and shook her head. She told me instead that Estes Sullivan lived eight miles out of town on County Road 23. By town she meant the half dozen grain elevators, the railroad spur, the two hardware stores, the Safeway shopping center, and Roy's Liquor and Gun Shop. I drove all the way through without getting lost and headed up 23.

"He's over to the delta," a woman in her 20s said when I rang the bell of the dilapidated farmhouse. The house was mid-Victorian, like most of the bigger ones in the Valley. The woman was not. She wore white tennis shorts and a red terry-cloth halter that was too flimsy and too loose to be a bra, and she was holding a tall glass of what could have been lemonade. Her face was small and brown and showed too many bones, like a bird's skull. I mopped my eyes with a handkerchief.

"Will he be back soon?"

"Oh hell no," she said, half-amused, her voice thick with Oklahoma or Texas. "He'll be out there until eight or nine o'clock. The tomato machines have gone over half the crop and now the Mexicans are cleaning up after them. He'll be working as long as they do." She eyed me brightly through the screen door and shifted the weight in the halter. "I'm his daughter-in-law."

"I wanted to ask him about someone who came here a few weeks ago."

She took the photograph I pried out of my notebook. "Tommy Shoults," she said promptly. "Are you from his firm?"

"He paid that bill," a high voice called from the next room. A woman, 65 or 70, with rinsed gray hair and wearing a faded sack dress waddled painfully through a door. Her ankles were swollen to the thickness of melons, and her pupils rolled up and almost out of sight as she spoke. "It's in the mail." She came closer and the young woman edged away, as if they were keeping territorial shells intact.

"He's asking about Mr. Shoults, mama." The older woman blinked uncomprehendingly. "The lawyer from San Francisco." Daughter-in-law turned back to me. "You didn't say if you were from his firm."

"Not exactly. I'm a private investigator working for them. Mr. Shoults has turned up missing, and I'm retracing his steps over the last few weeks."

She folded her arms carefully. Somewhere in the house a dog barked once. The heat drummed steadily on my temples. "I'll show you how to get to Estes," she said and with a glance at mama opened the screen door. We walked across the porch and down the steps to my car, which squatted in the shadow of a big Valley Oak, where the heat must have plummeted to 90 or 95, at the end of the driveway. Sweat trickled down her neck and shoulders and disappeared into the halter. She rubbed one red pouch casually.

"Where's old Tommy gone?" she asked as we stood beside the car. "Run away from the little wife?"

I leaned against the car window and took out a cigarette. "You sound as if you got to know him a bit, if you don't mind my saying so."

"I don't mind. Tommy likes a good time. He stayed over at the Best Western on Interstate 5. I get out some at nights in the summer. My old man is pretty tired after a day in the fields."

"I see."

"Flat tired. Tommy said he was here to check property lines and tax assessments for the company that owns this land. That's why he wanted to talk to Estes and drive around and all."

"That's right."

"Course his name wasn't Tommy Shoults, was it?

She licked a shred of lemon pulp from her lips. I studied my cigarette ash growing. "No, I guess it wasn't."

"George Webber. I like to go through people's things when I can. I don't know why. I just always have, from a little girl. It's like a secret. He took a shower and left his wallet on the table."

"Did you ask him why he was using another name?" She looked toward the porch, where the old woman had emerged and was staring at us with her wide, rolling eyes. "Did you tell your father-in-law?"

"Maybe if you're staying at the Best Western, we could have a drink and just talk about all that tonight." She took a step toward the house. "I usually go into the Corral Bar, about 10:30." She gestured north with her glass. "Estes is down that road to the end and turn toward the river." The road she had pointed toward disappeared into a quivering sheet of sunlight. There was no shadow higher than a tomato plant as far down it as I could see.

"He paid that bill," the old woman shouted from the porch. "He put it in the mail yesterday."

I drove for ten minutes before I came to the end of the roadway and could turn west toward the river. Everywhere, the sky seemed baked as hard and flat as the ground, streaked with metallic colors like the sides of an oven. Across the northern horizon three unevenly spaced columns of smoke mushroomed into the blistered air, as if the Valley had been silently bombed. Crop burnings. Everybody who drove through in the summer had seen them, gigantic pyres of leftover rice straw, tomato stalks, almond limbs, anything that wouldn't sell, cook, or decompose rapidly. I drove toward the column on the right, keeping the Mercedes' antiquated air conditioner whispering at nine. Once I passed a group of migrant workers, six or eight Mexican men and women in loose clothes and straw hats stooped over the broken plants, picking up scattered tomatoes and packing them in light wooden boxes. Minutes later a small plane whirred up from the end of a field like a bird started by hunters, flipped around and returned to spray twin jets of white smoke over the brown furrows. Otherwise the horizon was open in all directions. You could have driven north to Oregon or south to LA, hour after hour, without a curve or hill to interrupt you. I felt like a Lilliputian crawling through a bonfire.

The river she meant was a marshy irrigation canal that made its way west toward the Delta, and on, I supposed, to the Sacramento River, from there to the bay, and then to the empty Pacific. Water, water everywhere. I turned left into the full glare of the late afternoon sun and bounced blindly toward it.

Maybe a mile along the road, I stopped at a pyramid of metal drums stacked along the shoulder. Just behind it men moved in the fields, bleached shadows. One drum had been left nearly in the center of the road, its black stenciled label turned halfway toward me. Diazepam. That would be the pesticide, I told myself, feeling less citified every minute, and the brown cows give chocolate milk. I swung my front wheels left and squeezed past.

"Get off that goddam row, mister. You're crushing valuable plants!"

I backed the Mercedes a few feet, spun the wheels over a

rut, and turned off the motor. A big man in sweat-drenched ol-ive-drab workclothes walked toward me. He wore a wide-brim straw hat and a blue bandana around his neck. When I rolled down the window, he leaned in and stared, smelling of stale grass and kerosene. Fifty-five, sixty maybe. Who could tell? All the fat had been cooked off years ago, the flesh on his face hardened into stiff brown folds like a corrugated washboard.

"What the hell are you doing out here?"

The only people who keep the advantage by staying seated are monarchs and highway cops. I pushed the door open and got out. The heat beat up from the ground like the flames of hell.

"Are you Estes Sullivan?" I asked him. He was at least six-four and put together like a hickory cabinet. "Your daughter-in-law said I'd find you here."

"Did she tell you we're working our butts off out here too?" The same Oklahoma twang. There must be a tunnel or a pipe-line. What was it Hand had called the Valley? A cracker barrel? I showed him the license that the state of California had neatly typed and encased in clear plastic, and I explained that I had come on business. He took a long time reading the license.

"You're quite a ways from San Francisco," he said at last. "You must have got lost."

"It's not me that's lost, Mr. Sullivan." I handed him the photo. Behind him to the left another white man, younger than Sullivan, and two Chicanos started the motor on a gi-gantic, implausible contraption that I assumed was a tomato harvester. The sound shook the hot air in flapping waves, and I had to raise my voice to be heard. "I'm looking for Thomas Shoults, the lawyer who was out here a few weeks ago. He's disappeared and I've been hired to look for him."

"Is that so?" Sullivan twisted his neck and shouted at the Chicanos in Spanish and the motor softened its roar. The young white man left the machine and walked down a row of dusty plants toward us.

"He ain't here," Sullivan said. "He was, about a month ago. Spent the day and left."

"They should have told me, but they didn't. What exactly was he supposed to be doing?"

"He called up from the city and said he needed to check the lines." The younger man stepped over a short length of pipe and stopped beside Sullivan, who handed him the picture without speaking. Underneath the straw hats, their bony, long noses glistened in the sunlight, family noses passed from generation to generation like a baton from runner to runner. Their eyes were hidden by the shadow of the brims. I wiped sweat from mine.

"What kind of lines were those?"

The tomato harvester lurched off into the fields, straddling three rows of plants. Sullivan took a pack of Camels from his shirt pocket and shook out a cigarette.

"Property lines. The river shifts every once in a while over by Modesto, on account of the irrigation project. He wanted to see if our property lines had moved. Damn silly idea. You need a surveyor for that, like I told him. All he had were copies of the titles and maps from the courthouse."

"Did you just see him the one time, Mr. Sullivan?"

"Just the once."

"We got work to do, daddy." The younger man spat a gob of saliva into the ground between our feet. He had his father's height and several more inches across the torso. But his belly sagged with too many beer-and-chasers, and the menace of his shoulders curled out and flopped at the belt. One thick hand shoved the hat brim higher so that I looked into his face. The right eye was three-fourths closed in a permanent squint, as if ducking a long scar that started over his eyebrow and dug down toward the juncture of his ear and jawbone. The scar was recent, bright pink, and looked like the kind of split that runs across overripe fruit. Tomatoes, for example. I had seen faces I liked less and I tried to remember them.

"Did he call for the appointment, Mr. Sullivan, or a secretary?"

"Secretary."

The son put the photo in his shirt pocket and stooped to pick up the pipe from the ground. He tapped it against the palm of one hand in a slow rhythm.

"His office got the idea that he came back a second time, a kind of followup, maybe a week later."

"Just the once."

"You're sure you would have seen him?"

"He told you that," the son said. "Why don't you just move your ass off our property."

"I would of seen him," Sullivan said calmly. "He came the one day, drove around looking at fences and then went home."

"Your daughter-in-law says you don't own this place."

Junior kicked the open car door closed with a bang. A nearby bird squawked into the air.

"Now what's that got to do with your missing lawyer, friend?" Sullivan asked. He stuck the cigarette into a corner of his mouth and shoved his fists into the back pockets of his trousers. The Chicanos and their tomato machine were already half a mile into the hazy distance. I watched Junior edge closer, right hand tight around the pipe. There's a private eye handbook somewhere that says you get the best results when you push hard enough to be obnoxious. I had learned the same rule years ago when I had started out as a reporter, of course. What I seemed to have forgotten for a moment was the rule that tells you how to dodge a foot and a half of lead cinch irrigation pipe. Brain drain. It would probably come back to me.

Junior stepped in front of his father.

"He's better than you think, Bobby," Sullivan said. "He's professional. I don't want you to get hurt, boy."

"What the hell you doing talking to my wife?" Bobby said.

"She's friendly to strangers, Bobby."

The car window exploded into fragments as the pipe went through, but I was already two feet away and shuffling my feet in the dust like Muhammed Ali. Bobby pulled it back and turned to face me. The old man stood on the shoulder of the road and puffed at his Camel. Maybe everything takes place in slow motion, I thought, in so much heat. Bobby crept along the side of the car. I backed into the open space between the trunk and the pesticide drums. The sun in my eyes was painful and hot but Bobby wasn't thinking strategy. He raised the pipe level with his face, then swiped at the rear window of my poor wounded car, shattering it and filling the bright air with flying diamonds for a moment. I moved to my right. Bobby swung the pipe again and smashed the left taillight into blood-colored crystals. Sublimation, I figured. He really wanted to hit me.

"Stand still, you cocksucker."

Estes Sullivan came into view behind him. I felt my shoulders touch the scorching metal of a barrel and jumped forward with a gasp. Bobby swung the pipe high and hard, starting from behind his head, like a man trying to drive the last nail into a plank. Long before the arc turned down, I had bobbed and started to step inside, watching my fist and forearm traveling leftwards, remembering hot, dry fields like these, Texas variety, where at age 19 I had dodged the first punches ever thrown at me by an adult, a psychotic drill instructor from Atlanta who swung a lead-tipped billy club at us hour after hour, a demented glaze over his one brown, one blue eye. Fear is a fine teacher, superfine. I remembered his name as my hand knocked Bobby's wrist sideways. Alan Booth, T/Sgt. Ray Alan Booth. Maybe my mind had just skipped a dozen years, the way a radio signal will skip over half a continent, or maybe inner heat makes its own mirages. Ray Alan Booth's red Georgia-cracker face floated up as Bobby's pipe clanged harmlessly against a metal drum. I began a short, clean swing that rammed against the tender point of his jawbone just below the ear, and as the pipe dropped and he started to sag, I brought the left down and in, stretching my shoulder and digging deep into his gut. Bobby staggered backwards. The straw hat fell off, exposing a wide brow and thin, greasy hair that somebody had wasted time trying to style. His right arm dangled loosely away from his body, already numb from the impact of the pipe, but he wrenched up his face and launched a clumsy fist toward me anyway. I leaned my head back to let it pass, stepped inside again and hit him twice more in the belly, slow, deliberate punches that I put a lot of thought into. He started to hiss and deflate. I hit him once more under the ear and he went first to his knees, then to all fours.

The old man bent over Bobby. I turned to my car. There were five hours before my date at the Corral Bar and I decided I'd had enough of the sun.

CHAPTER 8

"WE COULD GO INTO BUSINESS AS A TEAM. DID YOU EVER think of that?" Dinah asked.

"Shrink and Vanish?"

"Maybe not." She wrinkled her nose in the way that always makes me want to jump over the table. "Sounds too much like a new detergent." She brought a plate of sandwiches over and sat down across from me. I picked up a salami and rye and poured the rest of a Dos Equis into the glass. Lunch had consisted of a glimpse of three McDonald's from the center of Interstate 80. It was three o'clock now, San Francisco time, and the cool gray fog was starting to cloud over the corner of sky I could see through Dinah's kitchen window. She went to the counter for more salad dressing.

"So what was she like?" Dinah asked with her back to me.

"Who?"

"The cute little housewife in the bandana bikini. The one you met last night in the Best Western tradition. Forgotten already?"

"*That* little housewife." I poured the dressing Dinah handed me onto my lettuce and pushed the tomato slices to one side. "She never showed up."

"No?"

"There may have been words at the Sullivan household."

"Um."

"Really. I sat around the Corral Bar until midnight, when they closed it up. Not a bandana in sight."

"And so you went cozily to bed to look at Johnny Carson. That doesn't sound like you, restless one." She walked behind me, leaned over my shoulder, and slurped some of my beer. I tried to jiggle my shoulders. "Stop that." She put down my glass and gave me a noisy kiss on the ear. "You went back to the farmhouse, didn't you?"

I settled for a shrug. "There was half a moon. I crept around on padded feet for a few hours, poking in the outbuildings. Webber had to have a reason for coming out, pretending to be a lawyer, looking at boundaries. Maybe I thought I'd see luminous fingerprints on the barn door, something, I don't know." I wadded up my purple paper napkin and tossed it on the plate. I hate explaining out loud what I'm doing badly, especially when Dinah puts on her analytic manner. She's always been partial to the idea that the first great detective was Freud. I like Oedipus for it myself.

"Did you see any?"

"No. I saw the Hound of the Valley instead, chained up by a big storage shed. And my pooch suppressants were in my trick belt back home. All I caught last night was the late show."

"Don't get your nose out of joint. What did you do all morning in that vacant little town? Pick another fight?" She abandoned my ear abruptly and wandered first to the counter and then over to the window. Her own evening had been spent at her brother's house across the bay in El Cerrito, where she likes to cast a nonprofessional eye over three nephews and a placid sister-in-law.

"This morning I asked around about the Sullivans," I told the back of her head, "and spent two hours in the County Records office bribing a nice grandmother named Alice who has carrot-colored hair and wears an apron to work."

"Maybe I'll cancel my subscription to *Ms*. What did you find out from all of this?"

"That the Sullivans are just what they look like—fairly poor tenant farmers, about medium efficient, who have been growing tomatoes there for ten years or so. The wife has been in and out of Vacaville Hospital for something, senility, I suppose. The old man goes to a local Chicano whorehouse once or twice a month, a mobile home called The Cherry Tree, believe it or not, highly recommended. I'm told they give green stamps. The boy doesn't get around much that way."

Dinah snorted from the window and bent her head to see something in the street. Her apartment faces south onto Union Street, one of the busier parts of town for pick-ups, muggings, drug sales, other urban niceties.

"Of course not. Bandana bod would murder him," she said.

"Yeah." I took out the one cigarette I had promised myself before I had to go. "But he has other amusements. A real bully, not nearly as popular as his old man. Lots of Saturday-night punchups, a little drag-racing. And a couple of years ago he was arrested for dumping pesticide from his cropduster onto a neighboring almond orchard. Killed all the bees apparently. People still talk about it in Truro."

"Somehow I don't see a San Francisco reporter going all the way to the Great Central Valley to investigate dead bees."

Whatever was happening on the street was over. She turned and folded her arms and looked at me. I got up and walked over to her, leaving the cigarette burning merrily away on the edge of the plate. Dinah is short, much shorter than I am, and plump, much plumper than I am, so I lifted her up until she sat on the window sill and I kissed the spot between her eyebrows where the light just catches a few delicate red hairs. She rubbed her face against my chest.

"I have to drive out to Hillsborough this afternoon," I said. She said something muffled that sounded like "Godzilla" and tightened her grip around my shoulders. "Mrs. Edison Browning has summoned me. The answering service calls."

"I had hoped you might not be busy." She slid off the window sill quite slowly, and I began to be busy.

"She wants to talk about George Webber," I said after a moment, and disengaged her hands. "And indirectly she's footing the bill."

"See if she gives green stamps," Dinah said and dodged away. I retrieved my cigarette and walked down her long dark hallway to the door.

"You never told me what you found out from the grandmother in aprons," Dinah said as I kissed her on the nose and started to turn the doorknob. "Were you trying to check property lines too?"

"Not really. I wanted to know who the Sullivans rent their farm from, who the real owner is."

"And did you find out?"

I nodded. "Frank Brazil."

Mrs. Browning was sitting beside the pool drinking tea. As I approached, she turned her head slowly toward me, like an old turtle in the sunlight, and gestured with her free hand to a chair.

"Millie will bring you tea," she announced, and made a

dry, snapping sound with her fingers. Millie's stout black legs disappeared around the corner of the house in a hurry. "Cream and sugar are already here," she said, dipping her cup in the direction of the table, "and wafers and bread and butter."

"Nobody could call me a fussy man," I said, "but I do like a bit of butter to my bread."

She sighted down her nose at me.

"Nursery rhyme," I said. "A joke."

She sat studying me while Millie deposited expensive, delicate porcelain gear in front of me. I studied her right back.

The whole effect was as carefree and Californian as opening night at the Met. She was dressed in a light brown, full-length dress with sleeves to the elbows. No long white gloves, but her wrists were weighted down by jangling bracelets decorated with gold and jade figures. Her gray hair had been twisted like a rubber band into a severe bun at the back fastened by a long black comb. Her skin was thickly matted with powder and rouge, but no amount of that could conceal the forest of wrinkles that criss-crossed her face in every direction. Her skin had not looked that way five years ago, according to the photo on Webber's wall. Maybe it had changed abruptly, the way a sick pine will turn yellow overnight.

"Carlton Hand told me that the newspaper had hired you to find George Webber."

Her voice was a monotonous, strained whisper. It reminded me of a gambler I knew in Daly City with the same kind of hoarseness, in his case caused by drinking a can of Sterno one afternoon outside Golden Gate Fields. I didn't think Mrs. Browning was behind in her vigorish. Twenty-two million was Herb Caen's estimate in his annual state of the city feature, and that probably didn't include her version of the little green toolbox. A laryngectomy for throat cancer would have had the same effect, and she was wearing a wide black ribbon around her neck that covered most of her skin. A clue.

"Actually, Mrs. Webber hired me," I said. "Not the paper."

"Don't be sentimental," she hissed. "It's my money. I pay his salary."

I spooned sugar unsentimentally into my cup and tasted. The pool looked peaceful in the late afternoon haze, a long blue-green rectangle bordered by heavy vases of ferns. I half expected to see a trout jump.

"Read this," she whispered after a moment. "It's from Julius Rawson. I expect you remember him."

She handed me a letter, electrically typed on creamy white stationery, from her Peninsula neighbor, popular pediatrician, and former client of mine. I glanced at it and nodded.

"He says he hired you to find his daughter and you did and then refused to tell him where she was."

I nodded again, a habit Mrs. Browning probably inspired. The Rawson girl, age 17, had run away from home last year, leaving a fake kidnap note and taking about $10,000 worth of jewelry and a sad little collection of stuffed animals that she was much too old to worry about. I never did figure out how she learned to fence the jewelry. Television, probably. Recess, maybe. I had found her in Hartford, Connecticut, three months pregnant, living fairly cheerfully with an older man, coping. I had also found that popular Doctor Rawson was given to fits of beating her and had twice managed to seduce her while Mrs. Rawson was drying out downstate. The girl had had an abortion three days before she ran away. She thought it was her father's. I had returned Rawson's fee, but not his daughter.

"He says that you made him appear outrageous to the police and that he is still seriously considering a lawsuit. Is all that correct?"

I took a fair-sized swallow while she talked. It was good tea. Some people can apparently distinguish countries and blends of tea, like oenologists with wine. I tried to think of a parallel word for tea experts, something to do with camellias if I remembered any Latin. George Webber would know; it might make a good column.

"That's roughly correct, Mrs. Browning, leaving out some of the high spots."

"Julius Rawson is a fool. I'm not surprised you had trouble. But I'm not a fool, Mr. Haller. I run three businesses. I sit on the boards of a dozen charities. I watch details and I know people. I've been doing this since my husband died 20 years ago." She took back the letter and dropped it on the table. "But there are two things I will not have from my employees. I will not have unauthorized publicity—as there was with that silly runaway girl—and I will not permit violence of any kind. Do you understand these points?"

There was something reptilian about her, the fierce hiss, the wrinkles, the rhythmic wagging of her head as she spoke. I slurped tea without answering.

"The district attorney of San Francisco tells me that your last case involved a double killing."

"I was there, Mrs. Browning, but the police did the shooting."

She jerked her head as if I had given a trick answer. "He told me that. But he also told me you have precipitated violence on more than one occasion."

She glowered at me across the table, pinching her face like Eddy Street Susan's about to do battle, although I didn't think she'd appreciate the comparison. "My son was killed in Vietnam, Mr. Haller, scouting a friendly village. The War Department gave me a medal to keep in his room and a coffin they told me not to open. My daughter was killed in a street incident, a nasty little race riot in Detroit where she was visiting. A mean, pointless, cruel death from a gun the police never found, shot by someone they never caught. She was there attending a conference on retarded children." I began a sentence, but she ran over it with her hoarse whisper, repeating a speech I imagined she had made often before. "I have suffered a great deal from senseless violence. I am not pitying myself, like some stupid Niobe, and I am not apologizing to you. I simply will not permit anyone in my pay to extend that kind of suffering. This country is insane enough to hand over firearms to every black, brown, and yellow child that can reach the counter. I belong to an older school. My newspaper and my television station are crusaders against this wicked permissive violence. It is repugnant to me to hire anyone at all who traffics in it, much less someone like you who I am told actually relishes it."

It was a long speech, especially for her voice. She seemed unaware of that. Her strong personality blasted anger across the table like a beam, a pent-up anger that made the folds on her old wrinkled skin tremble. I started to say something else, but she hadn't finished. "Carlton Hand said I would probably not like your manners. I don't."

She stood up abruptly. I did the same thing more slowly, balancing the expensive cup and saucer with one hand. Money wouldn't bring back her son or daughter or close down Grab's fights or even improve my manners. But she'd lived too long with a sense of its power to know that any more.

"My son-in-law will show you out."

As if on cue, a thin man in his late 30s had come out of the house, carrying an old-fashioned glass filled with something that wasn't tea. Mrs. Browning moved ponderously toward him, like an extinct beast, leaving me standing beside the pool and meditating on my manners. The son-in-law gave her a peck on the cheek, which she brushed away; he looked unhappily at me. I caught the murmured word "Mother"; then she vanished into the house and he slouched in my direction.

"Frederic Kingsley," he said when he got close enough. He put his glass down as he spoke, managing that way to avoid shaking my hand. "Mother has another appointment. Finish your tea if you like."

I put the cup down. "I'm finished, thanks."

Kingsley was staring through the glass table top at his shoes. He was largely bald, except for a few long wisps of yellow-brown hair combed straight across his head. He had gold octagonal glasses, a rubbery, boneless face coated with perspiration, and a peculiar way of looking both greasy and tweedy at the same time.

"I'll show you to your car."

"You work at the paper, don't you?" I asked. "I saw your name on the directory."

"Um, sort of general consultant. This way . . ." We started across the patio, diagonally toward the upper end of the house. "I've worked there since my wife died." He glanced at the house. "I expect you heard about that."

"I heard."

"Remarkable woman." He straightened himself to a kind of attention as he spoke. "Mother is a remarkable woman. This business upsets her very much." He gradually resumed his slouch. Orange mosquito lights went on around the pool. I thought we were going to enter the house, but he made a sudden turn, I followed, and in less than a minute we had walked around a pool shed and reached the graveled driveway in front. Servants' exit. My wounded Mercedes cowered under a hackberry tree, away from the line of bigger, newer cars by the main door.

"A remarkable woman," Kingsley said again. "She really has

a mission, the power and the mission." He turned his moist, neurotic eyes on me. "I tried to talk Carlton Hand out of this, I'll be frank. George Webber has undoubtedly gone off with a tramp; you must know the kind of man he is by now. Carlton is merely humoring his wife." Kingsley's voice was racing a little, and I was falling one or two pronouns behind. But he suddenly touched the sleeve of my jacket and altered his voice, making it sound weirdly like Mrs. Browning's whisper. "You must *not* involve her reputation." Then he regained his normal tone. "Her instructions are that you should report to me or Hand at least every other day. And we are very strict on expenses."

He shot out his hand and fumbled with mine. It was like shaking hands with a Kleenex. Then he was gone.

I got in the Mercedes and sat for a moment, watching the cirrus clouds blow in from the coast, 30 miles away. Precipitating violence, no doubt, Fred would like the phrase. It sounded like pompous cops' lingo, like a weather report. Like a reign of terror.

I started the car.

Two hours later, I was back in my office and reading for the 50th time George Webber's clipping about Martin Fells. I reached across the remains of a chicken taco and pulled the beer bottle closer to help my concentration. As far as I could tell, there was no other clipping in Webber's files, anywhere, from *The Chronicle of Higher Education;* there was no story on Professor Martin Fells of Berkeley in Webber's own file of his columns; there was no explanation on the clipping itself, except for the ballpoint scribble of five numbers: 5-0452. I got up from my chair in disgust and walked over to open the window. There weren't any more enraged or mutilated cats either. My shoulders jumped involuntarily as I remembered their harrowed faces, and I squeezed my hand hard across the back of my neck to loosen the memory. Webber had been snooping in the Sacramento Valley, not in the Berkeley hills. Nobody knew better than I did how newspapermen squirreled scraps of paper from every conceivable source. I told myself I was much more interested in Sullivan and Brazil.

I had just sat down again when the door jumped open with an ear-rattling bang.

"I keep forgetting to have the knocker fixed," I said.

Frank Brazil came into the room, followed by a square, heavyset man about 44 or 45, the same as a handgun caliber. The heavyset man wore a new tan loden coat, the kind with long wooden pegs instead of buttons, so I had to guess how much of the torso underneath was muscle and how much was fat. He planted himself on my floor, five or six inches shorter than I am, shoulders no wider than the front of a truck, and rolled his neck once to the left, like a boxer. I didn't guess a lot of fat. Brazil was a slighter figure about the same height, with a pale face the shape of a shovel and a look hard enough to crack glass. He wore a black, double-breasted overcoat with a brushed fur collar and a silver scarf, a rep tie that meant he had gone to Oxford or Cambridge or J. Press, and a dark business suit. His hair was combed straight back from his forehead and carried about half a pound of precious oils. He smiled a little, raising his lip just enough to show a sliver of teeth like a razor blade, and rapped one gloved hand against the open door.

"Apologies," he said, still smiling. "We thought maybe the building had been condemned."

They walked closer to the desk. The heavyset man kicked the door shut behind him without looking. The impact sounded like a gunshot. Two or three paperbacks toppled over in the shelf by the radiator.

"You've moved up in the world, Haller," Brazil said. "Central heating, a rug on the floor, a view of the bottom of the bridge." He pulled his left-hand glove off slowly, one finger at a time. "All it needs is a little roach powder."

"Now I know."

"Now you know." He looked at the filing cabinet in the corner. "Locked?" I nodded. "I might want to see if you've started a file on me, Haller."

"It's a locked cabinet, Frank."

"Kenny," He jerked his head at the other man, who walked around the corner of my desk and inspected the cabinet. I inspected Brazil. He looked more prosperous every year, much more prosperous than he had seven years ago when I had first seen him. Then he had been a lieutenant in the California Highway Patrol, pulling down about $16,000 a year and supervising patrol cars in the East Bay counties. He had resigned from the patrol, accused of "unnecessary brutality"—a legal phrase that Mrs. Browning would love—in the arrest and subsequent deaths of two black teenagers who had been pulled in for drunken driving on the Nimitz Freeway. It didn't help the blacks much that they had sideswiped a car and killed a middle-aged white tool salesman on his way to Hayward. But the trial had been a long, embittering business—the same one George Webber had covered for the Oakland *Tribune*—and afterward, with the help of some former colleagues, Brazil had started a new career. Bridgestone Security. Uniformed guards for all purposes, plainclothes, guards, alarm systems, electronic surveillance—anything at all to keep property secure. Like a lot of the security business, it wasn't over-honest. Twice during the past year, people working for Brazil, ex-cops mostly, had been accused of "popping," a very effective scam for big cities. In the classic form, a businessman, a shopkeeper, anybody with an office or something portable and valuable gets a phone call with a free offer—let us inspect your premises for security risks. Free of charge, a free written report, a discount on our services if you decide to hire them. All we want is your business. Strictly low-key. The pop was the free burglary that often followed a month or so after the customer had taken Brazil's people around the office, pointing out what was valuable and where it was kept.

Brazil had also started a Domestic Security Division, which patrolled private homes, arranged divorce evidence, tail jobs, and felony assaults. I didn't know if you could buy a hit man from Bridgestone, but everybody knew that you could buy harassment. Especially you could buy harassment to keep your neighborhood whatever color you wanted. It was a popular service in the East Bay, where blacks, whites and Chicanos lived jammed together in a melting pot that seemed always ready to boil. Brazil handled the opposite of block-busting for the white sections of Oakland and Contra Costa. He specialized in hardball demographics, the art of driving out unwelcome new buyers the fastest way possible, with paint on the walls, bricks in the windows, phone calls in the evening, baseball bats on the kneecap. The company motto was "To Have and to Hold."

He had made a lot of money at it. He had also become fairly prominent, in a grim kind of way, and lately he had taken to politics, making speeches on crime, permissiveness, and social disorder, speeches a little to the left of Attila the Hun but very effective in their way, and hugely applauded. Nobody thought he was ever going to be governor, but nobody denied that, last winter, he had delivered a hell of a lot of East Bay votes and campaign contributions.

The heavyset man pulled a small rat-tail file out of his jacket pocket and started to poke it into the filing cabinet lock.

"Key's going to be a lot easier," he said. "There's four drawers."

"Very good, Frankie," I said. "I didn't even see your lips move."

Kenny turned his face toward me. "What'd he say?"

"Give him the key, Haller."

"I called you a dummy, Kenny." His features were jammed together in a narrow space, leaving wide lanes of cheekbone and chin with a deserted look. The cheeks and nose reddened now, and the black pupils of his eyes dilated.

"You got a lot of mouth, Haller. Give him the key."

"I left it in my pajama pocket, Frankie. Why don't you use the one you wind Kenny up with?"

Kenny leaned over and gripped the side of the desk hard enough to leave pressure marks in the wood. I'd have to check it if I ever got the chance. His nose was three inches from mine; his breath was sour; his shoulders blocked the overhead light. "You want to cooperate with Mr. Brazil or you want to get folded in half?"

"Kenny," Brazil said.

"He's irritating me," Kenny said. "He's making me impatient."

"That's what he wants to do, Kenny. Use the file."

"Use the key, Kenny," I said. "It's in the drawer. Just promise not to breathe on me any more."

Kenny looked down. His eyes were gummy from this angle. I pulled the top drawer out. He stuck his right hand in it. I slammed the drawer as hard as I could and stood up at the same instant, bringing my right forearm down across his neck. His head bounced off the desk top and he rolled backwards onto the floor. One of the wooden pegs from his jacket ripped free and flew into the filing cabinet with a bright, pinging sound, like the snap of cartilage.

Brazil stood in the same place holding his gloves. I stepped around him, bent down, and took a .38 Smith and Wesson automatic from Kenny's hip pocket. He made a low noise and a bubble of saliva popped on his mouth.

"I hope you didn't concuss him," Brazil said in a level voice.

"I'd worry more about a bowling ball." I opened the pistol chamber and saw the rich glow of copper casing on the first bullet and left the safety on. Kenny made some more groaning noises.

"Did somebody give you a call from Truro, Frankie?"

"You make friends wherever you go, Haller."

"How come George Webber went out to look over your farm in the Valley?"

"Never heard of him."

"You make me very curious, Frankie. George Webber wrote a few unflattering stories about you, maybe six or seven years ago, before you became a constitutional expert. Now he goes down to look over your farm practices and he disappears."

"You're working for the *Constitution*, Haller. I could care less about some nickel reporter taking a walk. I don't want any stories in that shitrag about tenant farmers, absentee landlords, ecology, none of that. I pick my own publicity. You stick to peeping in motel windows and leave my organization out of your plans."

"You going to turn Kenny loose on me if I don't?"

"There's more and better than Kenny. You know that."

"Yeah. I know that." I had met some of them seven years ago when I had briefly represented the black kids' parents and tried to accumulate a little information about Brazil's arrest habits. Brazil had stood and watched, slicing his smile from time to time, while three of his boys had drummed a nightstick over my ribs. Then one of them had got out an electric cattle prod. "Do they still wear uniforms?"

"Either way," Brazil said. He kicked Kenny's shoulder, and Kenny got slowly to his knees, shaking his head. Brazil walked over and opened the door. Kenny got all the way up and looked around for me, blinking. I tossed him the peg from his sleeve and he fumbled and caught it. Brazil started to the elevator. Kenny hesitated, then turned and followed him with slow, short steps.

One way or another, this week or next, Brazil would be back. I looked down and saw that I had moved the safety of the pistol open.

CHAPTER 9

HE WAS IN," SHOULTS'S SECRETARY TOLD ME, "FOR ABOUT AN hour, real early. Then he went out just before nine."

She gave me a pleasant toothy smile and kept one finger tucked inside a Harold Robbins paperback by her typewriter. The other finger pointed to a page in a big loose-leaf log book, the kind in which lawyers record their work by the quarter hour for billing purposes. Her taste obviously ran to fiction.

"Did he tell you when he would be back?"

"No, sorry."

"Did he say where he was going?"

The smile dropped a few degrees. "I can tell him you called, if you like." She reached for a pad of paper.

"Would you like to see me do a one-arm pushup?" I asked. "What?"

"Never mind. It works for some of the guys." I gave her a card. "Mr. Shoults hired me to help out with Mr. Webber. I need to talk to him pretty quickly. Can you tell me where he's likely to be now or later today?"

She read the card with elaborate care several times, and I

began to wonder if I'd given her the one with disappearing ink. Then she stuck it under a corner of the desk blotter. "He didn't say he'd be away in the afternoon." A little hesitation. "There's a number I can use if it's really important. But he doesn't like me to." Her hand stole to the back of her neck and pushed a blonde curl higher.

"Private business, I suppose?"

"No." She blushed, but only a little. Secretaries and doctors are among the least shockable of human observers.

I pointed to an open space in the log book. "Will you put me down for half an hour at 1:00?"

The smile came back a little way. "Can you really do a one-arm pushup?"

"Nobody can. That's pure fiction."

But she let me use her telephone and then watched me leave the office, resting a big yellow pencil against her smile in an attitude of appraisal. I smiled back. Give or take 20 pounds, ten years, and the color of her hair and eyes, she reminded me a lot of Dinah.

I got off the Bay Bridge before ten and turned north on 1-80 toward Berkeley, losing sight for a few minutes of the big Spanish campanile that dominates the campus, then catching it again as I took the overpass and exited on University Avenue. The avenue itself crept through a couple of miles of broken-down hotels, bars with names like the Varsity, and the usual assortment of army surplus and occult bookstores you associate with higher learning, until it debouched at the bottom of the campanile.

I left the car in a parking lot on Telegraph Avenue—the rump parliament of hippiedom—and struggled past some sidewalk booths that seemed to be selling leather belts and por-nographic Easter eggs. Then, recalling that a detective travels on his stomach, I stopped for ten minutes at a dark, crowded shop that had "Expresso and Pastry" soaped on the window.

The coffee was good, the pastry tasted like shirtboard. I nibbled at its corners and admired the students.

Most of them wore the uniform of the California young—Levi's, sport shirt, running shoes—and they made me remember with sudden amusement my own college uniform from years ago: tweed jacket, dark tie, penny loafers, and crewcut. Pipe optional. Another era to these kids obviously, and about as imaginable as the Ice Age. Another era to me as well. It had been my father's college, his choice, an Ivy League school long on tradition and brutally short on informality, it seemed to me then, terminally pompous. When I weathered the first two semesters successfully enough, much to everybody's surprise, my pleased father had rewarded me with a summer on my own in Europe. There I promptly fell in love with a soprano in a third-rate Parisian opera company, lingered with her till well past the start of the new school year, and became almost by default an original '60s dropout. The singer, however, had led me through an education not to be found in Ivy League catalogues, and despite my father's letters and telegrams, I had pursued her happily up and down France for almost a year until she finally abandoned her American puppy for a minor shipping magnate from Toulon. By then I was accustomed to my freedom and scornful of college. I landed a full-time job with UPI in Paris and settled in to become a professional expatriate. Without Lyndon Johnson's draft, I might be there still.

I slurped the creamy top off the coffee and thought about Mitzi Charpentier and long summer evenings in Paris, about my father growing leaner and more angular every year in his lonely house in Brookline. Two of the kids got up from the next table and slouched toward the door, scruffy and cool. They had the curious ambivalent sexuality you see in California teenagers, beautiful warm flowers that just may turn out to be poisonous. Or possibly they were only AM-FM, as a funny writer named Peter DeVries says. I tried to picture myself at 19, shook my head. It had never been quite clear whether I had wanted to make the break from my father's New England iron or whether I was simply a born drifter and slider, an uncommitted soul. Drifter and slider, no doubt. Which is what makes me such a good Californian.

This morning, however, I knew where I was going. I left change on the table and walked up Telegraph to Sather Gate, famous once for tear gas and riots. Beyond it, next to a chromium-and-glass student union building, was a big plastic map for tourists. And beyond the plastic map, downhill over the tall, dignified redwoods and cypresses of the main campus, you could see the bay shining and Mount Tamalpais far to the north. There was a yellow line of smog just above that, smudged across the horizon like a bug on a windshield. I left the map alone with the view and followed a sloping pathway through a grove of trees with a dry streambed in the middle. On the other side of the grove squatted the massive modern bulk of the biochemistry building.

Dr. Fells was on the third floor. I walked up a wide staircase and down his hallway, peeking in the open doors of classrooms and labs as I went. A few students hurried by with knapsacks and bookbags, but for the most part, the building was oddly quiet. Fluorescent lights and air conditioners hummed together tonelessly. My heels made loud clicks on the hard linoleum floor.

The card outside his office said Martin Fells, Ph.D., Professor of Biochemistry. Summer Biochem. 128. Tu 11-1. That was all. Farther down the hall on the other side, a man in a suit leaned on crutches and watched me as he turned a ring of keys. I knocked and somebody said come in.

Fells was a short, thick man with a ferret's face, badly raked with acne, and reddish hair that ran in curling lines straight back from his forehead. Henry Kissinger 30 pounds lighter, grimmer looking. He was wearing a white lab jacket over a sports shirt and slacks and sitting at a gray metal desk littered with boxes of computer printouts and stacks of mimeographed forms. A number of chemical manuals stretched across one wall of bookshelves; there was a poster of Bobby Fischer hunched over a chess board on another wall; under it were a small laboratory tray with a filter coffee maker, hot plate, and a portable cassette recorder, which was playing chamber music quietly to itself. One window looked across a bleak courtyard to a line of other windows. The back of the office consisted of half wall paneling and half window, with a wooden veneer door at one end. Through the glass I could see a chemical laboratory that measured maybe 60 or 70 feet long, crammed with tables, microscopes, retorts, vials, coils, just like the set of a Bela Lugosi movie. In the far corner, next to a wire mesh animal cage, two young men with beards and ponytails were huddled around something on a table. Eye of newt and toe of frog, no doubt.

"Michael Haller, Doctor Fells. I telephoned you earlier this morning."

He frowned quickly, clamping his lips down hard over bad, yellowish teeth. "I must say you are persistent, Mr. Haller. I told you that I teach today, in 20 minutes' time in fact, and I really haven't time to discuss anything, even the disappearance of your friend."

"I know, Doctor, and I apologize. But there is some urgency about the matter. George Webber is not a friend. I'm a private detective hired by his wife to look for him."

He tapped a gold ballpoint pen against one of the boxes of printouts. "This is absurd. What can I say, Mr. Haller? I don't know this man, I have never spoken with him, I am at a loss to see how I can be of help. I told you that on the telephone."

"He may actually be in some danger, Doctor. I handed him my photograph of Webber and the clipping. He put down the pen and pulled out bifocals from behind some papers.

"The picture's familiar," he said after a moment.

"He writes a column for the *Constitution*. The picture runs at the top."

"Yes, the word man. I look at that sometimes." His voice had a clipped precision that I liked, a strong baritone with the slightest traces of a foreign accent. "This newspaper story," he said, picking it up, "is several years old. I've been at Berkeley for three years."

"You didn't send it to him?"

"Certainly not."

"Would some publicity office here have sent out such a clipping, as a routine procedure?"

"I doubt it. The public affairs office makes up its own press releases. I'm afraid I can't give you any more time, Mr. Haller." He leveled one finger at a wall clock that said 10:45.

"The clipping was in his working folder marked 'Current,' Doctor. Do you recognize the number written across the top—probably written by him?"

"That looks like a Berkeley extension," he said. "But it's obviously not mine." He stood up and hitched his trousers.

"All right. That helps, Doctor—do you happen to know whose number it is?"

"You're the detective, Mr. Haller, not I." He walked over and switched off the recorder. "I suggest you dial it and see who answers. Good day." He went through the door into the lab, and the two young men came toward him, carrying a bulky notebook.

I closed the door softly and stood in the hallway lighting a cigarette. The air was a little warmer there. The man on crutches was carrying a pitcher full of water and making his way painfully toward his office. He looked at me curiously as he passed.

"Met our star, did you?"

"All too briefly."

He chuckled and shifted the pitcher to his other hand. "Marty only teaches one day a week in the summer, like the rest of us. You picked the wrong day to sell him pharmaceuticals, that's all."

"That's not actually my line, Professor."

"Yes?" His eyes went a little brighter. "I sort of figured that, to tell the truth. We don't see many salesmen up here without sample cases. And with a build like Reggie Jackson."

"What makes Fells a star?"

"You really don't know who he is?" His face looked more pleased. "Have a cup of coffee and I'll tell you. I'm just killing time. I don't teach until Friday."

I took the pitcher and we went into his office together. The sign by the door said John B. Foreman, Associate Professor of Biochemistry, and gave his office hours and phone number. The typist had misspelled biochemistry.

There are people like Foreman everywhere, usually behind the raised curtain that drops when you stare at the window, usually older and frailer people but always curious, prying, faintly unhappy, displaced spirits in a busier world. I hadn't done very well with Fells. I had an urge to drift with his colleague for a minute.

"I do not like thee, Doctor Fells," he said as he hobbled into his office. I closed the door and he sat down heavily. A Chemex pot was on a hot plate. He wedged the crutches into a corner by the desk and swiveled to start measuring coffee. I put the pot with the water on the hot plate and plugged it in.

"Black all right?" he said.

"Fine."

"I hate paper cups," he said, handing me one, "but they're easier."

"What's that line you just said about Doctor Fells?"

"I do not like thee, Doctor Fells? That's an old student rhyme, originally about Doctor Fell of Cambridge. The reason why I cannot tell, But I do not like thee, Doctor Fell. You a NIMH type?"

He pronounced it "Nim-uh," and it could have been bio-chemistry or astrology as far as I knew.

"I never heard of it," I said.

The water rushed to a boil, and Foreman poured it care-fully into the filter paper, then after a minute poured coffee into the cup I held. I took a sip while he filled his own cup. The coffee was harsh and strong, and I made a face.

"You want me to smooth that out for you with a little Cremora?" he asked.

"I'm afraid you'd need a file to smooth it out for me. It's OK. What's NIMH?"

"I thought you weren't." He rocked around in his chair, bright and chirping as a bird, hopping from conversational limb to limb.

There were many more books in his office than in Fells's, some of them paperback novels stuck in alongside scientific texts. He had a poster of Janis Joplin, not Bobby Fischer, on the back of his door, and just to the left of his window another one of a blonde woman serving a tennis ball and wearing no shorts. There was no door or window to a lab, and the office itself was tiny and cluttered compared with Fells's. I deduced that Associate was considerably below Professor on the totem pole.

"National Institute of Mental Health," he said over his coffee cup. "That's where Fells came from a few years ago, and he gets visitations from them all the time. Bureaucrats."

"What's a biochemist got to do with mental health, Professor?"

"John." He smiled. "Good question. Old Marty is an expert in transmitter substances for neurons, brain cells, and they have an immediate effect on how our brains work and what we do—mental health. He also studies the links between certain transmitter substances and certain behavior patterns—mental health. He just might be the world's leading authority on two little chemicals in our heads called serotonin and norepinephrine." Foreman sipped coffee noisily. "Excuse the lecture," he said. "Teachers think everybody comes to hear them talk."

"What do these chemicals do?"

He cocked an eyebrow and smiled. "It's a little technical."

"Just smooth it out for me, John."

"Do you know what metabolites are?"

"No."

"OK. They're breakdown products from the normal metabolic processes of the brain. All of them are made from the protein in food, even Cremora. Now there are three very interesting metabolites that we find chiefly in the most primitive part of the brain, the limbic system, right in there." He tapped a finger against the back of his skull. "That's where we think the brain exercises control over its strongest physical impulses, like sex, appetite, territorial drives, aggression."

"Aggression?"

"Especially aggression. The three little metabolites at work there are called serotonin, norepinephrine, like I said, and one other called dopamine. What Marty apparently discovered is that people with the most aggressive behavior histories have very low levels of serotonin and very high levels of norepinephrine and dopamine. He did a lot of studies and got to the point of actually predicting violent behavior patterns on the basis of lab readouts." Foreman grinned. "Women have naturally high levels of serotonin, incidentally, which is what makes them so much less aggressive than men."

"Is that what you tell your female students?"

The grin spread. "Are you kidding? They'd tear me apart, limb from limb."

I put down my coffee and shook out a cigarette for Foreman, another for myself. He lit them with the same clumsy motions I had noticed before, as if his hands were heavy objects to be carried about. I wondered how he could function in a lab full of delicate instruments like the one across the hall.

"So why isn't Dr. Fells still back with the government?"

He made a face. "I don't know. He isn't that good, frankly. Or I don't think so anyway. You could get an argument. But there's a lot of uncertainty about his work. It's mostly conclusions drawn from animals and selected case histories that the Navy or somebody would send over to him in Washington. He wasn't really working with normal people, you know, your average neurotic. And anyway his funding ran out."

"And Berkeley just offered him a big job and all the dogs and cats he needed?"

"Monkeys, actually. Berkeley has the biggest collection of monkeys in the country."

"Yeah, I noticed that, coming in through Sather Gate."

He laughed and refilled his cup. I shook my head and sucked at the cigarette.

"If you're not from the government," he began.

I interrupted. "Why wouldn't the government fund him? I mean, it sounds like the kind of thing that would have all kinds of military implications—aggression, violence, territorial drives?"

"That's a common mistake," Foreman said. "There's absolutely no practical application. If there were, every terrorist group from the Pentagon to the Persian Gulf would be shoveling dollars into Fells's lab. Sure, you can imagine—just pump your soldiers full of dopamine and turn them into fighting monsters, absolutely fearless warriors, do anything, go anywhere, never stop. Christ, the World Boxing Association alone would support a lab, the NFL would bankroll all of Berkeley. But that's just science fiction. Drugs don't work like that. The same dose of the same thing will affect people in radically different ways. One guy can drink two beers and pass out, another can drink a case and go out and fly a jet plane. The truth is that nobody knows how a neuron transmits an electrical charge to another neuron, and that's the heart of the problem. All we know is that it happens and that the quantities of chemicals involved are unbelievably small—micro-microscopic. And like I say, the effects of a change in substance level will vary with body weight, physical condition, temperature, sex, a hundred things. The only thing we know for sure about nerve cells is how they stop working: you just cut off transmission of electrical charges." He gestured at his crutches. "That's what happened when I broke my back. Snapped the points of contact in all my spinal nerve cells, no more synapses—that's where two nerve cells meet. We can break them but we can't fix them. The only drug control that really works is poison."

I looked at my watch. "This is my card, John."

He read it and smacked his lips unpleasantly. "Some guys' wives never quit," he said. "I had no idea old Margie was so bitter."

"Not a divorce case, I'm afraid. I'm looking for a husband who's disappeared. Have you ever seen this man around here?"

"That's George Webber." He handed the picture back to

me. He's the writer for the *Constitution*." Foreman tilted his chair back and wrapped his arms around his torso, shoving one hand under each armpit. His thin face looked thinner.

"You know him?"

He shook his head firmly.

"Ever seen him around here?"

"With Fells, you mean?"

"Fells or anybody."

Headshake again. For a talkative kid professor, Foreman was suddenly acting like a mouth with a broken synapse. It might have been the effect of the dose of the oily coffee, but I didn't have time to see.

"I've got to be back in the city by one," I told him. "Thanks for the coffee and the talk. Maybe I'll stop by for another lecture sometime."

"Anytime but Friday," he said, and watched me carefully from the desk as I closed the door.

Shoults fired me 40 minutes later.

CHAPTER 10

WOULD YOU PAY THE SON-OF-A-BITCH $3,000,000?"
The wino was sitting on the far end of the bench, deep in a shadow, away from the chilly sunshine. The other one was sitting on the concrete beside him, legs stretched straight in front, face obscured by the brown paper bag he held up. I stepped around the legs and went into the phone booth. The paper bag came down and he shook his gray face hard.

"He's pitched his fucking arm out already," the first one said.

I closed the door of the booth and looked at traffic. The city had built this little piazza three years ago, to keep up the Mediterranean flavor of downtown, not thinking much about who would use it after the tourists had got properly mugged and warned off a few times. From the phone booth, I looked straight over the wino's legs and down Montgomery Street, a glass canyon of banks and offices. Wall Street West. The business center of California. Even the bums talked high finance.

I punched in a dime and dialed. Ten rings and no answer. I hung up. We've decided not to meet the expenses of such a search any longer, Shoults had said, looking down at a blank sheet of paper the whole time. We're convinced his disappearance was voluntary, he'd said. You're entitled to keep your retainer and fees to date, of course. Am I fired? I was just checking. We've just decided not to go on with this, Shoults read from the blank paper. And Mrs. Webber agrees? My last shot. There's no problem there, he assured me.

He was wearing the same gray suit, same button-down shirt, same solid manner. I noticed that the tie had yellow stripes today. Just send your report along with the bill.

Mrs. Webber wasn't home. I dialed my office and got Fred.

"Hoffman called again," he told me.

"What'd you say?"

"I took us off. The kid's not in the East Bay, Mike, be realistic. I told Hoffman the cops could do just as well now, for nothing."

"We should have waited, Fred."

"Bullcon. I just spent $200 of your money this morning over in Berkeley with the identity person for a big round zero. That was the last shot. You're not in this for charity, Mike. You got bills to pay. Me, for instance. A 62-year-old ex-cop eats a lot."

I heard the snap of a lighter over the telephone. "Who the hell is the identity person in Berkeley?"

"You know, Rita what's her face. You met her once. They used to call her the papermate, but she decided that's sexist. She put together the kit for that runaway Betty Jo Rule's after, driver's license, birth certificate, car registration. She even threw in a Sear's charge card, which is harder to get than all the rest put together, believe me."

"I remember her. What's she got?"

"Never heard of the kid. For $200. Never even sold him a stamp. For $200. He's gone, Mike. He's in Denver, or Nepal, or Burbank, or somewhere. You know how people take off, in this state particularly. Remember all those guys Juan Corona is supposed to have wasted up in the Valley. Nobody ever noticed them coming or going. Nobody ever missed them. Nobody saw Lenny Hoffman's kid either. Not in California."

"OK, OK. Just close up and leave the file out. I'll do the bill."

"I'm going to the ball game," he said. "Blue's pitching."

Beyond the phone booth in the shadow of a big redwood planter, another wino was propped up against a wall, knees bent and hands folded across them, tears running down his face.

"There's some dried blood on the side of your desk, Mike."

"I'll call you," I said and hung up.

A Muni bus rolled by, spraying the air with bluish hydro-carbons, like Bobby Sullivan's airplane. The Webber phone rang, rang itself off the wall for all I knew. The wino lifted his eyes in my direction. I left a quarter in the coin-return slot and started to walk to the *Constitution*.

"You can't," she bleated. "You just can't. He's getting his makeup on and he said *no* visitors."

"Watch it, Clyde." A burly black man with a shaved head wrestled a television camera through the reception door and pointed it toward me.

"This isn't my best side, you know."

"Save the jokes for the politicians, Clyde. Hold the door for me, sweetheart."

Carlton Hand's secretary came around the desk, fixed me with a reproachful look, and opened the door to Hand's of-fice. The cameraman wheeled the camera by me. Another man, wearing a blue knit cock cap and a pink tee-shirt that said "Hold These" came in the door and put two small kleig lights down with a thump.

"Hold these," he said and went out again.

"You can't see him," she told me.

I went around the camera and entered Hand's office. He was sitting in a straightbacked chair by the window with a blue-and-white-striped barber's apron around his neck. A small man in Levi's and sportshirt was straddling a reversed chair in front of him, leaning forward and patting Hand's face in brisk, pecking motions with a pad of orange gauze. Jars and mirrors and tubes of various sizes glittered in an open suitcase at his feet. A thin woman about 35 or 40 stood behind him frowning. She wore a sunbonnet and a white dress and carried a clipboard. Behind the varnished oak desk, another man was uncoiling wires attached to a pair of microphones. The makeup man put down the pad of gauze, and the woman handed him a painter's brush.

"Welcome to showbiz, Mike," Hand said.

"Please don't talk," the makeup man said. "Just hold your lips tight, compressed, like this." He dabbed the brush, smearing dark red.

"You going to have a minute after this, Carl? I'd like to talk."

"Please." The makeup man took another brush from the woman behind him without looking. The apron rose and fell in a shrug. The cameraman bumped me aside and moved the camera in front of the desk. I joined the group at the window studying Hand. "Rouge, Dianne." She handed him a jar.

"You favor the pointillist approach?" I asked. Hand chuckled. The woman gave me another dirty look for my collection.

"Just smack your lips a couple of times." Hand smacked his lips and winked at me and the woman. "Get the flake on his tooth, Dianne," the makeup man said and stood up. He stepped over the open suitcase and left the room, while Dianne bent forward and touched Hand's tooth delicately with a Kleenex, making her mouth into a big *O,* as if his face were a mirror. She went behind him and started to untie the barber's apron. I sat down on the chair.

"Webber's lawyer just fired me."

"You got another copy of this, Carl?" A man poked his head into the doorway.

"On the desk, Bernie." Hand rubbed his neck as the apron slid off. "Jeeze, Mike, I don't know what to tell you."

"You knew about it, Carl?"

"Oh, hell. Look—"

"You want to hold your head still, Mr. Hand?" Dianne had a steel comb almost a foot long and was smoothing down a reddish-brown cowlick.

"Did you OK it, Carl? Because if you did, there's something I think you ought to know about that trip to the Central Valley."

Hand's secretary materialized beside me and gave him a red mug full of coffee.

"No coffee," Dianne said from behind his head. "Not with the makeup already on."

"I think you're making a mistake, Carl."

"Mrs. Browning's on the phone." Hand turned to look at Bernie, who had reappeared in the doorway. Then he turned back to me. "They're doing a TV interview of me," he said.

"No kidding."

"For the six tonight. About the police series. The mayor is just shitting bricks, the son-of-a-bitch. We're going to hoist the vice squad by its own fucking petard."

"They'll love it. When can we talk?"

"Look, Mike, it's out of my hands. I can't do a thing for you, not a goddam thing."

"He was onto Frank Brazil."

From the doorway again: "Mrs. Browning's waiting, Carl."

"I'll talk with you later, Mike. I'll call you. I gotta do this, I gotta do that, the owner's on the phone." He spread his big hands wide in a classic gesture of supplication. The little chair groaned under his bulk and the cowlick jumped up again.

"Break a leg, Carl."

CHAPTER 11

A PAIR OF RED TIGHTS LAY HUDDLED IN THE GUTTER, NEXT TO the drain. I looked down at it curiously.

"Every stone has its story in the city," Dinah said.

We walked up the hill toward her apartment building. A blonde woman in her early 20s came jogging downhill, followed by a German shepherd wearing the cheerful, interested look of a tourist stepping out of a bus. We squeezed against the wall to let them pass, and the woman smiled and wiggled her fingers at me as she went by.

"Runner's hi," I said, taking the key Dinah held out and letting us in. "Have I mentioned that I love women athletes like that, keeping in shape, not going to the dogs?"

"You just like to think they're heaving and panting at the sight of you, tiger," Dinah said with her usual instinct for the jugular. And goosed me through the door.

Dinah is one of those rare psychiatrists who remains interested in medicine. She remains interested in everything, in fact. I took a bottle of the Cayumas Cabernet that she keeps in the closet—an ex-patient sends a case every fall—and sat down at the table while she worked in front of the stove. Conventional, liberated us. At the pop of the cork, she turned around, saw me watching her, wiggled her fanny, and winked.

"Let it breathe for 30 seconds," she said, turning back to the stove. "After that, it's just oxidation, same as rusting."

I poured wine for both of us and tasted mine. Rusty.

We had met in the morgue, of all places in the world, each of us on business, each of us coming out of the bone-bright, antiseptically cold room in the basement on Grove Street at a dead trot. I would probably have spoken to her anyway, because we had to stand together for five minutes in front of the elevator, because you tend to be talkative in a place like that, because I thought she had the most wonderful face I had ever seen. But she had spoken first, asking with concern if I was all right. "Your face was so grim and sad," she told me later, "like a little boy looking for his mommy." I had actually been looking for a fellow named Weatherall, missing for two weeks and thought by his wife to be suicidal. He turned up later in Phoenix with a peroxide waitress and $6,000 in stolen bonds. Dinah, on the other hand, there to identify the body of a patient who had disappeared weeks before, was the one who should have looked grim and sad. But then her feelings aren't for general consumption.

At that moment, she whooped something obscene from behind a cabinet door, and I watched the lines of muscle tighten in her short legs as she stretched to push tumbling cans and boxes back into place. A long way from Mitzi Charpentier in Paris, I thought, admiring. A long way from any of the women I had known in Europe or later in LA. Kiss the girls and make them cry. I sipped more wine. She had been married at 21 and, in her decisive way, divorced at 22. I had never been married at all, though once or twice I had been close enough to be scared.

"Ah, the woe that is in marriage," I quoted, standing up like a gracious male pig and helping her bring the steaks to the table.

"Cut the sweet talk," she said with one finger in her mouth, "and tell me about your medical morning."

So during dinner in her kitchenette, I described my morning in Berkeley and, in particular Foreman's lecture on drugs and behavior. She had never heard of him but one of Fells's papers was a classic, according to her required reading for medical students in neurology and psychiatry. On limbic neurotransmitter substances. I had missed it in *Reader's Digest,* of course.

"You know, what's ironic," she said, putting down her steak knife and picking up a glass of wine, "what's really funny is that dopamine used to be sold around Haight-Ashbury as an aphrodisiac. And now he's linked it to aggressive behavior instead of to sex."

"Some people never figure out the difference, Doc."

"Eat your steak."

"Is it an aphrodisiac?"

"No. And neither is dopamine. They were using it to treat Parkinson's disease at UC Medical Center, and it worked so well that some patients were able to resume their normal sex lives. But that was the result of just getting better, not of stimulating them. Rumors from some silly interns, that was all there was to it."

I leaned back and looked over her red hair at the gallery of pictures she had hung on the far wall. Dinah likes to buy from local artists—woodcuts, prints, small drawings—not avant-garde but complicated, serious work. There was a new ink drawing in the place of honor now a dark tangle of lines that began as a still-life of fruit, a bowl, a napkin and ended in one corner as a whirlpool of ink. Dinah said the artist had spent hours arranging the objects, shifting them, looking, rearranging before she had ever picked up a pen. I didn't really understand the drawing. I did understand the waiting, arranging, rearranging. There's a lot of artist in us detectives.

"Can a drug in fact make a person aggressive? I mean, wildly aggressive?" I asked.

"I don't know about drugs," she said, "but something else can. She got up from the table and walked across the dining nook to the living room, where another wall was covered with a white wooden bookshelf full of books and records She turned on a floor lamp, studied a shelf, then reached up and took down a thin black book, and came back to the table. "Where the bookmark is," she said.

I opened the book, *Mechanics of the Mind,* by Colin Blakemore. Dinah put a finger at the top of the page, on the word "process." I read:

> process yields an animal that is formidably ferocious . . . I finally had to decree that no one ever examine such a monkey alone, for . . . they attack to kill, and they single out the examiner's neck as their initial objective. The aggressive behavior comes in waves and is accompanied by salivation . . . baring of the teeth, and a kind of guttural vocalization that one seldom hears in a normal monkey.

"What was the process?" I asked, closing the book.

"Electrodes planted in the hypothalamus and the limbic system. A man at Yale once stopped a charging bull by pressing a switch connected to electrodes in the bull's brain. It was a demonstration for students. The bull was charging straight at him in the ring—they made a film of it—and the electrodes stopped him cold in his tracks. He just wandered off to look for grass or something, like Ferdinand."

"Must have disappointed a lot of students."

She picked up the little porcelain jug with the floral pattern she always uses and poured black coffee into two demitasses without comment. I pulled out a cigarette and lit it, then she took a puff and handed it back.

"I wish you'd switch to dope," she said.

"The name makes me uncomfortable," I said. "How could an electric switch stop a charging bull?"

"The brain is just one giant seething mass of electrical charges, humming away in your head. Each healthy cell passes a message to another cell with an electrical impulse, and the brain's cells are all connected to muscle cells that move your muscles. That's why they take electro-encephalograms after strokes—it's like reading a meter. And that's why smart folks wait until their alpha waves are predominant before they go solving mysteries."

"So our governor knows what he's talking about with his buzz words."

"He does indeed. And if you interrupt a circuit and change the message, you change the action. The electrical system was telling the bull to run, the electrodes flipped the impulse to a new circuit, and the system told the bull to go find food. They can interrupt a few specific circuits like that in primitive brains like animals'. It's as simple as turning off a light.

"I looked at those pictures from Webber's desk you left me," she went on after tasting her coffee. "Horrible things, but they're probably from some standard neuroanatomy textbook—the printing is cut off, so I can't tell which one. The cats are under anesthesia, having electrodes implanted in the cerebellum. Your friend could have gotten those pictures anywhere. In medical school, we had three cats like that in different cages in the anatomy lab. They all had parts of their brains altered surgically. One cat was normal, except that if you picked her up and dropped her, she wouldn't land on her feet, which is of course the god-given right of all cats. If you held her upside down and let go, she simply landed flat on her back. Her balance lobes had been severed."

"What about the other two?"

"One had been turned into a vegetable, absolutely no life, energy, cat-ness. Simply lay there, didn't even purr. The other one was like that monkey, only not quite so bad. It had been fixed so that the central area of the hypothalamus was constantly irritated, by an implanted magnesium tablet, I think. If you came near it, the poor thing went crazy wild, arching its back, spitting, screaming, clawing, completely insane. The only good thing was that it died after a few months—it just couldn't stand the strain of such constant aggressiveness."

"But they can't turn human brains on and off like that."

"Oh, they can do a few things, with severe epilepsy, for instance. But the important thing is that nobody really understands how the human brain works. We don't even understand something as basic as how the eye sends messages along the visual nerve path to the cortex. Look, you've seen pictures of pirates with their big gold earrings in their ears?" I nodded of course. "The pirates had a reason for wearing them. They claimed the earrings improved their vision, which helped them spot ships at sea. Now about a year ago, an acupuncture specialist showed that it probably *did* improve their eyesight. They usually pierced the earlobe just at the juncture of a branch of the optic nerve and a motor nerve along the skull, and an acupuncture needle there actually helps some myopic people. But the point isn't that all of a sudden we're all going to be wearing bifocal earrings. The point is that nobody knows *why* pressure there will help you see better, when pressure on another part of the brain will drive you crazy or wipe out your memory. As far as the brain goes, we're all in the dark. Except your friend Professor Fells." She gulped coffee and looked at her watch. "It's eight. I've got to be back at the hospital for the residents' seminar. Mendelsohn bugged out again. She says she'll scream if she hears one more session on mothers and daughters."

"What do women want?"

"Why are you so curious about brain waves, Haller? You're off the Webber hunt. You should let it drop."

"I didn't like Fells," I said, holding her coat. We turned the locks and went out into the chilly night air.

"And Foreman? You like Foreman?"

"I understand him. Mainly, I keep wondering what George Webber was doing with that clipping."

"Mainly, you're pissed at your newspaper friend for letting you get fired."

I sighed and kissed her on the nose. "I understand him too," I said. "Or I used to."

She put one finger gently against my cheek. "Probably you should get married," she said, "to stop the buzzing."

"Probably I should see a psychiatrist."

"Here." She pulled a ticket off the wiper of her car and handed it to me. I dropped it into the basket of a parked bicycle.

"I guess I was pressing too hard for some connection. I didn't like Fells and I thought Webber had been after some scandal with his drug research instead of the usual publicity gag. Black-market dopamine, maybe, I don't know. Foreman put the squelch on that anyway, of course." Dinah climbed in the car and rolled down the window. "He says it's harmless as mother's milk. There's no dose of anything that will work on everybody's buzz the same way."

"I don't want to argue with a Berkeley professor," she said, starting the engine and letting out the clutch, "but did you ever hear of aspirin?"

It took an hour and a half to walk the five blocks back to my apartment, largely because I went down Union Street. Perry's and all the other singles bars were just starting to heat up, taking in their nightly delivery of combustible account executives, sales executives, dental executives, florists, and pushers. Sucking the suburbs dry of the young and not-so-young, the single and the not-so-single. Union Street is a meat market too, like the Tenderloin, but not a butcher market. It runs to credit cards, styled hair, brand names on the handbags. And it may be the last island of heterosexuality in the city. All of the men stalking the bright sidewalks had caps on their teeth and shellac on their scalps, but nobody, as Fred liked to say, was light in his loafers.

I stopped for a minute and stared through a window, wondering what Grab would make of the fashion show inside, not to mention the wrestling matches. Then I went a few doors down to Modesto's, an actual digitless bar, which has been overlooked so far by the Chamber of Commerce and the Health Department, a bar with scars on the furniture and many of the patrons, with middle-aged waitresses in Dura-strength bras, bartenders sporting ear-length hair, ancient black writing gouged into the wooden booths, real sawdust on the floor. Perry's has sawdust too, but they ship it down from Marin County in sanitized plastic sacks. Modesto's seems to come with the gin.

It's an Irish place, of course. Named for a town in the San Joaquin Valley where the owner used to live, a pocket of Irish left stranded there when the great railroad-building days were over. I had two Irish whiskeys and a cup of coffee, thought bad thoughts, and watched the guy next to me drinking depth charges. From time to time, we both glanced up at the color photo of John Kennedy over the cash register or wiped our paper napkins along the slick wood of the bar. He was dropping his third jigger of rye into a stein of beer when I left and walked uphill to Green Street.

Ten minutes later the doorbell rang.

I turned off the record I had just started to play and went to the door. Carlton Hand boomed through, waving a bottle of red wine in each fist and flashing a grin into every corner of the room.

"I came to talk! Where's a fucking corkscrew?"

It took longer to talk than you might have guessed. The corkscrew was no problem, and there were even clean glasses, but Hand had to turn on the television first for the 10:00 news, to catch his interview again. Hand to mouth. I sat back against the couch and, after glancing at the set, watched the clouds of fog blowing in from the Pacific outside my window, big billows of gray and white tumbling slowly over and over, as if a giant breath were sending them toward us in puffs. Carl leaned forward on the couch and watched the six-inch figures of himself and two reporters talking gravely in his office about political corruption. Police corruption, in fact, the vice squad, the moral rot of which all this was the symptom, the need for integrity and competence in government, and a vision. The wind seemed to be blowing harder.

"Not too bad," Carl said, getting up and switching off the set. His grin was a little lopsided as he refilled our glasses. "Not too goddam bad."

"French wine is wasted on me, Carl."

"Don't be a shit, Mike," he said pleasantly.

"Where's Anne Webber? She hasn't answered the phone all day."

He took a long pull at the wine. "She's at Mrs. Browning's house," he said finally. "They didn't want you bugging her."

"Mrs. Browning all the way, right, Carl? Mrs. Browning and the boy consultant." He shrugged and finished his glass. I poured again for both of us. "Mrs. Browning didn't like my manners, so I figure she called Shoults or maybe called you to call Shoults. The backbone's connected to the jawbone."

"You're the detective, Mike."

"You couldn't stop her, Carl, talk her out of it? You don't want your star columnist found?"

"Webber's shacked up somewhere screwing his buns off, you know that's what I think. Anyway you got Kingsley nervous somehow—you must have talked too loud—and believe it or not he's the guy with the lady's ear. Kingsley called Shoults, Shoults called me, and Shoults called you."

I looked at him sprawled across the couch, his rumpled Harris tweed coat bright against the black leather couch, his belly folding over his belt, his big moon face flushed and friendly. Not fat, really, just big, just built along the lines of a steamer trunk in a seersucker suit. What the hell. It wasn't the first time a messenger boy wanted to be mayor. Or governor. Carl never thought small. And it costs money to package a vision.

"Tell me about that son-of-a-bitch Brazil," he said.

I told him. I pulled the cork out of the second bottle and told him about the Sullivans of Truro, Brazil's visit, Fells, Foreman, neurotransmitters. He listened and drank.

"Brazil really came around to see you?" he asked when I was through. "With a guy?"

I nodded. He shook his head. I got up and went to the record player while he poured the rest of the wine in his glass.

"What's that?"

"Luciano Pavarotti," I said. "Maybe the greatest singer

in the world." Pavarotti began the great entrance aria from *I Puritani,* the one that sends most tenors to their knees begging for breath.

"Is he fixed?" Carl asked. I stared. "Fixed, for Christ's sake, you know?" He wriggled his fingers in the direction of his crotch.

"Believe it or not, they stopped doing that in the eighteenth century, Carl. He's intact." I leaned against the stereo cabinet and looked at the next mayor and thought of the naive kid from Maryland by way of Inchon, remembered him grinding out those shrewd, brilliant stories and asking us questions like that—did anybody know what the Louvre was, was Milton a first or last name? We thought it was hilarious, until the first Pulitzer nomination came along.

"San Francisco," he muttered. "Half the fucking city is fixed. You got anything to drink? Bourbon?"

I went into the kitchen and made him a tall bourbon and me a brandy and came back to find him standing by my bookshelves, pulling out books, glancing at the covers and shoving them rapidly back into place like a library appraiser in a hurry. He took the bourbon and raised it high for a toast. I sat down in the chair by the window to be near the fog.

"Mike, we're talking."

"Carl, we are."

"How long has it been since we were talking to each other, Mike?" He took a noisy swallow. "Was it before or after I slugged you in the newsroom?"

"Before, I think."

"Yeah." He finished looking at books and started inspecting records. "Hell of a thing to fight about. Why'd you leave?"

I sipped my brandy. In the morning, my brain was going to feel like a raisin. "I wanted to write," I said.

Carl spluttered bourbon and waved his glass in the direction of my old Olympia. "What the fuck did you think you were doing? You had two stories a day, six days a week, 20-30 column inches—you weren't exactly digging goddam ditches."

"You wrote features, Carl, human-interest stuff, exposés. I wrote news stories, straight off the city desk, and any bozo can run a two-car freeway collision or a bank robbery through the format with half his brain shot out. You know that. Besides, I was younger then. I wanted to express myself."

"Christ." He came around the chair and sat down heavily in it, making die joints squeak a little. "You could have done something else. A column like Webber's." He thumped the coffee table with stiff fingers. "You're a lot like him, you know? Educated, kind of a wise guy. You could have done a column like the guy at the *Times* now, Jack Smith on the arts."

"I'm more like you, Carl."

He finished his bourbon and took off his glasses. Then he massaged the bridge of his nose, looked around the room with those careful, vivid blue eyes, and put the glasses back on. I found a crushed pack of cigarettes under some magazines on the table. Pall Malls that somebody had forgotten weeks ago. I lit one and pulled smoke down into my lungs, feeling it kick like a boot.

"Yeah," he said finally. "You want Brazil."

"And Webber."

"You're off Webber. Mrs. Browning wants you off Webber."

"There's going to be a connection, Carl. He went out to the Valley and drove around Brazil's farm pretending to be a lawyer—"

"Yeah, yeah, you don't have to draw a picture. On the other hand, if Webber is holed up in the Mustang Ranch like I say, then maybe Brazil is just reacting sensibly to you poking around. I took down the file on that Oakland business tonight, the thing with the black kids. You went after Brazil fairly hard."

"If I find Webber, I find out."

"I was surprised, you know, because most private eyes got politics that would make Genghis Khan nervous. I mean, talk about your law-and-order crowd." He leaned back suddenly in the chair and puffed air out of his cheeks like a beached whale. "Christ," he said. "Another couple of bottles and I'll be drunk. You got any more bourbon?"

I took the glass, maybe a little bit unsteadily, and went out into the kitchen. When I came back with two full hands he was up at the bookshelves again, restless and curious as a three-year-old.

"French," he said, waving a book I couldn't see. "I know ten words of whorehouse Korean and that's it, but I'll tell you something that's not in any of this, not straight out." He took the glass I held out and sagged into the chair. He worked his chin and jaw muscles loosely back and forth, silently, and then leaned forward. "What does he want? *What does he want?* You know how I started out on every one of those stories I did down in LA? You know how I got inside and got the story when the rest of you jokers were still scratching your nuts and reading your press card? You know what I ask myself every time somebody comes through the office door at the paper? What does he want? Sometimes, when I'm really sharp, I remember to say, *why* does he want it? There's not exactly an unlimited range of answers either way. But it's the only question that always works."

"You're asking that about Frank Brazil right now?"

"Hell, no. Frank Brazil wants to stick it to every spade and Chicano and Jap in California. The man's a freaking sadist with country-club connections and a mouth full of sugar. I know exactly what Frank Brazil wants. He's as simple as a bent poker to figure out. I'm asking what do you want?"

"Why not leave it at Frank Brazil?"

He poked a finger at me through the air, more and more energetic, the way some drinkers get. "That's just on the top. I look at you, I see a guy who goes out, takes unreal chances, gets punched at, shot at, slammed around by some punk D.A. in San Mateo on phony possession charges—yeah, I read about that. Hell, I printed it. That's why I called that dumb shylock Shoults—I think you were taking a fall for somebody else, by the way—and I don't figure any of it. I come here, I talk to you half the fucking night, I sniff around your crummy apartment like a cocker spaniel with a leaky kidney, I still don't get it. I don't see why you do it."

"There's a picture of J. Edgar Hoover around here somewhere."

"Jokes," he said in disgust. "If you had one, it'd be in the john. I take a few chances too, but I get paid $88,000 a year and nobody pushes me across some tomato patch." He looked around the room and pointed his glass accusingly toward the kitchen. "You're not even married."

"Maybe I should just go talk to Ed Barmby at the *Chronicle,* Carl."

He sighed and sat back. The cartridge made a soft popping noise and the turntable switched itself off. The little red power light blinked and slowly faded. There was something going wrong with the amplifier, and the whole thing would have to come out any day now, major surgery on a stereo.

"They'd love it too," Carl said. "They'd love it and they'd screw it up."

"Probably."

"They'd turn it into a hooker series as usual. 'Earthquake Levels City; Hookers' Prices Soar.'"

"Probably."

He rubbed the empty bourbon glass back and forth between his big palms. "What do you need?" he asked after a pause.

"I need to talk to Mrs. Webber again."

"She's going home tomorrow. Her and the daughters."

"I need my regular payment."

"Be goddam sure you got something hard on Brazil," he said, still watching the light on the stereo. "I'm not printing anything that doesn't hold tighter than a mosquito's ass, you understand."

"Sure. There's a lot of votes in the East Bay. I understand."

He made a choppy gesture of impatience and stood up. I got to get back to the paper. Bridget's picking me up at midnight after some recital." Bridget was Hand's wife, a delicate, small-boned Italian girl rarely seen in the old LA days, something of a famous hostess in San Francisco now. Nobody had ever figured out how she got named Bridget. "Send your bills to me direct. I'll run them through the plant-security budget. But keep them down and no goddam restaurant expenses. Mrs. Browning checks everything and anything when the mood hits her, and I don't want to do any explaining about you being unfired." He walked over to the door and we looked at each other for a minute, two men stumbling toward middle age together who had never quite trusted and never quite disliked each other.

"Thanks for the drinks," he said.

"Is she bankrolling your campaign for mayor or governor or whatever it is you want, Carl? The bottomless pit of breakfast food?"

He looked solemn for a moment, then flashed the grin again and I found myself smiling back. "I just want to fucking express myself," he said.

After he had gone, I sat back in my chair and watched the closed door for several minutes. Then I shifted slightly in order to see the dark bay through the window. What did I want? It was nice to puzzle somebody else for a change. The brandy tasted warm and alive in my throat. I wanted to give my inner violence an outward form, I should have told Hand. I wanted to find somebody and set him free. I wanted to marry Dinah and run away from her to Europe again. I wanted to be 19 and the grandson of Philip Marlowe.

The last of the brandy went down. On the end table, I could see the crumpled letter from my father, written as usual on the anniversary of my mother's death. "Dear Sonny," was just visible in the shadow. "It has been raining . . . "

I wanted another drink.

CHAPTER 12

DOCTOR CARTER IS A NEUROSURGEON," DINAH SAID AND winked at me. "Maybe he can treat a hangover."

Doctor Carter was at that moment cracking open a Dungeness crab with big, beefy hands that looked as if they'd just gone ten rounds with Ernie Shavers. I suppose I thought surgeons were all about 45, with wavy gray hair, leonine heads, matching Porsches, and fingers like Peter Duchin. Carter was on the wrong side of 60, short and dumpy, a round-faced little grandfather with bad teeth and drinker's veins tattooed across his nose and cheeks. Santa Claus in herringbone.

"Lack of oxygen," he announced. He had a large, hearty voice, like an Airedale, that made me squeeze my eyes shut for a moment. "Nothing in the world to do but drink lots of water."

"I told him that you had run into Professor Fells at Berkeley," Dinah said.

"How is the son-of-a-bitch?" Carter asked. "I've tried to call him a couple of times the last two days, but he's never in. You Californians don't stay still."

"You know him well?"

"I spent some time at the NIMH a few years ago." Carter leaned back to let the waitress deposit a huge plate of clams and scallops. "You people ought to have to live in Cleveland a little while, learn to suffer through real life." He gestured with a clam shell toward the window of the restaurant. "If it weren't for conferences like this one at your hospital, little lady, I'd probably die of boredom. The Cuyahoga never looked like that."

We all followed his shell and looked admiringly at the Golden Gate and at the huge white wall of midday fog rolling toward it from the Pacific. "You know the Cuyahoga River is so polluted it caught on fire once? Just after I had moved to Cleveland. Damndest sight you ever saw, a bunch of fire trucks trying to hose down a river."

"Fells and I didn't really have much of a chat, Doctor Carter."

"Evan. Call me Evan. Evan-rude, that's what the nurses call me." He sighed and peeled another clam. "Same old Marty, sounds like. Kind of a solemn joe, didn't you think?"

"Grave," I agreed, wondering if that was all right to say to surgeons.

"Evan and Professor Fells are rivals in a way, aren't you, Evan?" Dinah was picking delicately at a slightly overdone trout. Behind her, the fog had swallowed the bridge now and seemed to be turning in our direction, hunting.

"Fundamental difference of approach," Carter was saying. He wiped his thick fingers on his tie, leaving snail-like trails. "Neurosurgeons didn't think chemicals are the way to study the brain. Biochemists do, of course, poor suckers."

"Why is that, Evan?"

"Blood-brain barrier," he mumbled. "Most people don't know about the blood-brain barrier. You see, for reasons we don't understand, the brain doesn't absorb chemicals very well from the blood vessels that ran through it, the way other organs like the lungs and so forth do. Brain really takes only oxygen out of the blood. That's why you've got a hangover—alcohol mops up all the oxygen in sight. But if you've got a real problem, say a lesion in the cerebral cortex"—he pointed a clam at the top of Dinah's red head; she went on eating—"streptomycin's not going to do a damn bit of good, or oromycin, or any of those. Brain won't absorb more than a millionth of the drug that flows through it. You'd have to pump antibiotics in for days, constantly, just to get a little smidgen of it into the neurons. Meanwhile, of course, you'd have wiped out all the antibodies in your whole system and dropped dead of pneumonia or something else. Penicillin gets through fairly well, but a lot of people are allergic to it, and there's only one other antibiotic that has a chance. That's Chloromycetin, but it's a drug of choice only in meningitis when the patient is allergic to penicillin. Damn strong drug anyway. Until somebody breaks the blood-brain barrier, it's more reliable to stick with surgery." He paused to extract a piece of shell from his mouth. "Now why do you think some of us don't think we should even *try* to break it down?"

He leaned toward me like a kindly high school teacher, posing the last question before recess. I tried to please him.

"I'd say, if the brain doesn't want to absorb foreign chemicals, it must have a good reason."

"Bravo!" Carter turned to Dinah and beamed. "That's a smart young fellow you have there, Dinah girl. Not one medical student in a hundred goes right to the center like that. *Of course* the brain doesn't want foreign chemicals. They might be toxic, for one thing, and the brain needs to protect itself from poison. But mainly, the brain is a very complicated, very refined set of sequences of chemical reactions—and more chemicals just gum up the works. You don't jam a flashlight battery in a computer. I've had every bit as good success as Marty Fells in treating aggressive behavior with surgery."

I leaned forward, an obscure excitement stirring. Carter poured the last of the white wine in his glass and looked complacently around the room. "What do you do for aggression, Evan?"

"Operation called an amygdalectomy, removal of part of the limbic system. Very effective in some cases."

"Is that like a lobotomy?"

"Well, no. A lobotomy is a surgical procedure, a kind of waving of the knife through a hole in the skull to sever the prefrontal lobes. You don't take anything out. And it's kind of a funny operation. Supposed to leave the patient all calm and tranquil like a zombie." He chuckled. "Of course, there was the famous case where the lobotomized patient stabbed his surgeon two weeks later. Probably served him right. I'm talking about actual removal of brain tissue," he said cheerfully. "Amygdala, a little piece of brain in the limbic system shaped like an almond. A lot of aggressive impulses seem to start there—take it out and you pacify the patient almost instantly. Now a lot of your civil-rights agitators get unhappy with us for that and see some kind of plot. But we usually work on convicts and so on, people in some kind of institution, and of course we have to get their written permission before we operate, even if they're dangerously violent A lot of red tape. A few years ago, though, a chap in Detroit named Ervin proposed mass amygdalectomies for ghetto leaders after some riots, and that started a lot of fuss. Mostly died down now. Of course, the amygdala doesn't just control aggression. Seems to regulate hunger, too. I had one patient, young girl, with damage to it from a boating accident—got whacked with a boom in the temple—developed an uncontrollable appetite. Hyperplagia. Used to push other people aside at meals and shovel in food with both hands. Aggressive hunger, I guess." Carter's resemblance to Santa Claus had grown a little chilling in the last few moments. He drained the wine from his glass and belched softly. Evan-rude. According to Dinah he was famous for his temper tantrums after an operation. During an operation, Dinah said, he was supposed to be among the five or six best in the country.

"Civil-rights fellows thought we were embarked on mass brain-control surgery, which is ridiculous, naturally. There's only a couple of hundred surgeons in the country who know enough to do a good job on this kind of operation. You can only do a couple of operations a day, if that. What kind of threat? You don't see us dragging people in off the streets to cut open their skulls." He found one last clam in the refuse of his plate and cracked it, smiling slightly as if at the thought of white-gowned surgeons racing in and out of hospitals frantically, snatching victims from gas lines, offices, coffee breaks, like demented angels.

"Who supports this work, Evan? It doesn't sound like a typical hospital program."

"Oh, different groups. Your Human Relations Agency out here in Sacramento used to send us some cases—they run the prison system, you know. Wonderful name for it. And some government agencies—military, NIMH. Various foundations pony up, too. There's a police chiefs association out in the Midwest that underwrites some of our psychosurgical work. Law-enforcement groups in general are interested. And a few years ago, we were getting a lot of money from the big outfit in Oakland—Bridgestone Security. They came up with a hundred thousand one year. But not much lately, just a trickle. I've actually been thinking—you young people have got me off on this, I guess—but I ought to just give them a call while I'm here and see if they want to come back to table stakes. Look at that fog!"

We turned obediently toward the window and looked at the white roiling clouds, rubbing against the glass as if they wanted to come in.

"Wonderful," Carter said. "And it's like that all summer, isn't it? I don't remember the director's name, of the Bridgestone thing. Funny name, I think. An ex-cop of some sort. You wouldn't know, would you, Mike? Almost the same line of business really."

"Same line of business, I guess, Evan, but a fundamental difference of approach. It's Brazil, Frank Brazil owns Bridgestone Security."

"I thought so," he nodded happily. Dinah looked at me curiously. "Name of a country," Carter said.

"That's not a story."

I held the telephone receiver away from my ear for a moment and looked out the window. A listless breeze was kicking scraps of paper high into the air and making them drift. I could imagine Hand curling his mouth in disgust.

"That's not a story," he said again. "'Private Cops Bankroll Brain Research.' Brazil isn't going to waltz over with his trained ape and lean on you for that. Nobody's running up and down Eddy Street to hire some Superfly pistol because Webber finds that out. Jesus Christ. I run that kind of stuff every day, right next to the other hard news like Ann Landers and Cher's navel. I could fill a paper with features on how the government's poisoning us with nuclear reactors or how the jerkoffs in Saudi Arabia are putting fluoride in our crude oil. This is the age of fucking paranoia, Mike."

"Webber found something on him."

"And he found it in the goddam Central Valley, not in Oakland. Start thinking like a reporter, for Christ's sake."

He hung up hard.

"You get fired again?" Fred asked. He was sitting against the corner of the office, chair tilted back on two legs, watching the street as usual.

"Not quite."

"Then why don't you call that number on the clipping? You can solve the whole thing by telephone just like Nero Wolfe."

"You ever hear of serendipity?"

"Don't tell me. It's another word of the month from Webber's column."

I pointed my cigarette ash at the stack of papers and clippings we had been working through. "January," I said. "The Prince of Serendip. He had the gift of finding good things when he wasn't looking for them."

"Who is it?" His chair was down and he was reaching for his hat.

"Foreman," I said. I ground out the cigarette and stood up too. "It was written on his office door tag, right under his name."

CHAPTER 13

FROM THE SIDEWALK, THE BRIGHT GREEN LAWN SLANTED upward to the house. A pink, one-story stucco house with cheap wooden trimming and a low white picket fence on two sides. To the right was the garage, door open. In the flush of late afternoon sun, the lawn looked too green and too thick, like the toy lawns on a model railroad layout.

"You know a good dentist?" Fred asked.

"I know a dentist." There seemed to be lights on in two rooms, white spots against dark walls, but I hadn't seen anybody move yet. Foreman hadn't been at his office all day. Professors don't exactly punch a time clock, the secretary had sniffed, proudly or enviously I couldn't tell. And nobody had answered the phone when I called from the freeway an hour ago. A woman in a scarlet muumuu came out with a plastic sack two houses down and looked at us curiously before dropping it in the metal garbage can at the curb.

"Let's go look."

Fred got out of his side of the car and walked with me across the street. Quiet, very quiet up and down Alamo Street on a summer afternoon.

"I went to a new one yesterday," he told me. "Guy specializes in adult dentistry—that means over 60—and he turns out to be another California hippie." Fred was fourth-generation Californian himself. "Starts poking around and of course I gag—I've been gagging at the dentist for 62 years—and he sits back and looks at me very seriously and says, 'Have you had negative experiences with a dentist, Fred?'—they'd call you by your first name in the goddam funeral parlor—and he says, 'Maybe this is a time of particular stress for you in your life?'— and I shake my head no, with half a pound of plumbing hanging out my lip."

We reached the door and I pushed the bell. The house was smaller than it seemed from the street, probably five rooms, but most Berkeley tract houses are small.

"He says, 'Do you feel I'm violating your space, putting my fingers in your mouth like that?' I say, 'Mmn mmn mmn,' and gag again, and he says he thinks it would go better if I just talked about whatever traumatic experience it was I had with a dentist."

I pushed the bell again hard, leaning on it for maybe 30 seconds. "What'd you tell him?"

"I told him I used to bust so many dentists when I was on the vice squad I get nervous now." He peeped through the narrow window to the right of the door. "The back window's blown open."

"You got your keys?"

Fred pulled a heavy ring of keys from a silver reel on his belt and started sorting through them. The woman in the mumu had gone back in. A milk truck drove slowly down the street. On its side panel was a cartoon of a barn and silo in a pasture and over it a caption: "Cows in Berkeley?"

Fred's keys, about 20 in all, were long and flat with no

bulge or loop at the grip end. They were made out of gun metal and the bits were cut in various directions and angles on every side, indentations like rats' teeth would make. He had got them from a junkie in Delores Heights who had a brother in the FBI; the junkie also had a balloon of cocaine in his spare tire that Fred had decided to overlook in exchange. Once upon a time, of course, the bureau kept track of those keys like the crown jewels, but things had changed lately. Grab sold a couple of sets a month now. My laminated Visa card still worked on most locks, except not so fast and not so silently. The door swung open with a whisper and we went in.

"Jesus Christ."

The living room opened to our right, the kitchen to our left, joined by a narrow hallway. Strewn across the floor in both directions, as if blasted by a bomb, lay hundreds of pieces of cushions, papers, shattered bits of glass and wood.

I stepped into the living room.

A modern couch of rough beige material had been upended and ripped across the back with a knife, so that its stuffing spilled out in fluffy clusters. Two wing chairs had been tossed into a corner, their legs snapped off at different angles. A long, narrow painting had fallen from the wall and buried its face in the rug.

I picked up an overturned lamp and went slowly to the desk. The drawers had all been ransacked, emptied, and left sticking out like so many exhausted tongues. A little cardboard filing cabinet had been dumped into the fireplace along with a rack of phonograph records and a pile of blue-covered examination booklets. The only sound in the room came from a Chesterfield wooden clock on the mantle.

Fred walked toward the kitchen while I poked down a narrow corridor that ran in an L toward the street. The tiny bathroom was empty and messy, with no signs of violence. The bedroom was at the end of the corridor, also empty. But somebody had flung the blankets from the bed and onto the floor. I pushed one end of the water mattress and watched a ghostly wave ripple under the sheets to the other side. Clothes hung in disarray over a chair, a reading table, a bookcase. Miscellaneous small boxes had been emptied on a bureau. Tee-shirts curled in a heap on top of a little Sony television. The closet door was two-thirds shut. I pulled it open and saw more scattered clothes, shoe boxes, an old set of wooden crutches, and several cutouts from either *Penthouse* or a gynecological journal.

Fred came into the bedroom, glanced briefly in the usual cop way, dividing the room in half, then quarters, then eighths.

"You said the guy is on crutches?"

I nodded.

"There's footprints all over the kitchen table where somebody walked around opening shelves."

"Are you gentlemen from the police?"

The woman in the scarlet muumuu stood calmly beside the bedroom door, arms folded, looking from one to the other of us intelligently, carefully.

"Yes, ma'am. I'm Detective-sergeant Wrigly from SFPD. This man is my assistant."

"Have you some identification?"

Fred held out his shiny, worn wallet with his old photo-ID flopping down the bottom half. Unlike most people, she took the wallet and read the card through. Then she handed it back.

"You aren't in uniform, like the other men, so I thought I had better come ask. My son's over there watching." She gestured with one hand, and I stooped slightly to look. Across the street a towheaded boy, ten or 12, leaned against my car with his hands jammed into his pockets. "You never know anymore."

"You're talking about our people that came this morning, ma'am?"

Her big calm face turned slowly to scrutinize me. Faculty wife, I thought. Deliberate, assured, accustomed to asserting her presence to strange men. She had the healthy look and posture of a woman who had grown up a long way from any city.

"No, they came this afternoon, just before two."

"Oh, well," Fred began, "you know how slow things move."

"What I don't understand," she went on in her careful voice, "is why San Francisco police like you would be working here in Berkeley. This is a different district altogether."

"Just routine," Fred said.

"A former student is a suspect," I said. "Got a record of trashing, lives in the city."

She looked at me again and made a tisking sound. "Drugs, right?"

"What else?"

She turned her head to see if her son was still there. "I don't know what scares a parent more," she said. "My husband saw a girl break down in his class last quarter, literally. She had been taking quads—Quaaludes—and she just suddenly got up in the middle of the lecture and started walking around the room, crying and trying to brush imaginary things off her body, beetles and snakes and flies. It was terrible."

"You didn't happen to catch what precinct the Berkeley police were from, did you? It could save us a long drive."

"No." She shook her head deliberately. "I was in the kitchen. I haven't even seen John Foreman all day. He must be very upset. But that's the other thing I don't understand. They weren't Berkeley police. Why would Bridgestone Security be working up here instead of them?"

Where the hell was Foreman?

I put the Mercedes in gear and watched the rearview mirror as Fred padded up the stairs to his apartment. Then I drove a few blocks north, shivering in the cold from the window Bobby Sullivan had broken, and turned down Embarcadero.

He hadn't been seen in the biochemistry building all day. He had attended no meetings, met no students, done no work that we could trace. I glanced at my watch in the momentary glare of a street lamp. Almost 11. For five hours we had called and knocked all over Berkeley. The police had never heard of him. His friends and colleagues were indifferent, unexcited. People come and go so much in the summer, they said, sabbaticals to Europe, seminars to other labs, research to see if Paris really sizzles.

I reached the old part of Embarcadero and started to bump along the train tracks that still run up to the docks, servicing the ships. Not that many ships come to San Francisco these days. The giant freighters with their squat cargo containers and stainless steel piping all go straight to Oakland now, where trucks can unload them and scatter north and south without worrying about pencil-thin bridges, bottle-necked peninsulas, foggy, fixed cities. Others go through the Carquinez straits to Sacramento, where they pick up boxcars of rice to be shipped to Japan. Send us your poor, your tired, your huddled yen. Behind the big warehouse, a few lights gleamed on a tarted-up tourist cruiser.

You don't even really know he sent the clipping, Fred had pointed out. Or who wrote the number on it, or when. A jealous, bitchy guy according to my description, probably unstable—if he did have something to smear on Fells, there was no obvious connection, right? Webber had never printed a story, never started a file.

But Bridgestone Security had taken a rake to Foreman's home, I reminded myself. And Foreman was suddenly as inaccessible as the moon. As inaccessible as Webber.

I sighed and turned up Bush Street, away from the deserted docks. A Cadillac lumbered past me and into the darkness. If Cezanne could afford to spend hours rearranging his apple and his orange, I could go over Webber's folders one more time before heading for the Valley.

I crossed Montgomery and got caught in a snarl of traffic in Union Square. At the St. Francis, I waited while a flock of limousines unloaded a noisy party in evening dress, and I wondered, not for the first time, why they had named the fanciest hotel after the poorest saint. Then I crossed Market into the quiet.

It seemed cold, even for a San Francisco summer, when I got out and locked the car. Lights shone from a few first-floor windows in the police station down the block, and from the top floor of my building where some architects have an office. I went through the revolving door and walked over to the elevator, pressed the button and waited. Two Oriental men in business suits strolled up as the elevator arrived. I got in and reached for the button to hold the door open.

"Just in time," I said.

They smiled and one of them hit me very hard and expertly in the right kidney. The other grabbed my shoulders and held me up straight so that his friend could hit me again. My belly turned over with a sickening flop and my forehead slumped against the cold metal wall. He hit me a third time and I retched, letting little worms of bitter saliva crawl down my chin.

"That's enough," one of them said.

"He takes it pretty well."

One of their feet held the door open while they watched

me. Big, imperturbable men. Their clothes were ordinary, conservative; their breath was clean and lightly scented with mouthwash; their hair was short, their eyes were clear. Their faces were like two sacks of sand.

"We're supposed to use our own judgment."

"Why waste time? A loser. Just a two-bit peeper with a case of bad luck."

"Don't hurt my feelings," I said faintly.

They didn't like that. The puncher hit me in the same place and I vomited, splashing everybody's shoes.

"Dumb bastard." One of them wiped his soiled shoes on my trousers.

"Maybe we ought to take him out?"

"Bullshit."

I straightened an inch or two. The other one showed me the barrel of a pistol with a fat silencer clamped around it.

"Be over in a minute, smart ass," he said. The puncher jerked me up and spun me around, and I kept on spinning and drove my fist into the other man's belly while my left hand slapped the pistol high. He grunted and took a step back, not much damaged. The puncher bounced his knuckles off the back of my neck, just missing the right spot and taking my mind off my kidney. I hit his friend in the belly again hard. He started to club me with the pistol. I stepped inside and drove my knee up till he yelled with pain and I drove it again and again. The elevator shook wildly and the doors banged open and shut in a frantic rhythm. Puncher chopped twice more at my neck, but I was already slipping to one side, half-stunned, pulling the pistol down so that it went off close to his face with a little snap that even the best silencers can't stop, and suddenly blood was splattered in long, spidery lines all over the walls of the elevator, like the inside of an eye.

The puncher was sprawled outside the elevator, red hands pressed to his face. The other man slammed his elbow into my ribs, and I swung clumsily back at him, grazing his skull. He stumbled. I swung again and he went down to one knee just outside the door. His right hand went to his belt. I smashed my palm against the CLOSE button and stared helplessly while he pulled another pistol, flipped the safety and pointed in one wobbly motion.

The doors slid shut.

YOU COULD HAVE GONE TO A MOTEL," FRED SAID. "YOU love motels." He was standing in his narrow kitchen poking a spatula at a frying pan. I looked at the morning *Chronicle* on his coffee table and yawned.

"I wanted more protection than a hygenic wrapper on my glass, I guess."

Somebody was whistling in the next apartment and the sun was pitching fine black shadows through the window, warming up.

"They got your picture in that rag?" he asked. I watched him reach one stubby arm to a revolving tray of spices and pull out a tiny jar. The smell of thick, strong coffee settled over the room. A big plate of homemade biscuits cooled on a tray.

"Not a word."

"What's in the headline?"

"Same as usual. 'Ten Thousand Naked, Drug-Crazed Hippies Fail to Show Up at City Hall.'"

He chuckled and flipped an omelette over, shaking the pan as if it were filled with dice. "You sound like your buddy

Hand," he said. I tasted the coffee and wondered if I ought to introduce Fred to Connie Larkin.

"You going to see somebody about your elevator ride?" he asked as he brought the eggs over to the table.

"Maybe. As soon as I feel all better."

"You should have called Petrocelli at the precinct, you know."

"To do what? Scrub down the elevator? By the time I got down again the back way, they were both gone, and I had lost the urge to linger. I just wanted to get out of the way before some of their little friends came along."

"I would of looked for clues," Fred said through a mouthful of biscuit.

"You would have done just what I did. Find the goddam janitor and split."

"What'd you pay him?"

"I gave him a hundred."

Fred patted his pockets in mock alarm.

"Besides, what clues?" I went on. "Brazil's number's right there in the phone book, between Assault and Cadaver."

"Orientals are not his style, Mike boy."

I found a cigarette and lit it, one of the abandoned Pall Malls. I could always switch to hemp if my throat got sore. Fred poured more coffee into my cup from a red enamel pot. I mixed in a little cream and sugar.

"There's nobody else who could have sent them," I said after a while.

"And you're just going to drive your Batmobile over and tell him that, tell him not to be naughty?" He shrugged an elaborate seal-shrug. "Why not? It works on my two-year-old granddaughter."

"I'm going home to change and then see Mrs. Webber. You're going to Berkeley to see if Foreman shows up for class."

"You sure you don't want me to hang around?"

"You mean to help me in and out of elevators?"

He shrugged again. "I'm rough and I'm tough. I'll beat them over the head with an omelette while you call the cops." He pointed his cup at my trousers. "Hell of a lot easier on the clothes."

I stood up and rubbed the small of my back. "Just a little stiff in the middle," I told him. "I might go see the Chinaman too."

"There's ways to go stiff all over," he said and took the plates back to the kitchen.

Fred drove me to the garage on Van Ness where I had left my car last night, then followed me nine or ten blocks before giving an all-clear beep and peeling off toward Berkeley. I decided to believe him. Even if somebody had followed me from my office building, I couldn't have been seen leaving the service elevator around the corner on Sutter Street or taking the taxi from the line at the Jack Tar two blocks away. I left the Mercedes a couple of blocks down on Green Street and walked warily home.

Nobody looked suspicious except me, limping along in foul, rumpled clothes, one fist lumped ominously in my jacket pocket, as if over a .38 police revolver, say, or a volume of Baudelaire. The milkman drove his electric golf cart along, depositing cartons on the curb and whistling something loud and tuneless. Two young men with gold rings in their ears walked by, holding hands, and laughing in a non-piratical way. But then again, who knows? Long months at sea. Nothing but other pirates and an occasional albatross. I looked up and down the cheerful street and went in.

The apartment was as empty as ever. I put the pistol on the bathroom sink, took a shower, changed my clothes. One phone call later I was driving crosstown again to North Beach.

"Please?"

The young Chinese looked at me with heavy-lidded eyes and made a perfunctory bow from his shoulders. I handed him my .38 first, and he placed it carefully on a red lacquered table. Then he drew back a dark velvet curtain, opened a door, and showed me into Chan-lui's office.

"Ah, Michael. How pleasant to see you again. Let me pour tea before we talk."

He poured from a gold teapot and handed me a tiny cup, white and translucent as a silk handkerchief. He nodded slowly, which also meant closing his eyes for a moment, then poured himself a cup. I watched and took a sip of my own, rubbing my tongue against the delicate, unfamiliar taste. The little curls of steam smelled like the smoke of aromatic wood.

"I like to add rum to it in the evenings," he said, smiling. "It shocks my sons very much, I'm afraid," he added, and chuckled as if he were pleased. "They are not so flexible as I am. They do not know how to use things to their own advantage, however foreign. They sometimes act from impulse. The young are like that."

I sipped again in quiet agreement. He meant the Chinese young, like the ones who stood outside the curtained door with my pistol. I had heard that some of them were chafing lately under the old man's heavy hand. But beyond the dark office, the hallway, the two flights of steps, and the block-long tunnel to Grant Avenue, dozens of other young were still at work for him in much the same way, turning the wheels of vice in Chinatown at a smooth, profitable speed. Not all of them were Chinese, either.

The police called him "Louie" or the "Chinaman" and let him go on with it unmolested, mainly protection and prostitution, partly because they had never pinned anything worse than a parking ticket on him, partly because he ran too tight an organization to give them trouble. And a few years back, when rival teenage gangs had started gunning each other down in tourist spots and hurting business generally—reviving memories of the Tong Wars—Chan-lui Wa had quietly handed over names and addresses until, in a miracle of police efficiency, every single gang member had stumbled into custody, weighed down with incriminating evidence so good that even the California courts had convicted them. A few of the names, you sometimes heard, had had nothing to do with the Tong Wars at all but had been unlucky enemies of Chan-lui. If you break eggs, as Fred liked to say, you might as well make an omelette.

I was allowed to call him Chan-lui, as a privilege, thanks in return for a few small services. He liked my occasional visits, for reasons unclear to me. I liked to come to him because of what he knew about rackets, every racket in northern California; what he didn't know he always liked to find out, because, more than most people, Chan-lui had a lot of fluid cash that needed discreet investing.

He pushed the teapot to one side of his desk, letting the French cuffs and jade cufflinks flash in a reflection on it. He was the courtliest man I had ever seen, more aristocratic in manner than anyone I had known in the far-off days when I had covered southern France for UPI, more elegant than anybody I had ever spotted in London. As he should have been. He was born in Nanking, a prince of 26 generations, descended from the legendary emperor K'ang-hsi, and after he had fled China as a boy when the Communists had come to power, he had been educated at the Sorbonne and Harvard. He was now in his early 60s. I had never asked how he had come West or taken control of Chinatown's less picturesque half. I keep meaning to look it up in *Who's Who.*

"I'm sorry you haven't heard of him," Chan-lui said. We had passed the first ten minutes as always, discussing the book he was currently reading. This time it was *Portrait of Zelide,* a biography of an eighteenth-century Dutchwoman by someone named Geoffrey Scott. He let his long fingers caress the pages and lift the cover. His small hooded eyes never left my face.

"Not a word."

"How disappointing." He let the cover fall. "You are usually so well-read, Michael. Your intellectual eclecticism almost matches mine." He drank tea calmly, his monkey-like face moving up and down, not in a nod but according to some inner rhythm I knew nothing about. "He died in his early 30s, Mr. Scott," Chan-lui said. "Of pneumonia. A great pity."

"I know what you mean."

"Your question has not been forgotten, Michael. My brain is busy while my tongue is idle."

We stood up and walked around the desk and went to a beautiful standing cabinet, which was painted jet black and covered with broad yellow chips like the scales of a fish. Many men of his size would have kept the office small, to make their own physical presence more impressive, but Chan-lui kept visitors at a disadvantage in a subtler way. One window opened out on a southern view, toward the financial district; the rest of the room was filled, filled to the point of clutter, with antiques, glassware figurines, porcelain. Anything that could easily break.

He took several sheets of brilliant white paper from a shelf in the cabinet and carried them back to the desk. "Really, Michael, I think I can say nothing. If someone has tried to kill you for motives of revenge, they are not likely to be known to me. You do make enemies, after all. Good workers always do. If someone concerned with your present case

has made this attempt"—he spread his hands in a lovely gesture of helplessness—"I am in no position to speculate. I can only ask my sons to listen." He made a cold smile in my direction. "But the future, as the Koran says, is a hand that slowly closes."

Choosing one sheet of paper, he shunted the rest to the side of the desk. From an ebony cabinet on his right, he removed a long brown wooden brush and a bottle of ink.

"On summer days like this, Michael, when I was a boy, my brother and I used to climb to the top of our house in Nanking with our kites. They were handsome things, shaped like dragons, with sharp teeth made of light plaster and extra shafts of wood to reinforce the wings. My brother was older and so always claimed the privilege of launching the kite." He began to make circular motions over the paper with his brush. "I can still remember the view, the dry blue sky of Nanking, the rows of tile-roofed houses stretching in every direction as far as two little boys like us could see. Once he had sent the kite up and I had played the string out far enough, we would turn our attention to the rest of the sky. Because, you see, all over the city, from the tops of all those distant houses, other boys like ourselves were also sending up their dragon kites, filling the horizon as if an armada of paper and wood creatures had blown in from the sea." He dipped his brush in ink and studied the paper. "That was when the battle began. The whole sky seemed to me to shake with silent assault as kite fell upon kite, dueling high overhead, ripping at each other's wings and heads as we guided them below. A strange sight now, in retrospect. And what was strangest of all was that we never knew the names or saw the faces of our opponents. The battle began, so to speak, on enemies we never saw. We never even spoke of them, except once in a while when we were

repairing the wings of a kite or rebuilding a badly damaged one; and even then, of course, the boys never seemed as real to us as their kites." He looked up at me. "Your little skirmish reminds me of that."

I drank my tea.

"Have you ever studied Chinese calligraphy?" he went on after a moment.

I shook my head.

"You might find it amusing." I put my teacup on a side table and walked over to him. "It is the basis of all Chinese education and those who learn it well regard it as an art form rather than a system of handwriting." He took another sheet of paper and poised the brush inches above it, then let it dart forward like a diving beak. A run of his elegant cuff and a pagoda-like design glistened on the sheet in thick black ink. "That is my name," he said. "The first thing I learned to write. Here is my oldest son's name, King-su Wa. It looks rather like a boat, don't you think?" He dipped the brush in ink and poised again. "Some characters have different meanings, of course, depending upon the tone with which they are pronounced. There are six distinct tones in Mandarin. When this one"—he drew quickly—"is pronounced 'chaon,' it means 'friendship.'" His brush duplicated the character precisely. "Pronounced 'chaan' it means 'betrayal.'" His eyes looked up at me, two narrow black marks in skin as pale as dry parchment. "It was good of you to come, Michael."

The door opened and one of the sons walked respectfully in and waited for me. I looked at the figures on the paper again and nodded.

"Thank you, Chan-lui. I shall try to read up on Zelide."

He made a short, gracious bow and I went outside, where the other son looked at me once again with cold, unfriendly

eyes before he handed me my pistol. Then they led me through the long tunnel and up the stairs to a tiny courtyard a few steps off Grant. The same man gave me the bullets for the gun, bowed, and left.

CHAPTER 15

HE TOLD ME IT WASN'T BRAZIL."

"I told you that this morning. Brazil doesn't use them. For pete's sake, the guy's as lily white as the goddam HEW." Fred stopped barking and did something to the mouthpiece. Then his voice came back louder. "Did he say who had hired them?"

"He quoted the Koran."

"Christ."

"They were pros."

"Of course they were pros. They were hard guys. They were industrial-strength pros. But they were Chinese. And nobody hires Chinese for jobs like that without him knowing. You've been having tea and cookies with the Chinaman for as long as I've known you—he likes you—why the hell couldn't he show you a card?"

"The code of the Old West is inscrutable. Did Foreman show up?"

"Yeah. He came in this morning straight from the airport. I saw him just before his class. He was in Los Angeles visiting

friends for two days—can you believe it? No wonder the students riot."

I let my eyes wander. Tourists were swarming around the phone booth and into Union Square like summer locusts, obscuring everything but a few tubs of orange blossoms and the statue of Victory still celebrating Dewey's knockout in Manilla. I watched an elderly woman in a stylish blue dress, white pillbox hat, and white gloves step off the curb in the middle of the block. Traffic slowed, but not much.

"Did Foreman say anything about his house?"

"I didn't ask him. I don't think he knows. I just told him you wanted to talk."

The old woman had stopped in the middle of the street. Wide-eyed, she glanced in several directions, looked me full in the face, and started off again. "It's past one now," I told Fred. "I want to get to Foreman at his office."

"Mike, those guys weren't from Bridgestone. You don't bother Brazil enough for that much muscle. Not now. You got strictly nothing on him."

"It was a one-shot affair."

"Don't laugh. Last night smells like pro-am to me. Brazil could do it himself if he wanted to. But somebody hired from the Chinaman to do what he couldn't do himself. And there's nobody crazier than a guy who hires pistols."

I rubbed my face and watched the white pillbox disappear into Gump's. "All right, Fred. I'll be careful."

"The hell with you, boss. I was thinking about Dinah."

"Did you really lose your license?" Anne Webber put down her cup of tea.

"Misplaced it, say."

"Frederic Kingsley said you had been in trouble with the

District Attorney." She looked at me solemnly. "Several times."

"Just the once, and that was quickly settled." It was also six years ago. Kingsley had been busy.

"No, I mean Frederic Kingsley told me that several times. He made it quite clear that he never approved of you, of the whole idea of a detective. Mrs. Browning didn't even bother to talk about it. She hardly talked to us at all, in fact. My daughters called her a brontosaurus. You must have done something rather annoying to them both."

She had left the windows of the living room open and the thick blue curtains pulled apart, so that a great shaft of mid-afternoon sun fell on the couch where she sat, rather primly holding her knees together with both hands. I hoped that the sunlight would thaw her a little.

"I didn't exactly charm Frederic and his mother-in-law, Mrs. Webber. But they were set against the idea of somebody like me from the start. I don't square very well with sermons about nonviolence. Or with their notion of why your husband disappeared. I'm sorry for all the conflict."

"I think he was drunk about half the time I was there," she said after a moment. "Starting from quite early in the morning."

"Are you sure?" I asked, remembering my own brief conversation with Kingsley.

"Set a thief to catch a thief," she said cryptically and picked up her cup of tea again.

I fingered the Shell Oil bill she had given me. "Mrs. Webber, I'm pretty sure your husband has not gone off voluntarily." She bowed her head and studied her tea leaves. "He went to the Sacramento Valley once to interview some farmers. That was on June 21st. He posed as a lawyer and used a phony name."

"He does that sort of thing sometimes. Investigative reporters all do."

"He went back a second time, two days later. That's what this gasoline bill says. But nobody there saw him. He wasn't registered under either name in any of the local motels. He didn't buy gas anywhere along the route back to San Francisco. Whatever happened to him happened out there, out there in the Valley."

Her voice sounded small. "What do you think happened?"

"Did your husband ever talk about a man named Frank Brazil?"

"Oh, God." She had gone very stiff on the couch. "Oh, dear God. George wrote about him a long time ago in Oakland—he was working for the *Tribune* then—we lived in a little house near the zoo—Miranda was just five." She shook her head fiercely, scattering memories. "George despises him. Because of the killings of those two black boys. And his speeches now. George calls him the hangman, the fascist."

"Has he ever talked about a man named Fells, who teaches biochemistry at Berkeley?"

"No."

"Another man named Foreman, John Foreman?

"No. No. What is all this about? Who are all these people? All these men," she corrected herself, holding her voice down before it climbed too far.

"Your husband was apparently writing a story about Brazil again, or at least about the farm he owns in the Valley. But I don't know yet what he was uncovering or thought he was uncovering."

"Frank Brazil is behind his disappearance?"

I didn't answer.

"That violent man. All those bodyguards. All those speeches about punishing the criminal elements, preventive detention." In the harsh sunlight, I could see the wrinkles dug in her skin, little trenches sapping the fashionable tan. Beside her, on an end table, a clock shifted its hands toward three. She smoothed a fold from her skirt with trembling fingers. "You're trying to tell me that something violent might have happened to George, aren't you?"

I hadn't told her about Grab. I hadn't told her about the two Chinese last night, who may or may not have come around on her husband's account, who may have appeared for reasons all their own. She sat quietly, one hand turned palm up on her lap, the other hand gripped tightly around her wrist. Her eyes were quite still as she looked at me.

"Will you find him?" she asked in a whisper.

"Yes."

Foreman had left early. A headache, his departmental secretary told me in a voice of strict neutrality. He was going to do an hour's worth of shopping, then go home to rest.

I picked my way back across campus, swirled through the vortex of students around Sather Gate and went up Telegraph to my car. A group of street people were standing around it, dressed in the regulation Third World chic. Two tall black men in their middle 20s sat on the hood. I walked past them and started to open the door. They stayed on the hood.

"Hey, get off the man's car, motha. He got work to do. Got a nice coat and tie on."

"Fucking monster car, man."

"Got a busted window, too."

They started to clap their hands against the hood in bongo rhythm, and their friends on the sidewalk laughed and shouted. People walked by faster. I opened the door and got in.

"This car what you call *old,* man."

"Yeah, but this a *white car,* man."

"Heeeeey!"

They drummed faster, making the Mercedes rock as they swayed and kicked long legs against the fender. A white boy with a ragged beard shoved his face through the window on the driver's side, an inch from my ear, and howled obscenely like a wolf. Fells would have been interested in their dopamine. I got out of the car and the wolf boy scampered to the sidewalk, still howling, while a few others joined in. The two blacks drummed and grinned. I got back in the car and started the motor. Laughing, they slid off the hood. I backed the car a few feet until the wheels would turn out. The blacks had their arms around each other's shoulders and were slapping hands first against their knees and then together in the intricate, rubbery patterns of a hopped-up drill team.

Some fights can't stay started. I waved to them as I pulled into traffic. They stamped their feet and threw out their arms like Gene Kelly and gave me the finger.

"Do you want some coffee?" Foreman asked.

He was speaking with his eyes closed, his head back against the soft fabric of his chair. A cord of muscle twisted spasmodically across one cheek. Both hands lay motionless along his thighs, the fingers slightly curled and chalk white.

I turned in my chair and glanced through the curtained window toward the street. While Foreman had shopped his way slowly home, I had taken the Mercedes back to the city, double-checked my office for damage and corpses, and returned with Fred. Now he sat impassively in his fat, blue Chevrolet, looking for all the world like a seal in a porkpie hat, doing crosswords on the magazine in front of him.

"Sure. Coffee would be good."

He pulled himself slowly out of the upholstery, stumbling

once as he fit a crutch under his shoulder, and began a slow march to the kitchen. His dead legs dragged under him.

"Do you want some help?"

"I can manage." He reached the kitchen door and braced one hand against the jamb. "When I broke my back, it sent a bone splinter right up my gut. A couple of drinks now and my liver would end up like a softball."

"Coffee's fine, John."

He took a long time to make it, dropping utensils with a clatter, opening and slamming cabinet doors. I saw him spill grounds from his Chemex filter, big brother of the one in his office, then push them with trembling hands into the sink. But he emerged finally with two unmatched cups on a tray, and while he eased them onto the coffee table and himself down into the chair, I went into the kitchen for the pot and cream and sugar.

"I wouldn't be talking to you except for this," he said as I came back through the door. He was pointing to the piles of debris—cushions, wood, glass—swept up against the plaster walls, and his voice had the quivering tension of a child who wants to cry. "Mrs. Amberg from down the street came over to help. The police were here for all of ten minutes. Teachers get trashed in Berkely, that's all they said. They're going to call Bridgestone Security, but what are they going to say? Nobody even saw them except Mrs. Amberg, and I don't want to get her involved."

I sat down.

"I guess I wanted to draw a little attention to Fells," he said. He made a soft whoosh with his breath. "I didn't think the whole thing through too well, did I?"

"You connect this thing with Fells?"

Silence. Foreman's hands began to tremble again, and he used one of them to wipe coffee from his mouth.

"But you don't know what somebody was looking for, or why it would be Bridgestone Security doing the looking?"

Silence. The trembling hand went slowly back to his lap.

"Or is it that a little rampage like this just makes you think of Fells? I've been talking this week to a guy who specializes in psycho-surgery. He tells pretty scary stories about treating aggressive behavior this way." I thought of Carter's monologue on the way out of the restaurant. "He says there's a doctor in Mississippi who even performs amygdalectomies on hyperactive children, five or six years old. That kind of thing might interest a news reporter. On the other hand, you told me that what Fells does is harmless, impractical."

He shifted his weight in the chair, bent forward, and pulled up one stiff leg, which he crossed carefully over the other. The shiny blue overalls he was wearing, Berkeley haute couture, creaked with the movement and stood in little scallops at his knees, while his loafer slid off his heel. The hands resumed their tremor.

"That's right," he said at last, "what I told you about his work. I gave you the straight stuff on that. Neurosurgeons like the one you mean are interested in pacifying people. That's not exactly what Fells does. He studies how the brain sends chemical messages to the muscles to be angry, to be violent, to attack whatever comes close to you. Listen, I know about his work. Hell, I ought to. Before the accident, I was doing parallel work on one of the cranial hormones, melatonin."

"That controls aggressive behavior too?"

"No, melatonin inhibits the gonads, so to speak. It's what keeps us from growing up too fast. I was on my way to becoming an expert on the biochemistry of puberty." The quivering tones had relaxed. For the first time, his face took on animation and he looked at me directly. "Nobody quite knows why pu-

berty is coming earlier and earlier in all developing and indus-
trialized countries, independent of race, diet, climate."

I thought of the pictures in his closet. "OK."

"My work tends to prove that the effect of increased
amounts of light on the nerve paths of the brain is behind it.
Melatonin is not produced in the body as long as the pineal
gland in the brain is active. When it stops working—and it
doesn't seem to do any work at all in adult humans—then
sexual maturation begins. The more light the brain experiences, artificial or not, the sooner the gland stops working.
We probably grow up faster because of Thomas Edison. I was
just about to start work on the relationship between aging
processes and artificial illumination." His left hand flipped
over on the arm of the chair like a limp, white fish. "Seven
papers in one year," he said. "I haven't published two since I
got tenure. You can't exactly use an electrode with pinpoint
accuracy with hands like mine."

"You're jealous of Fells."

His voice came out matter-of-fact. "I'm jealous of everybody."

I glanced through the curtain again. Fred was still, holding
the magazine against the steering wheel. Little slanted lines of
sunlight were falling across a hackberry tree and into Foreman's
front yard. A delivery truck clattered by with a bump.

"You still haven't told me why you sent the clipping, John,
and the pictures of the cats."

"The cats were for shock value. Attention getters."

"They got it."

"People are funny about animals. You ever go to the race track?"

"Sometimes."

"I go down to Golden Gate Fields once in a while. I like to
see things that run." He puffed out his cheeks for a moment.
"There's certain horses you don't bet on, you know, not because

of anything real. Just because people talk, because there's some kind of whisper."

"So?"

"So there's that kind of thing about Fells. A very aloof personality—you saw that—there's talk about irregularities in his human subjects' permission sheets. You don't do anything in science to human tissues without a lot of paperwork. Strictly routine. Permission, reports, conclusions. People say Fells is slow with his sheets, makes them evasive, he's vague about procedures. But there's nothing substantial. Just plain dislike probably."

I looked at my watch. Not quite an hour before Dinah came off her shift.

"Get to it, John."

"I was coming out of the Co-op a few months ago and putting away groceries in my car. I use a special handicapped parking space in back, around by the delivery entrance. I saw Fells over in the corner of the back lot, sort of hidden by some trees where the lot abuts Ellsworth. He was talking to Frank Brazil."

I carefully pulled a cigarette out of my shirt pocket and lit it. I had switched to a filter brand that afternoon, in the interest of health. Health had been on my mind. But it was like trying to smoke Corfam. Foreman finished his coffee.

"How do you know it was Frank Brazil?"

"Christ, I've seen his picture in the paper dozens of times. The Berkeley *Barb* even made a foldout dart target out of one, with a big Nazi swastika for a bull's-eye."

"Did you speak to him? Or hear what they were saying?"

"They were too far off. And pretty absorbed. I got the impression they knew each other, though."

"And you thought Webber could make something out of that?"

He stirred uneasily. "I sent a note with the clipping. I thought Webber might give it a good slant. You know, university professor linked with repressive security forces, private army kind of thing. Maybe he could have shown that Brazil was looking for inside dope on how to make people more aggressive, and maybe Fells was going out of bounds for research money. I don't know. I just reacted. He passed a shaking hand across his face. Fells makes $12,600 more than I do. I guess I thought it wouldn't do him any good at promotion time to be associating with somebody like Brazil. Berkeley's a pretty intolerant place if you don't wear workshirts and Levi's and read the *Co-Evolution Quarterly.* He's always been a shit to me, because I haven't done any good work since . . ." His voice went away in a mutter, and he shifted the weight of his crossed leg with both hands. I killed the cigarette.

"Did you know that Webber knew Brazil too?

"No, did he?"

"A long time ago."

"I thought Webber would write it up, you know, right away. But he never used it. He called me about a week later with a question. But he never ran the story. And now you're telling me he's disappeared." Foreman hugged himself, as if he had suddenly shivered. "Jesus, I'm scared."

"What was the question, John?"

"He wanted to know if Fells ever went out to the Sacramento Valley."

Fred was fiddling with his police radio when I got back to the car, a long black metal rectangle slung under the dashboard that he plays constantly when he drives, listening with half his mind, he once told me, the way he used to listen to his wife.

"I got something," I said as I eased in beside him.

He started the Chevrolet and turned down the volume knob on the radio. "I got something too," he said over the low mutter of names and numbers at my knee. The Chevrolet slid around a bus and started down one of the steepest hills in Berkeley. A Volvo full of professors passed us.

"Fells knows Brazil," I told him, watching the flatlands come into view. "Foreman saw them talking together in the street."

Fred nodded and gunned through the light at San Pablo Avenue. "What time are you supposed to meet Dinah?"

"Her shift's over at seven. Why?"

"Will she mind if you're a little late?"

"No."

He leaned forward and turned the radio off with a snap. "I heard a homicide on there, just after you went in. Down at the Marina end of Lombard. White woman in her early 30s."

I felt my back stiffen, and I tasted the sour acid of Foreman's coffee again. "Did they give a name?"

Fred shook his head, cut over two lanes, and took the left lane away from three kids in a wound-up T-bird. They stared at us in disbelief as he cut back over them and sailed onto the freeway. "Same address, though," he said. "You want to look?"

I nodded and sat back in the cushioned seat. Reflected lights drifted out of the dusk, across the windshield, down the vinyl padding of the roof, over Fred's calm Irish face. He rubbed one palm against the back of his neck and with the other hand twirled us onto the bridge and toward San Francisco. I closed my eyes and tried to think what sort of things a man like Professor Fells would say to a man like Frank Brazil. I tried not to think about the last time I had been to the Marina.

"The tall guy's Hollister," Fred said abruptly, ten, 12 minutes later. I blinked open my eyes and saw two black-and-whites parked in front of Connie Larkin's apartment building, their red tops circling slowly. Next to one of them sat a square white ambulance shaped like a bakery van, all its doors open, and a young man in jeans and leather windbreaker slouched in the driver's seat, smoking a cigarette. A couple of uniformed cops stood by the front door and kept the little crowd back. Behind them, two men in suits were reading from a clipboard.

Fred pulled up beside the ambulance. "Hollister wants to be chief of detectives," he said as we left the car, "but they already got a chief of detectives." One of the uniformed cops spotted Fred and said something over his shoulder. Hollister walked forward, stopping us at the curb by the rear of the ambulance.

"You chasing lights, Fred, or just passing by?" Hollister had one of those soft Southern accents that seem to come from under a blanket. In the noise of the street, it was hard to catch every word. I pulled out a cigarette and lit it.

"Mr. Haller might know your victim, Lieutenant," Fred said, tilting his head in my direction.

Hollister looked over and studied me slowly, guessing my weight. A tall man, stooping already, though barely into his 40s. Long bony face, good-looking in a hard way, with brown freckles painted incongruously around arctic blue eyes. He had short hair, like all of them, a sandy stubble of crewcut, and narrow, flat sideburns climbing down past his ears country-singer fashion. Hollister was in his second or third year in the Homicide division, I knew, having worked his way through Burglary, Forgery, and Vice in record time. Most cops move from a beat into Vice, stay there while they're young and interested, then transfer one more time and grow old and sly in a specialty. But the ambitious ones transfer as fast as they can from division to division, over and over, burning right through the organizational chart until they finally scramble, lean and out of breath, into a paneled office at the Hall of Justice, as far from the streets as they can manage. Hollister had already made lieutenant six years faster than normal.

"Mr. Haller," he said with a flicker of sarcasm. "You've come to help us out with our case, Mr. Haller?"

"How did you guys ever get to be called fuzz?" I said, pointing my cigarette at his crewcut and clean-shaven jaw.

"He don't relate well to authority figures, Lieutenant," Fred said at my side.

"Yeah, I guess I heard that," Hollister said. He gave me the hard look again. I felt ten pounds lighter. Then he made his mouth relax a quarter of an inch at the corners, and forced his expression into something like armed neutrality, or pained, suspicious toleration. Churchill looks the same way in his pictures with Stalin. "Why don't we start all over again, Haller?" he said after a moment. "It's been a long day. You know something about this homicide?"

I exhaled smoke humbly toward my shoes. "Who's the victim, Lieutenant?" Pals all around.

"Name of Larkin. Constance Larkin. White female, early 30s, lived alone."

"I interviewed her for a client three days ago."

There was a shout from the door of the apartment building, and the crowd stirred into a murmur. Hollister looked over at the uniformed cops, both of whom saw him and hitched their shoulders like Officer Krupke, glowering up and down Lombard Street.

"Who's the client?" Hollister asked.

The man with the clipboard materialized, still writing. "They're coming downstairs now, Lieutenant," he said without raising his head.

"Who's the client, Haller? That's not privileged anymore and you know it."

"The San Francisco *Constitution*."

The clipboard jockey glanced up at that. Since Carlton Hand had started his new editorial sweep, there were cops who would like to paste his face all over the pistol range.

Hollister put a little iron back in his eyes. "Now what in the world does our next mayor Mr. Hand want to know about a semi-pro chippie down here in tomcat alley?" he said, keeping his voice soft but exaggerating the drawl.

"Maybe he wanted to take her to the policeman's ball. That part still is privileged unless in my judgment it pertains to the murder, and I don't know that it does. I was interviewing her about a missing-persons case that looked strictly routine. It still does."

"Pertains to the murder in your judgment." Hollister took out a tin box of little Dutch cigars and opened it. "They must pass out a phrase book when they peddle the license these days, Powers." The clipboard went down, a lighter came up, and Powers twisted nervously at the same time to see the front of the building, where a short, pudgy man in a blue suit and a rainhat had just appeared, carrying a black bag in one hand.

"Paulson's through, Lieutenant," Powers said.

"Pertains to the murder." Hollister looked at me admiringly. "Tell Hand that Miss Larkin either forgot to lock the door or else she met some playmate up on Union Street who got happy with a lead sap and played tattoo all over her face and tits. I didn't look under her skirt and I didn't want to. Maybe she died before the guy broke her neck or maybe not. Paulson's going to tell me all about it over coffee and doughnuts. You're going to come downtown and tell me what pertains to the goddam murder."

The doors of the apartment building sprang open, and a man in white pants and white short-sleeved jacket started to back out. We were only 15 or 20 feet from the door, so I could see the taut cords of his neck and wrist muscles as he maneuvered the stretcher out and down the three little steps to the sidewalk. The crowd made a pleased oohing noise and pushed against the two cops.

"Lieutenant, you know as well as I do that I don't have to come downtown with you."

They had the stretcher all the way out and tilted on the steps when the top half of the black rubber sheet pulled free and Connie Larkin's head rolled to one side, staring in our direction. At the sigh of the crowd, Hollister looked around. Her eyes were lost in swollen bulges of flesh, greenish-blue bruises made by the blackjack, and her long hair was sleek with dampness from the coroner's sponge; the round white line of her jaw hung stiffly from the rictus of her mouth. Red lights from the patrol cars swept slowly over her face, one after another. Then the stretcher handlers flipped the sheet back up and heaved her into the rear of the ambulance. Another goddam beautiful day.

Fred nudged my elbow and pointed toward the glass door swinging shut on the apartment building. I had seen it before. A six-inch silver decal of a shield with block letters underneath that said "Protected by Bridgestone Security."

CHAPTER 16

THE NURSE AT THE RECEPTION DESK TOLD ME THAT DINAH HAD gone to the cafeteria to wait. Fred tugged at the metal newspaper rack by the doorway, reached under, and pulled out a paper without depositing his quarter. He rolled it flat and stuck it in his coat pocket and started to follow me toward the bare concrete steps at the end of the lobby. The nurse glared after him.

"You ought to go downtown and see Hollister," he said, puffing a little behind me. "Even if you don't have to. You can be too damned independent for your own good sometimes. Pigheaded."

"Bullheaded. Hollister's pigheaded. I'll mail him a statement. That's all I have to do. I got no connection for him except a decal on a door and a queasy feeling in my belly."

He sighed long and loud, and we went through a door on the second-floor landing that said Emergency Exit, entering a wide corridor jammed with equipment trolleys and linen baskets. Overhead a loudspeaker bonged an electronic chime and started to list doctors wanted in surgery, doctors wanted in radiology, doctors wanted in psychiatry. They would have taken Connie Larkin down to the morgue on Grove Street, where Dinah and I had met, a squat, quiet building with fewer windows than usual on the first two floors and no loudspeakers in the hallways. The doctors who worked there didn't need to be paged and didn't need to hurry. I wondered whether it had happened the way Hollister wanted, the way it happens two or three nights a week in big American cities, and she had just picked the wrong guy at Perry's to help pay the rent. Or whether Brazil's people had been watching her apartment building the day I paid my visit.

"This place is like a bus station," Fred muttered, frowning up at the loudspeaker.

We went through a double door and found ourselves among all the wanted doctors, in a big, noisy barn of a room. At the far end was a food counter and a line of men and women carrying orange plastic trays. They eat at all hours in a hospital, and I had never seen the cafeteria when it didn't look like rush hour at Denny's. Near our door, a boy with a blonde beard and dirty green wrappers around his shoes leaned in a chair against the wall, snoring. At one of the formica-topped tables in the middle of the room, Dinah was sitting with her back partly turned to us, reading a paperback, a slice of cake in front of her, fork poised halfway to her mouth.

"Hello, little lady," Fred said. "I couldn't shake this goofus."

"Hello, Fred. Want some cake?"

"Well, actually no. I don't think so. I'll just get coffee. Maybe a sandwich. Mike?"

"Black." He gave a little salute and went down the room to the food line. I kissed Dinah hard and sat down in the plastic bucket beside her.

"I got your message," she said. "I was surprised. I thought you were out digging up Webber stuff like a beaver."

I turned over the book she was reading. *The Andromeda Strain*, by Michael Crichton.

"Truer than you'll ever know," she said with a smile. Fred came back and dealt us all paper cups of coffee and ham sandwiches for himself and me. Then he sat down on the other side of the table.

"You fellows are more than usually glum," she said as I dumped sugar into my cup. "Do hospitals make you nervous, Fred?"

"My son-in-law started medical school," Fred said. He picked up her book, turned it around, replaced it. "At UCLA. He dropped out after a year. Said he couldn't stand to be around sick people."

Dinah laughed, Fred laughed. I told her about my office last night, about Foreman, about Brazil. Then I told her about Connie Larkin. Two middle-aged men in hospital greens sat down near us while I talked and began to discuss intestinal hemorrhages and blood types. Dinah nodded to them and put her hand on top of mine.

"Mike wants you to have a bodyguard for a while," Fred told her. "Me, in fact."

"I'm afraid of more boys from Brazil," I said.

"I'm not afraid." She speared the last bit of cake with her fork. Angel food. "It's not your company, Fred. But I've got my own life to lead. And I'm just not going to take seriously a two-bit storm trooper with a compulsive inferiority complex. My daddy didn't raise any shrinking violets." Fred made a protest through his sandwich. "Mike likes puns," she grinned. "The sign of an impatient nature."

I lit a cigarette. One of the doctors in green looked at me and frowned. I shot him dead.

"Your father didn't raise any blockheads, either," I said. Dinah's father had retired from a mining company many years ago and bought a cattle ranch in Nevada. He had a legendary temper, even among miners, and a smile that could charm gold out of the pan. "Brazil has a couple of thousand people who work for him, not many of them even halfway scrupulous. Or squeamish. If he can get to me through you, he'll do it."

"I didn't think you knew enough to make anybody mad yet," she said.

"Tell her the rest," Fred said.

"Fred thinks the Chinese were hired by somebody else, not Brazil. An amateur, maybe connected with Webber, maybe not. Brazil is fairly predictable—he just wants to wipe me off his shoe. A crazy with a grudge is not."

She set her face stubbornly, lifted her chin, and finished the cake. Fred looked at her, then at me.

"I'm going to bring the car around front, Mike." He stood up and hiked his belt over his belly. "You two lovebirds work it out and tell me what to do then."

He picked up the rest of his sandwich and strolled under the No Exit sign toward the stairs.

"I think hospitals do make him nervous," she said, looking after him.

"Brazil's not a joke, Dinah. He's got no taste for legal niceties. In his own way, he's a real vigilante."

"Like you, fond lover."

I looked up in surprise.

"Don't look like that," she said. "You're a cop of sorts, yes. But I've watched you for four years and four months, in action, at work. You have your own private code as well. Some inscrutable combination of New England Puritan and bleeding heart."

I watched cigarette smoke drift higher and begin to branch out, like the ghost of a tree. "Most PIs do," I said.

"Probably. Probably it goes with being private, not wearing a uniform, not really working for the system. In your case, it comes out in the way you don't do divorces, the way you worried over that miserable Hoffman kid, the way you didn't give that girl's address that time in San Mateo. You may not spell it out, but you won't play follow the leader either."

"What makes you think my private code's any better than Brazil's?"

She smiled an odd, shy smile and touched my mouth with two fingers. "Honor is not won/Until some honorable deed be done," she said. "You'd better eat your tomatoes and go meet Fred."

I looked down and noticed that I'd separated tomato slices from the sandwich and stacked them on the side of the paper plate.

"New habit. I don't think I've eaten a tomato since I drove down to Truro and saw all those barrels of diazepam waiting to be sprayed on the fields."

Dinah had taken her purse and started to get up. Now she stopped halfway.

"Am I pronouncing it wrong?" I asked.

"You'd better do your freshman chemistry all over, Mike. Diazepam isn't a pesticide."

"It was labeled on the barrels. One of them anyway. In nice white stencil." She sat down slowly, her brow wrinkled. "I have a clear memory for the scene whenever somebody's waving an irrigation pipe at my skull."

She pulled a ballpoint from her purse and wrote the name of the chemical out on a napkin in tall block letters.

"Is this what you saw?"

"Yes."

"That's not a pesticide, Mike. That's the basic ingredient in tranquilizers."

Dinah let Fred drive her back to her apartment. I took a cab from the hospital to the St. Francis and got out at the Mason entrance, around the corner from Union Square. Nobody showed unusual interest, except a derelict stumbling south toward the Tenderloin. I gave him a buck. Along the side of the hotel, neatly spaced about every ten feet, like baby owls on a limb, lounged a file of male whores, some with painted faces and frizzed hair, others in leather shirts and dungarees. One way or another, it's always been a sailor's town. I went through the main lobby of the hotel to a second, smaller one, where the elevators for the new tower addition run. On the 39th floor, in something called the Fountain Room, Carlton Hand was giving a speech to the University Club of San Francisco.

I opened the door at the back just as a flashbulb went off with a loud crack. He was standing behind a lectern at the center of a banquet table, a serious expression on his big red face, one finger lightly touching the microphone on the lectern as he listened to somebody at the far corner of the room ask a question. Other tables ran at right angles toward me in crisp white rows, and around them, leaning back with cigarettes, bending over coffee cups, were several hundred men, mostly in evening dress. Waiters moved respectfully among the tables, clearing and pouring.

A tall man with a tuxedo hanging from his neck motioned me rather angrily toward the cluster of reporters and photographers in ordinary coats and ties, halfway up the banquet room along one wall. By the time I reached them, dodging the inevitable television camera from Mrs. Browning's own station, Hand had answered the question and was pointing to the audience for another one. From the wall, I could see the jewelry-draped bulk of Mrs. Browning herself, several seats down the head table to Hand's left, one of the few women in the room. At a lesser table in front, Frederic Kingsley was pouring something amber into a tumbler.

"So I don't really see the environmental cost as a factor," Hand said. "There was a gentleman in the back?"

Somebody else stood up and started a long question about preventive detention for suspected criminals. Hand scanned the room, spotted me, and looked unhappy. I pushed by the newsmen and went into a little room at the corner, a speaker's waiting room or utility storage room.

"Now there can be constitutional objections," Hand's amplified voice began. I closed the door, sat down on a straight-backed chair by a table stacked with empty coffee urns, and waited.

Fred was with Dinah. Or at least seeing her home. Brazil was across the bay. Somewhere outside Truro, in the light of the moon, Billy Sullivan was looking at his little cropduster loaded with 20-gallon drums of tranquilizer. One drum. Don't exaggerate. You had to ingest diazepam, Dinah had said, swallow it or get an injection. Just breathing it in would kick off a headache and make some people's ears ring, but not lay them out, not make them lie down in neat little furrows across the Central Valley.

I lit a cigarette.

On the other hand, if you combined it with certain common water-soluble chemicals, she said, on the army's principle of nerve gas, then you could spray it with considerable effect, anywhere from drowsiness to stupefaction. To death.

I sprayed some smoke into the little room.

And it wasn't hard to make the new chemical solution. It was the kind of thing that all the Princeton sophomores were writing up this year for *Popular Mechanics.*

Maybe Billy just kept the stuff around for the bees, in case the mood struck him again. Apiscide. George Webber would like the word. Just the chemical to have around the place, if the place were being overrun with unusually aggressive people. Even a private army of them. But Fells had never mentioned the Central Valley in his life, Foreman claimed. He thought he spent most of his spare time at the shore.

Applause rumbled through the fiberglass walls. Hand was going to like the story. He wasn't going to like the price.

"What the hell do you think you're doing?" Hand closed the

door gently and shouted again. "You want Mrs. Browning to see you out there?"

"She didn't."

"Or Kingsley?"

"Kingsley was blinding himself. Everybody was watching you. You had them by the balls."

"Jesus." He looked around the little room. "I thought this was the can. What's so goddam important you couldn't use the goddam telephone? You find Webber?"

I told him about the visitors to my office. He paced back and forth, twisting the spigots on all the empty coffee urns. I told him about Chan-lui.

"He's about as trustworthy as Brazil. Hurry up, dammit. This room stinks."

I told him about Foreman, about Fells, about tranquil Truro. Then I told him about Connie Larkin and her broken neck, her head flopping sideways off the edge of the stretcher, underneath the Bridgestone decal. Finally I told him what I wanted to do about it all.

He sat down in one of the hard chairs, then stood up again. His face was still flushed from the applause, the banquet, but under the buzz of fluorescent lights, it looked older and wearier too, like a crumpled ball of paper.

"I've got to get back to the office," he said. "We're short 20 tons of newsprint for Sunday. Truckers taking a goddam job action again." He put his hand on the door knob. "Getting like the frigging English, call something a job action when it means you don't move your butt. Action!" He snorted in disgust, then released the knob. "I don't know, Mike. I just don't know. The police series is going beautifully—some of the people out there, the big people with the big money, are talking about me . . . This is a risk. I don't care about paying for it. But you could blow me right out of the water if you're wrong. Crusader is one thing. Scandalmonger is another. They're talking about the governorship right now. But not if I turn the paper into the goddam *National Enquirer.*" He took a deep breath and opened the door part way. "Do you see what I'm talking about?"

I nodded.

"I never heard of you if you fuck up."

"Yes or no, Carl?"

He rubbed his nose and looked at the floor.

"See how far you can get," he said.

Through the door, the banquet room appeared almost deserted, except for waiters and busboys picking up at the head table. A group of men were lingering by the main exit, laughing at something.

"Walk me back to the paper," he said. "I told everybody I had to get back anyway."

He stopped at the door to shake hands with the group and talk for a moment. I walked ahead and waited at the elevator rank. Hand caught up with me just as the bell rang, and we stepped inside together.

In this section of the hotel, they use glass-walled elevators that climb up and down outside the walls before going inside a conventional shaft. A press agent's dream, an acrophobe's nightmare.

"Like riding in a goddam bubble," Hand said irritably, looking around. "I always think the thing's going to come loose and I'm going to float across San Francisco like a bubble."

"You're getting poetic, Carl."

"It means I'm horny." He leaned against the wooden rail and stared out as the elevator started its slow descent. Outside, the city stretched toward the bay, toward the mountains, the Valley. Lights blinked and moved in every direction, like the inside of a computer, I imagined, or the inside of a brain. Fog blew in ruffles below us, and the moon was coming up over Berkeley, fat and orange.

"I miss the east," Hand said. "I miss the hot summer nights without goddam fog. I miss it when it doesn't rain out here until December. I miss the goddam crickets." He turned his face to me, pale in the artificial light. "You've forgotten. You're like a native out here. You don't know how goddam strange this is."

We slid down the throat of the building.

CHAPTER 17

THE ALARM IS SUPPOSED TO BE FOOLPROOF.

Twelve hundred dollars, the landlord had told us, the best system money could buy. He hadn't wanted any alarm at all, until burglars had broken into the basement storage rooms and found Dr. Susen's old black bag packed away in a suitcase, and then he had no choice. Let the junkies of any big American city know there's a doctor living in a building and you might as well forget about ordinary security. Black bag equals doctor equals drugs. Six break-ins later, including two in the landlord's ground floor flat, and we had the alarm.

I looked at the light seeping out from under my apartment door like a puddle.

The door itself was cracked open about a quarter of an inch, its hinges creaking slightly in the draft. Upstairs somebody flushed a toilet. Downstairs the street light from the sidewalk just reached the first stairs, brightening the faded green runner; just reached that far and stopped, as if poised to listen.

I pushed the foolproof front door open a little farther. My fist pulled the butt of the .38 above my jacket pocket. The envelope of money that Hand had given me dragged at the other pocket. A photo-electric beam shoots knee-high across the hallway right behind the door. The switch to turn it off is located above the frame of the door and to the left, an awkward spot to reach even if you know exactly where the tiny lever is. Once you open the door, you have seven seconds to flip the switch off. After that, the alarm sounds automatically in the nearest police station, nine blocks away. The hinges creaked again. I nudged the door farther open with my shoe. The only other way to get past is to cut off the electric power of the whole building, which also triggers the alarm at the police station. For 1,200 bucks, you get quality, reliability, peace of mind. For 1,200 bucks, I had an open door and a burgled apartment.

Or maybe more.

I pushed the door completely open and looked down the hallway. The umbrella stand I had brought up from Los Angeles, a bright orange tube with Mexican parrots painted on it, lay against the bedroom door where it had fallen. I drew the pistol free and stepped inside.

Inside the apartment, the draft felt stronger. I glanced to my left, through the bedroom door, at the usual jumble of furniture and clothes. Nobody was hiding under the bed.

I moved silently down the hall, stopping to peer through the open door on my right into the kitchen. It looked as undisturbed as ever. A few plates in the drainer. Some miscellaneous bottles and glasses on the counter. A box of cereal. The barrel of the pistol cast a long black shadow across the white walls, a bony finger pointing.

"You must *live* on granola, man. Shee-it. Good Scotch, though." Grab showed me a full glass and a grin. "Up yours."

He was sitting in the brown leather easy chair by the windows, looking out at the night and the water. He wore a light blue vicuna shirt that hung over his hips and was cut in a V halfway to his navel. The pants were orange, made out of a material that shimmered as he wagged his legs. His loafers were tasseled and white, brilliantly white, and he wore no socks.

"Anybody else here?" I gestured toward the rest of the apartment. "Or are you drinking alone?"

"Some of the brothers down on the street. Nobody here. You got problems?"

I looked down at the pistol, tried to feel angry, ended up feeling tired and thirsty.

"Hey, man, have some Scotch, relax, live a little, work your way in. Show a little hospitality."

I got a glass from the kitchen and poured a handful of Scotch over two cubes. Grab was fiddling with my binoculars, holding them up to his eyes, looking out at the bay, then re-adjusting them.

"Nice place here," he told me while he twirled one eyepiece and looked. "You seen the fox across that roof? Some kind of nurse, man."

"How'd you get in, Grab?"

"Guy who put in that little number kinda owes me a favor. I stay pretty tight with the alarm-sters. I been trying to reach you at your office."

"You want to sell me a better alarm?"

"Naw. Got a deal for you, man," he said, putting down the binoculars.

"Tell."

"You remember I told you about those two evil brothers got an offer to waste the dude in your picture?"

"I remember."

"One of them just had his memory jogged, how about that?"

"Yeah? How?"

"Down in San Jose. Got himself another felony—and that makes two. So he needs money now."

"What'd he do?"

"He playful. He tried to shampoo another brother with some kind of battery acid, down in a bar."

"Boys will be boys."

"Right on, right on. But this boy I'm talking about needs bail to get out and get clear. You follow what I'm saying?"

"How much?"

"Judge set it at 50. Stiff little cocksucker. Wants to clean up San Jose. Gonna have better luck flyin'. Hey!" He giggled, picked up his glass and drank loudly.

"If it's 50,000 bail, he only needs 2,500 to get out. You must have that in the glove compartment of your El Dorado, Grab. Why the favor?"

"No favor, man. I got the bread for sure. But, like I say, this one evil brother. He liable to skip out on the bail, you know what I mean. So it's only five I'm out, but you know how it is. I got to go after the son-of-a-bitch, he skips out on my money. Got to give him a conk where everybody knows it, or else the troops get the wrong idea, they say, hey old Grab's gettin' ripe, he pass up five for this one, he sure to forget two for that one, three for that one, 15 for that one. You see how it is when you got responsibility, right, Sherlock? You got trouble too."

"Uneasy lies the head that wears the crown." I drained my Scotch and poured us both another.

"So right, man. But now look. He skip out on *you*, that's no trouble for *me*. And you don't mind losing the green too much, 'cause you going to talk with him before he takes to drifting. I'll give you that much. Hey, man, you got five in the monster stereo right now."

"Have you got a bailsman?"

"You know Will He Wash?"

I nodded and chewed some ice. Most bailsmen in California cities are black or Chicano these days, and they run their pictures in the yellow pages to prove it. Wilson E. Washington was a well-known bailsman down in the Tenderloin.

"He put up the stuff if I tell him it's OK. Only thing, Sherlock, he going to want the five in cash."

"I was thinking of using my Visa card."

He chuckled and got up. "You never stop, man. I wrote the name here." He gave me a memo sheet with the letterhead of the San Francisco Warriors. I didn't even want to think about that. "Call Will He in the morning, work it out."

Grab walked to the end of the room, put my binoculars on a book shelf, and pointed to the piles of books and papers on the floor I hadn't finished shelving.

"You got mice, man, or you got rats?"

"Rats."

"Yeah, that's what I thought when you walk in with that cannon sticking out your sleeve." He picked up a black leather wide-brimmed hat which I hadn't seen, lying on a table by the door. "You a straight guy, Sherlock, and you got pretty damned good moves. But you know what? I could have blown your head off the minute you came in."

He went down the hallway whistling.

CHAPTER 18

THE IDENTITY PERSON WAS IN.

In the middle of a stand of redwoods in the Berkeley hills is a little house so carefully blended into the lot that it seemed to have arisen by spontaneous construction. From the front door, not another house or person could be seen.

"Describe her."

I described Betty Jo Rule.

"You got a buzzer?"

I took out my wallet and showed her my license. She gave it a close reading, then took out my driver's license too, and glanced at the back.

"All right. You can come in." She turned and waddled into the living room, making the whole house shake on its supporting poles. "Button up the hardware," she said over her shoulder. I buttoned my jacket over the pistol.

"In there."

She stood at the door to a fair-sized room that looked out onto the backyard and a maze of trees and vines. The room itself contained a beat-up wooden desk scattered with scraps of paper, paper of all colors and sizes, and many small bottles of paste and glue. Behind the desk was a wide-framed upholstered chair; behind that an olive-green filing cabinet and a stack of cardboard liquor boxes. Three walls were hung with dry bamboo matting. Along the fourth stood a spindly metal bookcase cluttered with paperbacks, Kleenex boxes, pharmacist's jars, and five or six small mirrors on wooden tri-leg stands. The floor was completely covered with a dark brown rug that had the consistency and smell of dog hair.

I sat down in the chair in front of the desk. The papermate, as she used to be called, looked at me briefly, grunted, and left.

A minute or two afterward, through the window behind the desk, I could see her easing herself onto the redwood deck that ran the width of the house. A tall, skinny man with a beard and apostolic haircut sprawled half out of a hot tub, listening to disco music on a radio. She spoke to him and he slowly got up, spilling water and steam. He picked up a white towel and wiped his face, then, completely naked, he went into the house. The papermate started back.

While I waited, I looked at the wall directly behind my chair. It was covered with photographs, all of her, carefully mounted in various expensive frames. No two photographs were alike. The nearest to my head showed her in a bright caftan, standing on a beach, long hair blown out by the breeze. The one above it showed her in front of a car on a San Francisco street, unsmiling, wearing a mannish suit, close-cropped hair, and carrying a big shoulder-strap purse. Others showed her at various weights, in various costumes, here and there in California. She was always alone in the pictures.

When I had met her before, two or three years back, the identity person had been thin, almost dainty looking, and her hair had been fussed into a fashionable Berkeley frizz. Now she came back through the door as fat as somebody could get, fat enough to resemble one of those huge balloon characters in a Macy's parade, so fat that she seemed lighter than air somehow, puffed up to bursting and ready to float away. She wheezed into the chair behind the desk, and I thought of a favorite remark of my grandmother's: she was taller lying down than standing up.

"You brought cash, I assume."

"It's not a complicated job. What I want is privacy for it."

"Let's see the cash."

I counted out 20 fifty-dollar bills on her desk. As she watched with small black eyes, her mouth was sucking in a creamy marshmallow cookie she had taken from a drawer in the desk.

"This is the guy," I said when she had moved the money to the center of the desk and squared the stack. She took the clipping with the photograph of Fells and studied it. "You've still got a little bit of Boston accent," she said matter-of-factly, without looking up. "You want this superimposed on a glossy?"

"That's right. Somebody is out taking the glossy right now, of a man standing in a field. I want the picture to show him talking to this man, in the field."

"You're going to need another picture of this guy." She snapped a finger against Fells's solemn face. "Too grainy. And what am I going to use for full-length? You've only got the guy's head here."

"Fred said you could fake a full-length out of files."

"Sure, I can fake it. I can make it look pretty good. But anybody who knows about cameras is going to spot the lines and the glue marks. Under an ordinary glass, he could see glue. I mean, it depends on whether you're dealing with a turkey or somebody who knows what he's doing. That goes for the other stuff too."

"Can you fix it another way?"

She popped a cookie and considered. An orange cat stalked along the window sill behind her and dropped silently to the floor. I looked it over for batteries and wires.

"Can you go another thou?"

"If I have to."

"Mickey can go down to the university and snap him coming or going. We use a little Minolta Spymaster, about this big." She held up a marshmallow cookie for me to see, then ate it. "You tell me where, he'll wait outside, get a whole roll of him, moving, standing, everything. Whatever I need. Then I put it on top of the glossy you bring me."

"Can you do that today?"

She shook her head. "Negative. I wait till you bring me the glossy so I can match exposures and film type with the Minolta." The cat squeezed under the desk and looked up at me, licking its lips. "I also wait for the other thou."

I pulled the envelope out of my jacket pocket again and counted another thousand onto the desk. Plant security at the *Constitution* was going to look impregnable on the books this month.

"Is it Fred taking the picture?"

"Yeah."

"Busy boy. He was looking for some kid named Hoffman last week. Tell him to bring the film here and we'll develop it."

"He should be back by four or five." I stood up. She wiped her fingers clean on a tissue and looked at me as if I were an empty box of cookies.

"You going to screw the guy in the picture?"

"Yep."

She pulled a blue U.S. passport folder from the center drawer of the desk and dismissed me with her eyes. The last cookie made a bulge the size of a golfball in the smooth surface of her cheek. "Good," she said with another grunt. "Off the fucking pigs."

Twenty minutes and half a world away, three blocks past Sather Gate, I sat down in a gloomy booth against the back wall of Tony O's.

"I couldn't talk to you in the building," Bartus said. He was wearing a dark blue workshirt with "University of California" sewn in white thread over one pocket. "This place is OK, though."

Sunlight had never reached the line of booths we sat in, apparently. I moved one foot over the sticky floor. Or brooms. Next to my leg the wide gray tape on the vinyl upholstery had peeled back over the years, and now a thin coil of spring poked a couple of inches up toward the table edge, like a rusty snake. On the table top itself, in the midst of initials and dates, someone had carved a large reclining amazon; very near her, at a suggestive angle, somebody else had carved an outline of the campanile.

"This place is fine," I said.

A blonde boy in a long white apron slid a disc of pizza onto the table between us and picked up the two empty beer bottles.

"You want another beer?" Bartus asked.

I nodded and gave the kid a five while Bartus drained his glass. Then he picked up a triangle of pizza, chewing fast on the little strings of cheese that slipped slowly toward his lap. When the kid brought back the beer and change, Bartus stopped eating, glanced up and down, and patted the top of the octagonal box beside him.

"More than a week is going to have to cost you extra," he said.

"I'll have them back by Wednesday."

He looked disappointed. Little bits of cheese had caught in his beard, and he sent his tongue out on a search-and-destroy mission. I missed Tommy Shoults.

"You probably already got a projector and shit," he said.

"All I need."

"Yeah." He aimed a crust at the rest of the room. "These college kids never do anything at regular hours, do they? Three in the goddam afternoon they're having Coke and pizza for breakfast."

I saw the shadow before he did because he was still talking. But he suddenly put the crust down on the table and rasped at me under his breath, "Oh, hey, be cool."

The cop's bulk blocked the dim light for a long moment, then his tan uniform emerged out of the corner and started moving slowly in our direction. I picked up a slice of pizza and ate an anchovy.

"I know this guy," Bartus whispered.

None of the students straightened in their chairs as the cop strolled slowly by, looking them over. Most slouched a little lower and stopped talking. Bartus and I were by 20 years the oldest pair in the restaurant. He came through the tables toward us at a deliberate pace, sandy-haired, middle-aged, a comfortable roll of fat around his hips, just above the regulation gunbelt and Mace can. His eyes were hidden behind reflecting sunglasses, but they would be regulation eyes, too, warm and soft as pebbles.

"You don't like anchovy, I'll take 'em," Bartus told me.

"Who's this?"

The nightstick fell gently across the table, just brushing the edge of the pizza dish, as if he were measuring it to slice.

"He's OK."

"You work at the audiovisual, don't you?" the cop said to Bartus.

"This guy's a tape salesman. He's taking back some defective tape to see can they fix it."

The cop looked at me, but all I saw were two little reflections of myself staring back. Across his breast pocket a black rectangle spelled out the name Marcus in letters about the size of the health warning on a pack of cigarettes. They have a name-tag law in Berkeley, but the cops don't like it any better than in other places.

"If you know him," the cop said.

"Sure."

"We see somebody your age in a place like this," the cop explained to me, "we don't know him, we think drugs right away."

"I understand."

Marcus dropped his nightstick through the loop on his belt and picked up a slice of pizza.

"I busted a guy yesterday who was selling angel dust down in the BART station. The guy was so doped up himself, he tried to sell the shit to a priest."

"I ask you," Bartus said.

The cop talked a minute longer, then swaggered off toward the street. When he had disappeared, Bartus belched. I took out a roll of 20s, which he stuffed into the top of his pants before reluctantly handing me the octagonal case.

"I wish I knew what the hell good that stuff is to you," he said.

Fred called about six from the papermate's house.

"Do you know how *hot* it is out there?"

"It's all in your mind. Can she work the film?"

"They're developing it now, her and Mickey. A hundred and eight. I almost burned out the air conditioner on the car. I'm pouring a can of beer down my shirt right now."

"Did Sullivan buy your story?"

"You bet. I had the press card, the letter, the works, three different cameras. *California Today* wants to do a story on farmers in the Valley, just like you said, and I was out taking pictures for the writers. The old man didn't seem to care too much one way or the other, but the good-looking kid stood right up by the tractor and let me snap all I wanted. They didn't even call the neighbors to check me out. I wasted two rolls of film on some guy up the road in a mobile home."

"Do you still have that friend in Motor Vehicles?"

"Henry Beek, yeah."

I looked across my desk at the huge black man standing by my window. Watching the police station, I assumed. His shoulders spanned the window, his thighs and buttocks bulged out of the khaki trousers, massive as tree trunks. A razor had sheared his skull of all hair whatsoever, and it gleamed under the fluorescent light with a slick polish. On one side of his neck, the corners of a white bandage were already uncurling, a present from the San Jose PD, he had said, along with a few thumps lower down that didn't leave marks. He turned to face me, showing small, narrow eyes, yellow as a muddy flatland river.

"I've got a license number to look up," I told Fred.

"Beek is only there mornings now. They shut down the computer at night anyway to save money. Give it to me, I'll call him in the morning."

I read from my memo pad. 912 KEX. Fred read it back and then hung up.

"You done with me?" my visitor grunted.

"If you can't remember anything else, yeah."

"I gave you the number. Blue Buick Skylark, nothin' special."

"You also gave me middle-aged, medium height, clean shaven—that wouldn't pick him out of a phone booth."

"I ain't plannin' on police school, man."

I could see that. I could also see that I would have to wait till morning for my information. I thanked him. He scowled and left the office slowly, looking back as if he might pull it down in splinters after all. Samson C. Baker. Eddy Street, drifter. Samson with the shaved head. Two hundred and thirty-five pounds of walking felony assault, second-time loser, official bailee of the state of California. He had forgotten to thank me for the bail. Whoever had been waiting in the hall joined him, and I heard the elevator ring them down.

"That was about nine on the Richter scale," Dinah said.

I fumbled on the bureau top and found my cigarettes. Dinah turned over on her side, propping her face on a pillow, and watched while I lit one and walked back to the window by the head of the bed. Through the part in the curtains, you could see a dark gray line high up, then lower down a black one where the next apartment building started. I drew the curtains back and saw the great clouds of fog moving in slow motion, scrubbing the city. I tried to make my mind lie down and be still.

"Are you a grump?" Dinah asked from the bed.

"Hand is so nervous all of a sudden he makes me nervous."

"Man is the worrying animal," she said sleepily. She stretched her legs and looked at her toes arching slowly under the sheets.

"The thing ought to work," I said. "If the identity person did her stuff right. If Fred's friend in Motor Vehicles is on the ball. If Hand doesn't lose his nerve. There's really nothing else to do." I exhaled smoke and watched it flatten against the window panes, the little sister of the fog. "But I don't like plans, even ones that I make up myself. I don't like the constraint. I like to leave room for impulse, flexibility. Plans are ruts."

"You're getting self-righteous about your flaws," Dinah yawned.

"Don't you ever get tired of analyzing?" I snapped, looking at her quickly.

"Don't you ever get tired of being so damned independent you can't even live with a simple plan for 24 hours?"

She sat up stiffly against the headboard and we glared at each other across the faint light. I looked away and tapped ash into the ceramic ashtray one of Dinah's patients had made for her last year. Under it lay a blue manila hospital folder, probably a case history she had brought home to read before I arrived. I could see the name "Tracy" typed on a label in one corner. Dinah's friends are divided on the issue. Half of them think that, although I can read and write and take my hat off indoors, she should drop me like a hot potato and marry another head doctor, or another professional, or at least a college graduate. The other half think that a liberated woman and a "rogue male," as Shirley Mendelsohn had called me, are poor bets for anything more substantial than a two-week stand in the summer doldrums. Especially when the woman makes $54,000 and the man clears $18,000 or $19,000 in a good year. We had actually been together for four and a half years. It surprised her friends that there was anything so conventional as fidelity in our relationship. Or fights.

I drew in more cigarette smoke and watched dawn hurrying into the sky. My eyes felt tired, sticky, my throat tense with anger. I saw a light go in the other building and then go off again.

"Remember how you used to talk about the army?" she asked after a time from the bed.

I nodded and continued to look out the window. I had hated the army.

"You used to say you had no quarrel with human nature, but you thought the army tried to press it into molds it was never meant to fit."

"I remember." I dropped more ash into the ashtray and wondered if "Tracy" was the little girl who had burst into tears every time she saw her father.

"You are the least class-conscious person I have ever known," Dinah said. "In a way the most tolerant. I think the kind of threat Brazil poses to somebody like your friend Grab or even that mysterious Chinaman—that gets to you more than you think. It's molding again. And it puts an extra burden on a vigilante."

Dinah likes to peel things to the core. Which is why she's a shrink. I took another breath and then put out the cigarette.

"I'm sorry about snapping," I said, more or less graciously.

"Grump," she said.

I looked across the room toward her. Always, from the moment I had first met her, Dinah had had that quality of self-confident, challenging sexuality that a few lucky women seem born with. A lioness, not a deer.

"I'm sorry," I said again.

She kicked the sheet halfway off and rolled toward the center of the bed. Her fingertips just grazed my hips as she turned.

"Did you know that the Richter scale is open-ended?" she asked.

CHAPTER 19

DOWN? THE COMPUTER IS *DOWN?*" HAND'S VOICE MIMICKED Fred's. "Why the hell do they talk about machines like that?" He switched to a mincing feminine pitch. "The computer is depressed and wants to be alone. The computer wants to sulk."

Fred spread both hands in front of him, palms facing the floor, and appeared to be inspecting his nails.

Hand walked a few paces back and forth in front of his chair. "So when do they get it up?" he asked in his normal voice.

"Early in the week, the fellow says."

"Early in the week. Meantime, Haller here has the occasional armed hood coming in the door, nobody knows why, we have the license of the guy who wanted to kill George Webber, but the computer won't tell us who he is, and Haller also has the bright idea that Brazil is marching some doped-up super army all over the goddam Central Valley. Play that thing again, will you?" he said abruptly.

Fred leaned forward and hit the rewind switch on the recorder. We listened to it squeal for half a minute, then he pressed the Play button.

". . . reciprocal centers of the brain for rage and fear. You can remove the amygdala and control these centers to some extent—the amygdala seems to control dominance and submission too—but that's impractical on any large scale." Fells's voice was scratchy but unmistakable. There was a muffled thud, as if the microphone had moved. "And in some cases *increased* aggressiveness has followed the removal of the amygdala."

"So you decided to use chemicals?" My own voice was a little louder on the tape and sounded high to me. Fred readjusted a dial. Hand continued to pace.

"Yes." Fells sounded contrite. "Certain new peptide molecules have been shown to pass through the blood-brain barrier into the cortex, but only in combination with other, sometimes toxic, chemicals."

My voice: "You mean poisonous?"

Fells: "Yes."

My voice: "What happens if you do penetrate the blood-brain barrier?"

Fells: "If you rearrange the coding mechanisms in the synaptic/dendritic network . . ." He seemed to hesitate. ". . . You can reprogram the activity of the limbic system. In other words, you can make people wildly, suicidally aggressive in their behavior. With such aggression usually comes a temporary increase in physical strength, because of unrestrained neural signals to the adrenal gland. We have a laboratory monkey now, a fairly small specimen, a lemur, about 14 inches tall, six pounds in weight, the size of many newborn human babies, who strangled to death a dog after receiving peptides in his water."

My voice: "Is this research legal?"

Fells: "No." Pause. "It is quite illegal and very dangerous. That is why I have decided to break it off. And to make public what has been happening."

My voice: "You have been doing this research where? Berkeley?"

Fells: "No. In the Central Valley. In special laboratories." The tape scratched again here, more loudly than before, but Fells's words were clear enough.

My voice: "Is all this on the Sullivan farm in Truro?"

Fells: "Yes."

My voice: "With the knowledge and support of the owner of the farm? For his own political purposes."

Fells: "Yes."

My voice: "Who is that?"

Fells: "Frank Brazil."

Hand switched off the machine.

"She's terrific, isn't she?" Fred said. "She had me say the Gettysburg Address into the machine, diddled around with some splices and made it start out, 'Off the fucking pigs.' She even rearranges single syllables, her and Mickey. It took them an hour to get 'Brazil,' but it sounds terrific."

"Yeah. Terrific," Hand said sourly.

He took a cigar about the size of a tommy gun out of a metal tube and jammed it into his mouth. I lit another cigarette and remembered my own surprise at the tapes. I had written the basic script, of course, a patchwork of guesses. But using only my voice and two or three reels of Fells's videotaped lectures from Berkeley—"Biochem. 161a, The Chemistry of the Brain"—Rita the papermate had created a whole conversation. A whole confession, in fact. Or betrayal, if you took Brazil's point of view. For once, I saw the advantage in having a university of 28,000 students, most of whom glimpsed their famous professors only on television screens in scattered classrooms. An expert would catch the doctoring she had done, of course. It's become a commonplace kind of fraud in the gim-mick-minded world of industrial espionage—Pinkerton's and some of the other big agencies have whole divisions devoted to polygraphy and voice analysis—but we didn't expect to be dealing with experts. We had in mind an audience of one.

"This is totally impossible—I mean, you're talking about fraud?"

Nobody looked at Frederic Kingsley. Nobody had been looking at him for the past half hour, since he had come in the door with Hand, an uninvited, jittery observer, skittish as a bug. Now I made myself turn slowly to face him.

"What's the problem, Kingsley?"

"What isn't!"

He uncoiled from his chair in the corner and slouched to-ward the desk.

"You can't involve the newspaper in intimidation—and forgery." He turned his pouty face toward Hand, who was chewing the cigar and studying the floor. "I told you to be careful two nights ago, when I saw you talking to this man outside the office." I thought he was going to wag his finger at me. "You can't let the disappearance of one neurotic reporter—who's probably gone off drunk with some tramp anyway—you can't let that drive you to these wild extremes. Fake tapes! Fake photographs! Frank Brazil and a respected, highly respected Berkeley scientist in collusion on secret research!"

"What's the other explanation, dammit?" Hand kept his voice down with difficulty. "What else fits the facts?" He pulled the cigar out of his mouth and began ticking off points on his fingers. "Brazil owns this farm in the Valley. And a huge tract of land with it, that goes all the hell up into the foothills. Haller said so, but I had it double-checked. Fact. George Web-ber, who's had his knife out for Brazil since the year one, goes out to this same goddam farm, sniffing for something. Second time out, he disappears—poof! Gone. Unless Haller here has gone to the trouble of forging some gas company receipts too, the last place we got Webber is on his way back to the Valley. Fact." His gaze came back to me, bleak, unfriendly. "Now he tells me he's got a witness, another highly goddam respected Berkeley faculty member that says Brazil talks with this guy Fells. And he tells me this guy Fells is an expert in how to make people behave violently. And he tells me that out on the farm, they've got enough tranquilizer to stun an army. Fact, fact, superfucking fact!"

He started to march across the office, away from Kingsley.

"Who the hell knows what's really happening out there?" he growled. I couldn't decide if he was talking to me or to Kingsley or to himself.

"Look," he said, turning on his heel and coming back. "You know the kind of man Brazil is. We all know." He was looking hard at Kingsley, pleading. "Brazil's a vigilante. He's got a mind that thinks in terms of baseball bats, nightsticks, acid baths, spades, niggers, greasers. He makes speeches about preventive detention and the yellow-black-and-blue peril. Those goddam security guards of his have kept the East Bay in a fucking racial uproar. Now I'm hearing that we got a crippled professor with a ransacked house, and Bridgestone Security stopping by. I'm hearing that Webber's girlfriend gets herself knocked dead by a prowler in a house his people protect. Maybe there's a connection, maybe not. But most of all, I'm hearing that he's got a violence expert working for him, maybe, just maybe pumping up his troops with monkey glands or whatever else is going to turn them into the fucking Hulk—you know how many security guards he has in that Bridgestone racket of his? Four hundred! Four hundred!"

He started pacing again. "That son of a bitch scares me.

I can see him coming up with something dynamite, I mean something that could blow the top off law enforcement in this country. Who knows? Supercops, maybe. Cops so strong, so mean and wild you're going to send a dozen of them through Watts or Harlem or South Oakland keeping law and order like a fucking buzzsaw. Or the other way around—provoking riots so he can take the chains off his troops and let them really wade in. Who knows if he can?" He wheeled and leveled the cigar at Kingsley. "*The story is that he's trying.* And you're telling me, don't play dirty to get it, don't try to fool nice Dr. Fells into squealing on Brazil. There's a Pulitzer on every fucking page of this!"

Kingsley had been holding himself stiff while Hand talked, the fingers of one hand holding down his glasses' rim as if they would blow off. He started to follow Hand up and down the room.

"You're hearing," he said scornfully, glowering at me as they passed the desk. Fred lifted his feet for them. "You're hearing everything from one source, a two-bit private detective. A do-nothing with a record at the district attorney's office"—Hand waved cigar smoke away in disgust—"all right, all right," Kingsley amended, almost scampering to keep up with the big man's steps. "Forget that. But look at him. A failed reporter, years out of the business, makes ten, fifteen thousand a year at most, but finally gets his fingers into an expense account—how much has he touched you for already? Three, four thousand?"

Hand stopped pacing and looked first at me, then at the wall.

"Mother's going to like that a lot, you bet. Money down the drain, no receipts, only his word that this tape woman cost such and such. Him and an ex-cop who ought to be working school crossings."

Fred winked at me. I began to think there was iron in Kingsley's slouch after all.

Hand and Kingsley ignored us. They were face to face now in the middle of the room. Kingsley's skin had gone pale red with anger, his arms jerked at his sides, his Adam's apple bobbed like a cork. Hand was motionless, a look of pain digging itself across his big moon face. He squinted as if something were too bright.

"The reason he's only hearing me," I said, "is that Brazil and Fells won't talk to us. You know that, Kingsley. We've tried, I've tried. We've telephoned, written—nothing. These tapes are a fraud, I grant you, and the photographs." I tapped the top one on my desk. In it Bobby Sullivan and Martin Fells, Ph.D., stood talking to one another beside a tractor and several drums of pesticide. Behind them the flat skies of the Central Valley lay like a sheet of glowing metal. The papermate had done a flawless job. "But if we show them to Fells, the weak link, and play him the tape and threaten to send them to Brazil, I think we'll get cooperation. He knows what Brazil is, too. If Brazil thought Fells had sold out, gone over, broke down, whatever, he'd do more than write a letter—"

"That's exactly the problem," Kingsley interrupted in a shrill voice. "You're talking about provoking Brazil—to what? Beatings? Assault? Murder? Suppose Fells does say something incriminating—I don't believe for an instant he will—suppose he does and you print it: what then? Is this violent Frank Brazil going to lie down and let the paper print story after story, walk all over him? He's not going to be in jail. He's got lawyers to guarantee he's not going to be in jail. What's going to happen to Fells then? What's going to happen to the paper—the delivery trucks, the reporters, even you? Are 400 thugs going to sit still? Do you owe Mother that kind of possibility? After what's she's done for you?" He stood up straight, with the air of a man about to fire his best shot. "After what she plans to do for you?"

Hand came around a chair and moved slowly toward me,

fists still jammed in pockets. He took the cigar and rubbed it out savagely in the ashtray on my desk.

"I'm a newspaperman," he spat, looking at me, talking to Kingsley. "I need that story." He glared at the cigar and let it go. "Haller will go to the *Chronicle* with it if we stop now."

"You're not just a newspaperman," Kingsley said urgently. His slight, nervous figure somehow brought an outsized passion to whatever he said. I was quickly revising all my notions about his insignificance. "You've got a future. You've got support, momentum, money. But not if you do this. Not if you bring down everything Mother's been working for this last ten years, not if the paper starts a war."

Hand was leaning stiff-armed on the desk, the weight of his shoulders pressing so hard that the knuckles were white with tension. A cord of muscle in his neck quivered like a bowstring.

"And this man has a record of precipitating violence," Kingsley began after a moment, pointing at me. Then he suddenly went quiet, as if unwilling to risk another sentence, and we all looked at Hand, waiting.

He slowly raised his eyes from the desk to meet mine. His voice came out thin as a dime.

"I need time to think, Mike. I want you to hold off sending that tape."

I looked at him. He might as well have had AMBITION flashing across his forehead in colored lights. He looked like Faust about to shake hands with the Devil. Mrs. Browning's withered claws were devil enough. He had seen me fired to please her. He would let a story die to oblige her nonviolent principles. And maybe to keep his political future where he could see it, nursing away at $10,000,000 or so. On the other hand, I was still working for him, and he was asking me as much as telling.

I sighed.

"This can't sit on ice, Carl. Brazil knows we're pressing. I want to send them today if I can."

He rolled his head to the right and looked at Kingsley. Fred scuffed his feet and made a noise that could have been clearing his throat.

"I'll talk to Mrs. Browning," Hand said.

"Not from here," Kingsley said. His body had begun to sink back into its usual slouch. His face looked as if he'd passed through a fever.

"I'll go see her." To me: "I'll get back to you by six."

He reached for the tape and photographs, found my hands there first.

"Leave those here, Carl. I won't do anything until I hear from you."

He moved his eyes from me to Fred, back again. "All right," he said. "I'll call you."

"By six."

"Yeah." He shook his shoulders loose for a second, then headed for the door. Fred got up and opened it. Hand and Kingsley went out without a word, and Fred closed it softly.

I walked to the window. After about two minutes, Kingsley and Hand emerged and started down the sidewalk, Kingsley gesturing energetically as they walked, Hand stooped, listening, eyes on the pavement. They passed out of sight. I looked at my watch. Ten-twenty on a cold, foggy Saturday morning.

"What does he want?" Fred asked at my shoulder. We both knew he didn't mean Kingsley. "What the hell does he want?"

CHAPTER 20

FRED GOT HUNGRY AGAIN ABOUT THREE.

He put down the paper he had been reading at the desk and looked over at me. I was sitting in the easy chair that's the one with the cushion from Ocean Park—and reading Webber's secondhand copy of *Organic Chemistry.* Webber's columns and files covered the floor around my feet. I looked like an aging sophomore at a cram session.

"I don't know why your pal Hand thinks this is baseball news," he said, pointing at the green sheet.

"What's the matter?"

"Guy named Dopey Fernandez urinated on a birthday cake in the locker room at Toronto."

"Trying to put out the candles?"

"He started a hell of a fight. Why do they even report that kind of thing? Now it's going to be a statistic, a new item in the goddam record book. Name the first lefthander to pee on a cake in the AL East."

"Too bad it wasn't Fireman Lyle," I said, opening *Organic Chemistry* again.

"You think he's going to call?" Fred asked.

"He'll call."

"Is he going along?"

I shrugged.

"You're a worrier, that's what I like about you." He refolded the paper and lined it up on the blotter. "Who's set up to deliver if he says OK?"

"Rocket Delivery Company, serving the Bay Area since 1940. They never sleep."

"Yeah. I was like that in 1940 too." He shoved back the chair, scraping the legs against the hardwood floor. In the glare of the overhead light, his skin looked drained, gray. Behind him, the window showed more gray, in the form of thick, milky fog from a low-pressure center that had camped outside the Golden Gate. Earlier it had been drizzling. Typical San Francisco summer. The coldest winter I ever spent, Mark Twain was supposed to have said, was one July in San Francisco.

"I'm going back out to get some doughnuts," Fred said. He drew his stout body up to his full five-foot-eight and patted his waist indulgently, as he might pat a grandchild. "Maybe I'll jog down there this time. You want some?"

"Just coffee, please."

He pulled his old tan trenchcoat off the hook and went out the door. I rescued one of Webber's clippings from the floor, wondering if Webber was ever going to be around to read them again himself. In the corridor, there was a muffled sound, like the elevator doors closing.

But not quite like that.

I put down the clipping and stood up. Outside, cars hissed by. Inside, silence. I walked quietly to the door, hand on hip, near my holster, and opened it.

"Mike! Go!"

Fred was wriggling in the far corner of the corridor, pinned down by two figures in raincoats. A third one pointed a pistol at my face. Kenny.

As he fired, I flung myself to the left of the elevators and rolled, flinching at the dull thump of the silencer. I pulled my own gun free. Kenny fired again, and hot splinters of something stung my face. I grabbed the handle of the fire door into the staircase and stumbled through.

"Stop!"

I collided first with the metal bannister, bounced back, and collided again with the fat man coming up the stairs. My gun clattered against one slippery step and soared into the air as he kicked it. A moment later, it banged like a gong four stories down.

It wasn't much of a fight. He kicked me awkwardly in the cheek. I hooked his calf and dropped him headfirst on the landing, sprawling backwards. I lunged forward and grabbed the big pistol spilling from his jacket. He sat up and I hit him with the barrel, hard across the temple. The door started to open and I scrambled around him, tripping on his feet, grasping the bannister with one hand, looking for a place to stand and shoot.

Kenny poked his head through the crack. I fired twice, missed. The hollow stairwell jumped with sound. I began to vault downward, step after step. Somebody shouted overhead. I ricocheted off two narrow corners, descending in tighter and tighter circles. The steps swam under my feet. I rammed against the door on the third-floor landing, pushed the bar down—Fred shouted.

I looked up.

Kenny held Fred over the stairwell, upside down, head pointing toward the concrete floor far below. The trench-coat flapped from his shoulders like brown bats' wings. He twisted once in Kenny's grip, then hung very still.

"Put it down, Haller."

I raised the gun. In the poorly lit stairwell, with an unfamiliar pistol, at the outline of Kenny's head behind Fred's legs—it would have to be a better shot than I was likely to make. Good shot, bad shot, neither one was going to help Fred much.

I raised the barrel higher, balanced Kenny's ear on the sight. Then lowered the pistol and dropped it to the floor. Another man came rapidly down the stairs.

CHAPTER 21

A LOUD BUMP JOLTED ME AWAKE, AND MY HEAD FLOATED OFF. Heat. Unending heat. Heat that pressed down like a weight from every direction, a tight, thick coffin of heat.

Against their will, my eyes unstuck themselves. Heat and darkness.

The floor bumped again and swayed. I moved my head tenderly. Somebody groaned, probably me.

I blinked a few times mid propped myself on my elbows, banging the back of my head painfully on a wall. I was inside a small service van apparently, the kind that delivers diapers and pizzas and cadavers. There were no windows along the sides, only occasional cracks of light from tiny rips in the metal, much longer cracks along the outline of the back door. I sat all the way up, clenching my teeth to keep my stomach in, and extended my hands to both sides of the van. There was a smell of gasoline, stale straw, something else that was likely roasting flesh. I bent forward and patted both hands in little circles, like a blind man, stopping suddenly when I touched short, moist hair. Fred made a low noise and shook his head.

We were still in our San Francisco clothes, I realized, and the temperature inside the bouncing van must have been far over a hundred. I pulled off his coat and loosened his collar, then did the same for myself. It helped not at all.

Fred coughed and rolled over onto his stomach. Greasy with sweat, I rocked forward on my knees, bracing my hands against the hot metal of the right side of the van. Through the largest tear, a clean rupture about two inches wide, one inch long, I could see the brilliant glow of sunshine and the unmistakable wide, brown horizon of the Central Valley.

We hit a bump, Fred rolled like a loose bottle, and I pawed the hot metal with slippery fingers. Then the van resumed its steady speed, running along a paved road in a straight line, through rows of green plants, tomatoes or rice. In the distance, along the jolting horizon, giant smoky fingers probed the sky. Crop foes again, huge mounds of burning straw. The van couldn't have got much hotter if we had driven through them.

I slumped back against the front panel. My left arm twinged insistently, so I ran my fingers over a swollen area on the triceps, a little spot the size of a quarter, just where doctors are trained to place a needle. The hot air hunkered down on me like an incubus, my eyes clamped shut, my mouth slacked open. I could pass out again, or I could hum the fire scene from *Gotterdamerung*. Fred didn't stir. With my eyes closed, I watched a long black wave of nothing roll toward me and break.

When I woke up again, it was night. Or early morning.

I sat up very slowly. The space I now found myself in was cooler by far than the van, and standing still. Overhead, pale beams of light penciled their way through a series of irregular cracks. I felt a dirt floor, wooden walls, no Fred. I stood up, letting the nausea drain out of my belly.

It was a shed of some kind. My trained detective's nose, tamped with dust, could still distinguish the smells of hay and animals and motor oil. By standing against the wall and peering through the widest of the cracks, I could also see stars, the black shadow of a tree; other shadows to one side of my spot could have been a truck or the corner of another building. I sat down again, weakly.

My watch was gone, as was my belt. My mouth felt as if an owl had slept in it. A dog barked once in the distance and was quiet. I swallowed cool air. Half remembering as I slumped back, I rubbed my left arm and felt for the swollen point where a needle had gone in. Before I found it, I was asleep again.

I was awakened by a boot in the ribs.

I coughed and turned over, protesting. The boot landed again, hard, and I opened my eyes.

"He's OK."

Flat Oklahoma twang, nasal and brassy. I had heard it before. I focused more clearly. Bobby Sullivan squinted down at me from a great height, a lopsided grin slitting his fat face. His bad eye still looked like a fresh scratch. The rest of his face looked like a free-way accident.

"Give him some water," Bobby said, and the bright red scar down his cheek moved like a snake when he spoke.

One of the men who had been holding Fred in the corridor years ago came through the door, still wearing a black suit and white shirt, unbuttoned at the collar, no tie. He carried an aluminum feed bucket full of dirty water, which he poured slowly over my head, making Bobby Sullivan laugh and making me sit up with a jump. While his laugh wound down to a gritty hack, I rubbed water from my eyes and tried unsuccessfully to lick it from the corners of my mouth. My swollen tongue worked in and out like a broom handle.

Bobby had a gun. I spotted it right away, a double-barreled, well-oiled heavy-gauge shotgun, with "Weatherby" printed in gold across the walnut stock and a tan canvas strap pulled tight as a nerve, the big size bore that a farmer might use to shoot vermin or clear a tree stump. It lay comfortably in the crook of his right arm like a child's doll, barrels pointed casually in the general direction of my feet. But it wouldn't have to travel far to reach my middle. I drew my knees up cautiously.

"Enjoy your breakfast?" Bobby sneered.

Some of us are morning people, some are not. I concentrated on clearing my eyes and ventilating my mouth, and didn't say anything. Bobby watched me for a minute, then suddenly hooked one boot under my knees and threw a glancing kick at my crotch. I fell to one side, gasping.

"They want him over there right away, Bobby."

"They can blow it out their ass," Bobby said. But he stepped back to the door and let the other man come forward to lift me up by my armpits. I rocked for a moment, letting the waves of nausea and pain slosh back and forth in the bowl of my head. Then I straightened. The well-dressed fellow clamped a pair of handcuffs around my wrists and used both hands to snap them shut. When Bobby gestured with the shotgun, he stepped behind me and poked something into my back, probably not his finger. I stumbled through the narrow door into the daylight.

It was a farm all right. And still the Great Central Valley. But it wasn't the Sullivan farm that I had visited before.

Instead we were in a bare space between two isolated buildings. Behind us was the little shed where I had slept, made of weathered lumber that had once been painted white and a corrugated tin roof. Ahead of us, beyond a parked white van and a stack of wooden crates, stood a typical Valley barn—three stories high, at least a hundred feet long, almost half a football field. It too was wooden, but the planks fit perfectly and the rust-red paint looked nearly new. A few big oak trees watched us from one end of the barn. At the other end, a dirt road ran straight into the limitless rows of stubby plants, dark green and drooping already in the fierce sun, though it couldn't have been later than eight or nine. A mile away, maybe farther, rose a bright yellow hill, a crop-burning stack I assumed, waiting for the torch. Otherwise there was nothing, not even a farmhouse across the horizon, itself dissolved in haze, nothing except the heat, which rippled up from the ground in every direction and put the whole scene in crazy motion. I blinked and raised my hands to shade my eyes. Bobby's friend jabbed my back hard, and we both followed Bobby in a quick march toward the barn.

The first door was a conventional sliding arrangement, wide enough and tall enough for a small truck to roll through. Ten feet inside it was a second door, built into a solid wooden wall that extended about 20 feet on either side of it. The roof of this structure stopped three feet over the door, so that above us, stretching into cobwebbed darkness, the beams of the barn roof hung like ribs in the vault of a cathedral. As far as I could tell, the smaller building nestled in the shell of the basin like a miniature piece in a Chinese box. The second door was painted dull blue, made of metal, and it hissed as Bobby worked it open, letting out a rush of cool, dry air. Somewhere in the recesses, an air conditioner shifted gears. We went in and the man behind me closed and locked the door.

"Throw the sonabitch down there while I go find the boss," Bobby said. His friend swept a heavy foot through my ankles and pushed, sending me to the floor on handcuffed wrists. That gave me a chance to inspect the floor for clues. It was made of cheap white linoleum strips, like the floor of a supermarket, and smelled of manure and Lysol. The wooden walls had been lined with plasterboard and sprayed a brilliant green. There weren't any clues.

I looked up to find that the ceiling was very low, not quite two feet above the top of the door frame, and insulated with acoustical tile. Blank. I twisted my forearms to hold up the cuffs for viewing. Peerless Heavy Duty, the standard police brand up and down California. Single key, two locks, tubular stainless steel bracelets, six-inch chain, all the parts glossed with shiny reflecting chrome. Bridgestone Security would buy them by the truckload.

"Keep still," Bobby's friend said, showing me a pistol barrel as wide as a coal chute. A Walther PPK, to my surprise.

"Don't you know one of those things jammed last year when a guy tried to shoot the Queen?" I asked. "Even James Bond gave them up."

He kicked me, knowledgeably, in the kneecap, and I yelled once as the pain bounced up and down the big sciatic nerve in my thigh. Then we waited in companionable silence for Bobby.

"No, he don't show no effects," Bobby said as the door at the other end of the room hissed open. Bright light made me blink, and by the time my eyes were clear I was looking up at Bobby, Bobby's shotgun, Bobby's boss.

"You had to be a smartass, Haller."

Frank Brazil walked past me to the outer door and checked the handle. I suppose I wasn't surprised. I hurt in too many places to give much time to being surprised, and I had expected to have another chat with Brazil anyway, sooner or later, one place or another. What I hadn't expected was to see him strolling about the inside of a Central Valley barn dressed like a mannequin at the boat show. He strutted back from the door slowly, letting us admire the expensive brown poplin trousers, the cream-colored linen sports coat, the red Lacoste shirt, the gold oyster watch, the Gucci loafers. The resort effect, very dapper as always. Except that around the loafers were little green paper bags, cut low and held in place by elastic.

"You always double-check that door, Cassidy. Always."

Cassidy bobbed his head obediently. The Walther stayed pointed at my chest.

Brazil stared down at me, exuding sheer physical menace in a way that made my muscles tighten. His pale face, flat and pointed as a shovel, shone with perspiration despite the coolness of the room. He continued to look without speaking. I could have been a rare flower he was admiring. I could have been a cockroach he was deciding how to squash.

"You'll know me when you see me again, Frankie," I said. It was either wisecrack myself off my belly or else give up altogether. Give up on getting loose, give up on finding Fred. Besides, my knee hurt like hell.

Brazil made a spitting motion with his lips that I took for a smile. "I would of been happy to give you a tour of the bottom of the bay, Haller, with a boxcar on your back."

"Still merry as a cricket, aren't you, Frankie?"

Bobby swung the fine Weatherby shotgun into my face, and I rolled and sprawled. Wit and the unconscious. My cuffed hands went to my right ear. A trickle of warm, frothy blood ran down my cheek and started to drip onto the hardwood floor. Brazil's sport coat had real buttons at the cuffs, I noticed, gold oblongs that actually held the split sleeves together. He buttoned and unbuttoned one cuff while he watched me bleed. Then he shook the cuff out and looked up.

"Bring him on back. Cassidy, you stay here. Keep checking with whoever's outside."

"Kenny is."

"So keep checking," Brazil growled. His green-clad feet flopped back toward the inner door. Bobby hauled me up, and as

I stumbled and turned, I could see Cassidy open a box mounted on the wall by the door and take out a military-style telephone handset. My ears kept ringing.

The inner door led into a narrow corridor lined with other doors, and the corridor itself ended in a short hallway that made the crossbar of a T. The walls were still plasterboard, the low ceiling still acoustical tile with a string of fluorescent lights down the middle. A cheap plywood door stood closed on the left. From behind the plasterboard on the right came the steady pumping noise that a diesel generator might make. We turned left at the T and faced a white door with "OR" painted on it in neat black letters.

"Don't look up, Bobby," Brazil said.

He opened the door with a key and we followed him through, passing under a momentary flash of heat from the top of the door-frame. Once past, I craned back and saw a narrow black bar with a long slit in it, out of which streamed lines of purple light that blended midway to the floor into a shimmering, transparent curtain.

We were in a fairly spacious room, same low ceiling, windowless, furnished with a sink, tall white metal cabinets, shelves of jars and pharmaceutical instruments that had been pegged into the green plasterboard at various heights, and several stools and chairs. On a counter by the sink, next to a small stack of clear plastic boxes, sat a big microscope with a wrinkled black finish and three thick wires running out of it into the wall. Under the counter, several dark blue cylinders of gas stood on their ends, a black rubber hose dangling from each neck. The whole room reeked of disinfectant. We were about as far away from a barn in the Central Valley as we could possibly be.

Brazil walked over to the double doors that led out in another direction, and placed his face against one of the glass windows in them. Then he rapped on the glass. A loudspeaker over the door crackled and a faint voice said something that ended in "minutes."

"Let him take a look, Bobby. I want smartass to see it com-ing." He smiled his baby shark's smile at me and stepped aside. I took two steps to the door.

Space helmets.

Inside the next room were two men wearing space helmets. I blinked my eyes clear. They were hunched over a long, stainless steel table. Green hospital gowns covered their clothes, green pa-per bags their shoes. And on their heads, looking like Armstrong and Aldrin in the Eagle, they wore regulation NASA helmets.

The nearer one walked toward the head of the table. They were both examining the naked body of a Mexican man, older than me, I guess, but it was hard to be sure because his head and genitals had been completely shaved and his complexion was the color of dirty bathwater. Two clear plastic tubes ran from his nos-trils to the other side of the table and disappeared. There was no anesthetic mask on his face. He made no movement at all.

The shorter figure reached for a tray and came up with an in-strument that looked like an ordinary carpenter's drill, except that the bit in the chuck was as long and narrow as a knitting needle.

"Keep watching, peeper," Brazil said behind me. "You want to watch now, so you can dream about it later."

The short man positioned the drill at the top of the Mexican's bare skull. The other man adjusted the bit slightly with one fin-ger. The first one rose on his toes, turned the drill, and suddenly jammed his weight forward, driving the metal into the bone with a grunt.

Behind me, Bobby made a sound that could have been a sigh. I felt my stomach clench, like a fist. Blood spurted slowly from the skull, splattering the green gown, then died away to a trickle. My hands automatically went to my cheek. Bobby rapped me in the kidney with the shotgun and they went down again.

To my left, Brazil pressed his face close to the other window, mouth slightly open, lips flecked with saliva. In the operating room, the first man had reversed the drill and was now waving it gently back and forth as he withdrew. No more blood came out of the hole, but the drill bit was bright red and coated with shiny mucus. The second man said something through his space helmet—we heard the crackle of his radio—and water sprayed from the raised edge of the big table, washing the little lines of blood into a hidden drain. He took a long section of very narrow plastic tubing and started to work it into the hole the drill had made. Brazil's breath rasped and he wiped fog from the glass with the side of his hand. The shorter man spoke through his radio, nodded in approval at something, and at last raised his head to look at us. Through the bubble of plastic I could see the red hair, the rake marks of childhood acne, the quick, intelligent eyes of Martin Fells.

"Did you give him another injection?" Fells asked through his helmet.

"You said just the one," Bobby answered. "He's still a little wobbly."

Fells took off the space helmet and put it on a counter-top. "Most people would still be on their hands and knees," he said in his normal clipped baritone. "He's got the constitution of an ox." His arms slid out of the green surgical gown. He reached in back, flipped the sash loose, and dropped the gown into a laundry hamper. Then he came over and peered at my face. Up close, his skin had the texture of coarse sand. "I told you not to abuse this man."

Bobby glanced over at Brazil, who was leaning against the counter, buttoning and unbuttoning his cuffs. "He gave us some lip," Bobby said apologetically when Brazil didn't speak. "So we had to slap him around a little."

"Just a boyish romp," I said.

"Shut up." Brazil folded his arms deliberately, high on his chest.

Fells inspected my ear with a medical frown, breathing out a sweet-smelling mouthwash that was probably meant to annihilate bacteria left and right. It made the nausea of the morning start to churn again in my throat. "Superficial," he announced.

"I love your bedside manner," I said, fighting to stand straight, "but I miss the poster of Bobby Fischer."

"I remember you," he said, stepping back. "Never fear. I remember you, Mr. Haller."

"Never fear." Brazil's lips curled back in disgust. Fells ignored him, walked over to the sink and began to wash his hands with a rapid, wringing motion under the running water.

"Where's Fred?" I asked anyone.

"Happy as a clam," Brazil said. "Right, Doc?"

Fells continued washing his hands.

"Why the space helmets?"

Fells turned slowly from the sink, caressing his hands with a soft white towel.

"Brain surgery is the most delicate of all medical procedures," he said. The water continued to run from the tap behind him. His ferret's face showed no emotion at all. His voice hovered over the words and picked them out precisely, deliberately, like tidbits at a banquet. Bobby looked unhappily at the running water but made no move to stop it. Fells looked steadily at me.

"Of all human organs," he said, "the brain is the most susceptible to infection. In the old days, not so long ago"—he smiled at his joke showing the bad teeth—"in the old days, brain surgeons were not even permitted to speak in the operating room. During an operation, they used sign language to the nurses and each other like mutes. Medical mutes." He liked that too. "Even so, most patients developed some form of corticular infection."

"You're no doctor."

"But we march along. These ultraviolet lights over the door sterilize anything coming into this room quite effectively. The operating room is completely sterile. We have a Lanimer recirculating air system that blows air up and through those big overhead vents and along a totally enclosed circuit. They use it at Massachusetts General and quite a few other hospitals now. And also in the Lascaux caves in France, to protect the prehistoric paintings. The space helmets were worked out at Houston and Northwestern University to permit us to talk to each other without breathing on the open wound. Fairly common now, actually." He put down the towel. "Of course I'm not a doctor. But it doesn't really matter in an autopsy."

I turned my head and looked through the windows of the door again. The other man in surgical green was extracting a long, thin copper spoon from the cavity the drill had made.

"He's scooping out cortical tissue for biopsy," Fells said in the same tone he'd use to describe a carburetor or the GNP. "Gray matter. Spinal taps don't tell us very much in detail about what's happening in the brain, so we like to get right in and see for ourselves."

"You want to show him the rest of the zoo?" Brazil had been watching me while Fells talked. His face was moist, and his eyes were wide and bulging, probably with excitement. I couldn't tell for sure without a biopsy.

"You really are a sadist, aren't you, Brazil?" Fells took off the shoe covers with a snap and flipped them into a white plastic trash pail. Brazil watched him, expressionless, silent. Not a partnership made in heaven. Some lazy afternoon, I'd try to figure out what to do about that. "You may as well bring him along," Fells said. He picked up a metal clipboard and opened the door back into the T-shaped corridor. We followed, stepping through the ultraviolet curtain.

"Show him that one first," Brazil said.

Fells gave a scornful look over his shoulder. Behind me, Bobby laughed with pleasure, the pure laugh of a little child. Fells took out a key chain and turned the lock of the center door, but didn't open it.

"Take a look around, smartass," Brazil said. "Maybe your old pal is there."

Bobby thumped me hard with the barrel of the shotgun again or maybe just a crowbar. I turned the door handle and pushed.

A German shepherd lunged for my face with a howl, teeth flashing, paws drumming insanely against the bars of its cage. He fell back snarling and instantly threw himself forward again, cracking bone against metal. One paw swiped between the bars at my eyes. His snout thrust after it. His teeth ground and clattered against the metal. With another lunge, he twisted and fell end over end, jumped again, his whole body jerking in convulsions, his fur standing high, matted with blood and filth. He dropped back once more and hurled himself up, like a ball slammed against a wall.

Bobby shoved me closer. I drew back.

"Look at him sweating," Bobby said. "Like a fucking pig."

I pointed trembling hands toward empty cages behind the dog.

"I thought you'd have monkeys, too," I said, trying to sound smartass and coming out scared.

"We did," Brazil said over the howl of the dog. "But they died."

The room at the other end of the T was a tiny hospital ward. Windowless, of course, green plasterboard and linoleum like every other room I'd seen so far. And without doctors, nurses, or Gray Ladies. But there were beds. And there were patients.

Eight standard hospital beds in a row. The last one on the right was empty. In the others lay five Chicano men, one white teenage boy, and Fred.

They were flat on their backs, pinned down at their chests and ankles by wide, dark blue canvas straps. Intravenous feeding bottles and tubes hung over each bedside, dripping clear fluid down the tubes, to disappear into bandaged arms. All of them had shaved heads. Fred and the boy had their eyes closed and sighed in long, slow patterns of breath. The five Chicanos had closed eyes as well, but their faces and trunks moved restlessly, in grotesque, involuntary rhythms, and their lips made loud smacking noises at the air. Under the sheets and canvas straps, their legs jerked uncontrollably, as if shocked by an electrical charge.

"Tardive dyskinesia," Fells said in a bored voice. "Iatrogenic." He went to the farthest bed on the left and started methodically to read the chart on the end. I knew what the last word meant. I had seen it on enough coroner reports and death certificates, in and out of the line of business. Doctor-caused.

"What are you doing to Fred?"

Fells went to the next bed and picked up the chart. "Your friend is going to be helpful," he said without looking up. "Unfortunately, I have plenty of men about his age. I require more variety."

Bobby snickered.

"Is the boy named Hoffman?" I asked. It was hard to tell from the shaved head and pallid face. But he looked like the picture.

"I haven't the slightest idea," Fells said. He made a mark on the chart with his gold Cross pen and moved on to the next. "Mr. Brazil supplied him."

Mr. Brazil shrugged at nobody in particular and took out a pack of mentholated cigarettes. "So what?" he said.

"I'd rather you didn't smoke in here," Fells said.

Brazil gave him a smile you could slice ham with and lit the cigarette. Fells looked at him, at Bobby, and then turned back to his charts. Bobby's glance wavered between the two men.

"We found him in Oakland," Brazil said after a moment. The anger never very far beneath the surface with him rushed suddenly into his voice. "Some of the boys did, when he was trying to bust into a warehouse Bridgestone does. I tell my people to keep an eye out for kids like him—dogsmeat I call them, because they're what's wrong with California, what's wrong with the whole lousy, screwed-up country. No discipline, no order. Your kind of guys, Haller. Smartasses. Loners. Gets a few pimples, feels sorry for himself, starts pumping drugs up both arms like a fucking hose. This one was looped to the gills with quads, acid, angel dust, something. Had a .22 target piece he shot himself in the foot with, and my people found him passed out in the toilet." The tension slipped slowly out of his voice, and he looked at Bobby with a sly, sideways glance. "The kid holds up pretty good against the professor's brew, though. He's been sucking it up for two weeks now. Of course, the young ones usually do. The old ones can go out like a candle, just like that." He puffed smoke out in an exaggerated motion. "You're probably going to fall right in between, Haller." Bobby snickered on cue, Brazil looked at me defiantly.

"What's in the I.V.?" I asked. There was no point, now or ever, in arguing with Brazil.

Fells glanced at me and went back to his charts. "Don't bother with what you don't understand." Dynamite in the classroom.

"Is it dopamine?" I asked him.

He gave me his full attention. "Who have you been talking to?"

It didn't seem like the time to work on his grammar. "Dopamine would account for the straps," I told him. "Maybe for the jerking too."

"It's a solution of serotonin and carbolic peptides," he said mechanically, then glowered at Brazil. "You told me he didn't know anything except that George Webber had been here."

"In a few more hours, it's not going to matter if he took a Ph.D. in this shit."

"It might if he talked to somebody besides the old man."

Brazil inspected his cigarette and frowned. "We'll talk about it when they get here. Let's get him out and get him ready. I just wanted to let him see the fun coming."

"The serotonin should make them listless and drowsy," I said quickly, "like a trance."

"Did Webber write that down?" Fells demanded.

"What do you give Snoopy? Overdoses of dopamine and norepinephrine?"

"Brazil, I want you to check this out first, check this out right away."

"We'll check when I say so."

"Why is Fred's I.V. darker than the others?" I would get high marks for persistence anyway.

Fells pulled his glare away from Brazil. His face had flushed the color of wet clay. He jammed his hands into the pockets of the lab smock he was wearing. "These men are on massive doses of neuroleptics—tranquilizers to you—that cause blockade of the dopaminergic receptors. It should tranquilize them completely, but in fact it usually creates overactivity of dopamine at the limbic receptor sites. The result is the tardive dyskinesia, the jerking and twitching you see. Many psychotic patients in mental wards have the same disease, but only after prolonged periods of medication. I am inducing it in a period of about a week." His speech slowed down. "His I.V. is cloudy because it contains a three-percent solution of heroin as well."

I kept my face blank. And only Bobby appeared to notice my hands suddenly straining the steel chain between the handcuffs taut. He raised the muzzle of the shotgun slightly.

"Don't worry, smartass," Brazil said. "He's not going to have time to get hooked." He picked up a needle from a tray beside the nearest bed. "You want to give Haller a sample too?"

"Put that down." Fells snapped at him.

"Fuck yourself, Doc."

I slid my feet two short steps back toward the door.. The low ceiling seemed only inches above my head. The plasterboard walls closed in.

"How do you get your volunteers, Fells, when the meat wagon isn't running from Oakland? Have Bobby spray the fields with Mace?"

Bobby chuckled. Fells came up close to me. "Don't underestimate him, Brazil. I don't need him that much."

"You need a pop of your own shit, Doc."

"It's called DMSO," Fells said to me in his condescending, lecturing tone of voice. "And it is in fact something like Mace. It penetrates the skin—which very few gases do—and it carries an extremely powerful tranquilizer to the cortex in a matter of seconds."

"Diazepam."

His eyes flicked to Brazil and back to me. Brazil tapped cigarette ash onto the spotless floor.

"Diazepam," Fells said. "DMSO was developed at the Biological Warfare Center in Fort Mead. Not far from the National Institute of Mental Health where I once worked. As I'm sure you already know," he added drily. "They were looking for gases that paralyze and kill—Mace is actually a by-product of their research—and they came up with DMSO as an agent for carrying live bacteria. Unfortunately, it is now an illegal drug in this country, since it also causes cataracts of the eye after a few exposures. It is still used experimentally in Eastern Europe. And it carries the tranquilizer I have made out of diazepam very nicely. Sullivan sprays small groups of workers with it when they've separated from everyone else, out of an auxiliary tank on his plane."

I nodded. I had seen how far apart the field hands worked from each other in the Valley.

"How do you choose them?" I asked. My breath seemed to race in my chest. Bobby was looking at an I.V. bottle. The door to the corridor stood halfway open. "They've all got families to report them missing."

"We only take unmarried males—wetbacks, here illegally,

supporting somebody far across the border. Bobby and his father pick out the new arrivals before they become known to the others, and assign them to remote fields. He smiled, showing the inside of his upper lip. As warm-blooded as an oyster. "This is California, Haller. Half the population is wandering around in a daze, the other half couldn't care less about what happens to a couple of dozen Chicano field hands."

"What happened to George Webber?"

Brazil snorted and looked around from the bed where he was standing, toying with a chart. "Is he still in the cooler, Doc? Or did we send him out?"

Fells kept looking at my face. "You're a fool, Brazil. People did care about George Webber, and that's why we've got this problem now."

"This particular problem," Brazil said coldly, "is wearing handcuffs and heading for the number-eight bed."

"He talked to Foreman. And your goons didn't find the cassette."

I calculated three steps to the door. Run, rabbit, run. Brazil said something to Fells. I tried to guess how fast Bobby could move his gun if I shoved Fells toward him first. Or if he'd just shoot through him.

Not a bad idea in any case. Fells's narrow eyes never left my face while he argued with Brazil. Ferret or not, he was more cautious, more methodical than the other two. I wanted to run my knuckles through his wavy red hair.

"You don't worry about being outside the law?" I asked. My toes turned an inch toward the door.

"I think of myself as being ahead of the law," Fells said. "And in his own crude way, Brazil is actually part of the law. Don't make a mistake about us. Despite our differences, we both believe in the same thing. We both believe in the inability of certain races to live peacefully in a democracy—Brazil because he has actually suf-

fered from that inability; myself"—he showed the yellow teeth—
"myself because I have eyes to see."

"But you're not really interested in making people violently aggressive, like the dog, are you? Not even cops. That's just a front."
Up on the balls of my feet, calves tightening.

"You are uncomfortably perceptive," he said, not looking uncomfortable. "Aggression is always uncontrollable. Violence is always unpredictable. There is no point in creating what you can't
control. We are working here on techniques for mass social control." The smile rode a little higher. "The opposite of aggression.
Techniques for mass pacification."

Bobby Sullivan stepped behind me with his shotgun and
waved me toward the door.

CHAPTER 22

I OWE YOU," KENNY SAID, AND POUNDED ONE FIST AGAINST MY LEFT temple. I saw it coming in plenty of time, like a boom swinging, and my shoulder took most of the impact. It hurt anyway. Brazil stood in the doorway of the shed, a pistol in his hand, the smile unzipped.

"You still owe him, Kenny," he said.

Kenny hit me again, hard on the neck, and sent me spinning against the side of the shed. With practice, he might drive me right through the wall. He threw two more left jabs into my diaphragm, ducking them under the handcuffs, then stepped back to let me slide to the ground. I kept the anger out of my face and stayed there, looking up at him blankly, gasping for breath.

The tan loden coat was gone, of course. Now half-moons of sweat swung under each armpit and his neck dribbled over the loose collar in round folds. Beneath the thin sports shirt, pillows of blubber stretched across his torso. Not much for muscle tone or definition, our Kenny, but after the injection and the joy ride through the Central Valley sunshine, a pair of kittens could have worked me over.

He looked at Brazil. "The Doc don't want his face abused," Brazil said and jerked the pistol toward me. Kenny took two steps, bent over, and hoisted me to my feet. As he stood back and cocked his arms, I got a good look at his fists, about the size and color of footballs, then he hit me again, jabs and crosses in the gut, until I sank down on my hands and knees and spat blood into the dust.

"You're gonna spend the day out here, Haller," Brazil told me, buttoning and unbuttoning his right sleeve with the free hand. "You're gonna cook in this dump until the Doc finishes with the dead greaser and some people double-check your tape shit back in the city. You're gonna fry like a piece of country bacon. Then Kenny's gonna come and take you back to the barn and tuck you in that nice clean bed you saw."

I rocked back on my knees and swallowed the last of the blood. Kenny kept his gummy, undersized eyes on me, worked his big jaw a little, like a garage door sliding shut, and hitched his belt. I could see the metal key ring that hung from one belt loop, inches past the holster where a snubnosed .38 Police Special rested. Cracked leather holster, dirty along the rims. Kenny didn't take good care of his equipment. Kenny was careless by nature, careless and slow.

"The heat's not so bad," I said hoarsely. "It's the humidity."

"You're gonna be a smartass right into the grave, Haller."

Kenny snorted and they both went outside, closing the door and snapping a padlock behind them.

After a minute or two, I propped myself against a wall and looked around my oven. The shed was about six by six, 12 or 14 feet high, topped by a rusty corrugated roof; the rest of it seemed to be solidly built of ancient redwood planks, soaked first in cattle sweat and pelted with bits of straw and cobweb.

I sat for a few minutes longer, letting the heat close in and grow friendly. Then I stood up awkwardly and began to go around it, feeling for loose boards, broken nails, anything weak or disconnected to push or pry. The handcuffs gnawed at my wrists as I worked, spitting out little bits of skin and blood, my eyes grew blurry, and twice I paused and rested on my knees. The only thing weak or disconnected I found was me. I sat back down and waited for the shed to collapse all by itself.

Windows wouldn't have helped. Enough light filtered through the old plank fittings to let me see. And there was no breeze to come through a window anyway, no wind anywhere in the world, nothing but murderous, implacable heat.

As near as I could figure, it was only early afternoon, nowhere near the worst. Soil takes longer than water to heat, I dimly remembered. An elementary physical principle, like capillary action or the equal and opposite reaction that follows a fist in the belly. But soil, once started, stores heat longer than water does and releases it more slowly. In San Francisco, with ocean on three sides, the summer comes out fog; 50 or 60 miles east, between the two reflecting ranges of mountains, it comes out sizzle. Five or six o'clock would be the peak, I guessed. A hundred or more outside. I licked my lips dry and stared at the metal ceiling. A hundred and twenty or more inside.

I slumped farther down the blood-hot wall. Motes of dust flickered and burned in front of my eyes. They had to have a partner, I thought. Brazil was only the supplier, glad to deliver the odd lot of flesh whenever his security people picked up a stray, glad to rent out a remote stretch of his farmland for the barn people. In it for his own crude sense of politics. In it for the money too, no doubt, but taking his change in miscellaneous acts of sadism. Fells. I didn't know what the hell Fells was in it for. Less sadistic than Brazil, less obviously racist, but only because he didn't seem to notice any of his victims as people. Persons. We the persons. The heat wriggled its sharp fingers down into my scalp. I tossed to the other wall. At least Brazil took pleasure in pain, identified in some perverse way with what he caused. Fells was a technician.

There had to be somebody else. Somebody who had put the whole insane scheme together, a synthesizer, a visionary. Dinah would have a name for him. I shook off the thought of Dinah. What were they going to do—take the Eddy Street fillies and turn them into Avon ladies? Mass pacification, Fells had said. The end of aggression. Of black, brown, and yellow aggression anyway. America the tranquil. Indivisible. With liberty and serotonin for all. For most. My mind swam. It would be somebody who knew about the identity person's recording. My throat made a harsh, faraway sound. I stretched full-length on the ground. I would think about who when it was cooler. Darker and cooler. My tongue crawled out of my mouth. My eyes caught fire, and I closed them slowly.

Long before Kenny returned, I was awake again.

There had been noises in the driveway outside: car doors slamming. I stood up, stretching my hands forward in the darkness like a sleepwalker, and took two stiff steps to the door. The temperature in the little shed had dropped into the 90s, the balmy 80s maybe, and we were well into the Central Valley evening. No light came in through the fittings. I pressed my forehead against the wood and peered through a long crack over the padlock at dim, unmoving shapes, shadows of shadows. I waited, letting my eyes adjust, the sweat congeal over my body in a greasy coat.

My stomach rumbled, and I snapped off a long splinter from the door and started to chew it. If I had the constitution of an ox, I also felt like eating one. Maybe Kenny would bring a sandwich and a bottle of beer when he came. Maybe Bobby would come instead. Bobby was quicker, smarter, meaner. I hoped it would be Kenny, careless and slow.

Something flapped in the sky just beyond the door, and I

shivered. A vulture, probably, with a hot tip. My mind drifted with the lightheaded buoyancy of someone who's just passed through a fever. I peeled another splinter. Or it might be a bat. I thought of Fred hanging upside down over the stairwell, coat flapping, I thought of him across the way in the barn, flat on his back with a fruit jar full of witches' brew dripping into his veins. How long did it take to become addicted to heroin? My hand-cuffs scraped the dry wood. Maybe Dinah was right, and I had become a vigilante, a maverick with a streak of self-righteousness who enjoyed putting other people back into place. But right now all I cared about was unhooking Fred from that needle. Then I could worry about vigilanting Fells and Brazil. The bats flurried by again. Mass tranquilization, they wanted. A nation of game-show watchers and Stepin Fetchits. The splinter broke and I spat out the pieces. They teach the kids in the army a new move these days with the heel of the hand, a lethal kung-fu blow that would stagger an armed water buffalo. More cross-cultural fertilization from the Vietnam incursion. Betty Jo Rule had used it once, and later told me it was outlawed in karate tournaments. I pulled the six inches of chain tight between my wrists and thought slowly about impromptu kung-fu.

It could have been an hour, or only ten minutes later when light splashed out in a pool from the door of the barn. I peered through the crack. A big shadow moved across the light, circling a flashlight on the ground. Kenny's voice grumbled something and the light stayed on. Then I heard his feet scratching the path on the other side of the door.

"How ya doing, Haller?"

I sat down in my original corner.

"Boss wants me to check you out again. You make him nervous."

"Come on in. The door's open."

He rattled the lock hastily. The door lurched outward. The

flashlight beam jumped at my eyes. He sighed and came in a half step. "It's going to be a pleasure, Haller. A hell of a pleasure." One hand held the flashlight. The other one I couldn't see. In the distorted glow, his nose looked like the bumper on a bus.

He moved the light across the little room, up and down. The left hand seemed to hang loosely near the holster.

"It's a shame Brazil picked somebody as inexperienced as you, Kenny. He's going to sulk himself right into a pet when he learns about it."

"Can the garbage," Kenny said. "What the hell are you talking about?" he asked after a moment.

He who bites gets bitten. I sat up straight and showed the cuffs, keeping my elbows close to my sides, palms up. He put die light on them.

"You left these way too high, Kenny. I've already snapped two links in the chain."

"You're full of shit," he said, bending over to look. "I left these things—"

I never found out where he left them, because I rammed the cuffs straight up, hands stretched as far apart as I could hold them, the chain taut as an axle. The chain caught him at the base of the nose and drove the bone up with a sound like snapping your fingers, and blood cascaded down my arms.

I hadn't killed him. Bruce Lee could drive the nasal bone straight back into the brain with the heel of his hand, but Kenny was still gushing blood and trying to sit up. I fumbled with bloody hands around his holster and pulled the pistol out. With my right hand, I reversed the pistol clumsily, felt for the occipital bulge on the back of his head with my left. I swung the pistol in a short, hard, tranquilizing arc. He flopped back with a grunt.

They would be coming out in another minute or two, if

Kenny didn't return. Somebody would. Somebody with both hands free and a bigger gun.

I found the flashlight against one wall and brought it up beside his trousers, next to the key ring, grabbed the ring and ripped the belt loop free. Kenny groaned and pumped more blood from his torn nose. The light in front of the barn was still untouched by shadow. Kenny tried to roll over.

He carried more keys than a janitor. I held the ring in front of the flashlight and rubbed slippery fingers along the metal, feeling for the short, stubby shape that fits a Peerless. Maybe he didn't carry the key for the handcuffs after all. Something moved across the entrance to the barn.

Fred would have found it in an instant. Fred with his set of FBI twirls, his calm, sure moves. Fred with his veins full of cloudy white dope.

There were two short keys. I took a precious second to wipe my fingers against my trousers, selected the first key and put it in the left cuff. A voice said something from the barn.

The key fit. But didn't turn. The ring slipped out of my fingers, and both key and ring sank into darkness. I bumped the flashlight around, fished them out of the dirt, spread the keys. The second one fit, too. I wrenched my fingers against the metal loop, leaning my weight on Kenny's thigh and turning. He bucked and tried to roll. Two shadows blocked the light from the barn door, moving fast. The key clicked and my left wrist dropped free.

I got up with a lurch, wobbling on legs like straws. Then I plunged sideways past the open door an instant before the first round of buckshot blew it off its hinges.

The next ten minutes were spent in an elaborate ballet across the fields.

First I loped a few yards through the darkness, over foot-high tomato plants that clawed at my ankles, stumbling in and out of furrows, sawing the air with my breath. Then stopped and listened. Shadows moved forward, beaters thumping the earth, firing an occasional shot low and straight to move me out. One shadow ran back to the barn. More shadows emerged, shouting.

I fell once, climbed up, ran to my left. There was no light at all, except from the barn door now almost a hundred yards away and the orange rind of the moon almost gone under the western mountains. Not much silhouette to aim for, only the wheeze of my lungs, the sound of my clumsy feet. On the other hand, a shotgun is not exactly a precision killer. Buckshot rained on tomato leaves to my right, and I sprawled full length.

Near the shed somebody waved a flashlight. The idea caught on. Two more appeared a minute later, fanning slowly. Another appeared farther out, almost directly in front of me, and they all began to move forward at different paces.

I counted slowly, from left to right, as if it would be nice to know. Five lights coming toward me like ghostly dancers, swaying to the drumbeat in my ears.

I put Kenny's pistol down on the warm, hard ground and twisted my right hand up so that my left hand could put the key into the other slot and turn. The cuff slipped easily off, and I shoved the pair under a tomato plant. My hands were sticky with Kenny's blood and came back matted with dirt. The tomatoes were hard as baseballs, designed by California agribusiness to fall off a truck without a bruise. I could always stand up and pelt them with tomatoes, Vida Blue gunning down the opposition. Two lights angled off far to my left. The one in front kept coming.

I swallowed something cold and sour and felt it slide down inside my chest, spreading a ripple of fear. It would not do to die face down, on my belly, in the goddam Central Valley. The handcuffs glinted under the plant. I took the pistol with my right hand, with my left pulled the cuffs out again and draped them across the top of the leaves, balanced, two silver circles. Then I began to inch backwards, still on my stomach.

Twenty yards away, the closest flashlight waved slowly back and forth. I looked sideways at it, the way you're supposed to in the dark, and saw nothing but a blur. I turned my face back. The flashlight swung to the left. I gripped both hands hard around the pistol and took a long, deep breath. Time passed like a Chinese dynasty. I heard feet crunching earth. The little rib sight of the pistol rode just above the light, now ten yards away. Five. The light found the handcuffs and stopped. I let my breath go slack . . . squeezed the trigger . . . three steady shots making whomps like somebody beating a rug. The flashlight spun end over end into the air and vanished. People shouted. Lights bounced wildly in my direction, then abruptly went out.

I rolled to my right, crushing tomatoes, and ran at a stoop for 30 or 40 yards as fast as I could. Nobody shouted, nobody shot. I clumped down beside the fat mound of an irrigation ditch and looked back. The moon had run for cover. The light in the doorway of the barn had gone. Leaves whispered excitedly to each other as a breeze went by. A white spot in the far distance, a shirt maybe, moved and dropped. I lowered my head and vomited silently into the dirt.

After a little while, I raised my head again and looked around. Nothing had changed. I crawled sideways a few feet. I had no idea at all where I was, no idea how far it was to a highway, to other people, how long it would take to reach them. At points, the Central Valley is 50 miles wide, as empty as a desert. If I were still wandering around the fields about four hours from now, when the first sunlight came sliding down the Sierra, Brazil would pick me like the cherry off a cheesecake.

And while I wandered, Fred and the others would still lie in that restructured barn, watching bubbles plop down a plastic tube.

I trailed the fingers of my left hand into the ditch, scooped tepid water to rub against my face.

They would expect me to head into the Valley, away from them. The only reasonable thing to do. And all of them would be out looking now, straining for the first glimmer of light, even Bobby in his jacked-up Piper Cub. How many more of them? Six? Seven? A dozen?

It wouldn't really matter, I thought as I pulled my sore body up. I had already decided to go back to the barn.

CHAPTER 23

THE GOOD NEWS WAS THAT THEY HAD LEFT THE BARN DOOR OPEN. A faint light glowed inside it, the only light in the Valley, probably coming from the hallway behind the blue door. That meant that nothing to that point was locked, that anybody with two free hands and a lot of useless curiosity could slip right through the door, pass Go, and collect Fred. Of course, that was the bad news too.

I crouched in the darkness against the barn wall and watched. I could stroll through the open door like a debutante in heat, expecting nobody to lay a hand on me. That was in fact all I could do. First, however, I'd have to walk up to the semicircle of light, show myself, and step inside blind, where Fells or Brazil or the boys' auxiliary of Bridgestone Security might be waiting for all I could tell.

I inhaled warm, soupy air. Maybe the power company would foreclose suddenly, leaving us an in the dark. Maybe the Hound of the Baskervilles in there would break out of his cage and run berserk. Maybe I could hotwire the white van and find the nearest freeway. I craned my head in the direction of the van, still parked in the driveway between the barn and the little shed. The light reached to its left front wheel, halfway across its cab. I stared at it for a long moment, thinking. Then I slid my feet along the black ground, shifting the pistol grip in my hand carefully and still thinking.

From this angle, behind the van I could see another shape, lower, wider. Sedan-sized. A few more steps showed me the slanted reflection of light on blue metal and glass, light on a windshield. I remembered the car doors slamming.

The light stopped short of the other side of the sedan. If a window had been left open, I could reach inside and switch off the interior light that went on when a door was opened. If the key had been left there, gift-wrapped, I could start it up and travel off. If it hadn't, I could still start the motor.

I looked at the lighted barn door, then back at the car. The car made more sense than my original idea to barge into the barn and rescue Fred with the four bullets left in Kenny's automatic. I thought, why not check the car at least? A foolish consistency is the hobgoblin of little minds. And I was the guy who distrusted plans, who liked to go with the flow, trust his luck.

I straightened painfully and brought the pistol up waist-high. I took three steps toward the car.

My luck ran out

The high beams of the sedan exploded in my eyes, the horn sounded long and hard, and Brazil stepped out of the barn.

I wheeled and began to bound away, caught in the blazing lights like a startled deer. Brazil took two running paces and shouted. Footsteps pounded toward me in the darkness from the direction of the fields. I came to a full stop blinking in the harsh light and turned to see Brazil standing very still, body sideways to me, both arms outstretched and holding the pistol high and steady, just the way they teach you at police school.

"Put it down, Haller. I don't miss for shit at ten yards."

I turned the other way. Somebody else was standing beside the van, aiming another pistol. Beautiful form all around. Next to him the lights of the sedan stayed on, obscuring the face of whoever was sitting in the driver's seat.

"Put it down."

I dropped Kenny's pistol at my feet, and that was that.

A face came out of the darkness. Bobby Sullivan, carrying a very big, very solid Colt Single Action .44, the kind of gun that California sheriffs used to pack in the gold rush, the kind that is sold now mostly to gun buffs and western ranchers and other parties who like a weapon that will blow a hole in a man's chest the size of a two-car garage. Not a city gun. Some people who carry a .44 like to file down the hammer so they can fan and fire like Wyatt Earp. Maybe Bobby would show me trick shots later.

Brazil slowly lowered his pistol, a triumphant look on his face. Fells appeared at the door, not looking bored for once. The lights of the sedan still framed me like a spotlight, but as Bobby walked carefully toward me and blocked part of the glare with his shoulder, I could see the license plate on the car for a moment. I saw pretty much what I had expected to see.

912KEX

The car door opened, and a man got out from behind the steering wheel, and he too was pretty much what I had expected to see.

"Have you got his gun?" squeaked Frederic Kingsley.

"The heat didn't soften you up too much after all, did it, Haller? You left Kenny half dead out there."

"I was already hard-boiled, Frankie. Get to whatever you got in mind."

"They didn't find the tapes in your office," he said softly.

He was sitting on a wooden office chair turned around backwards. His arms lay folded across the top of it in a relaxed, country-store kind of pose, one hand fingering the thick button on his cuff. Behind him, Bobby Sullivan watched me carefully, rubbing the scar on his cheek with one hand, holding the Colt like a rock with the other. I didn't give a lot of thought to jumping them, partly because I was sitting the right way in a second wooden chair with my arms pushed back through the slats and handcuffed. Partly because I was too tired and sore. Tired and sleepy. I wanted to go to my room.

Brazil lit another of his mentholated cigarettes and threw the paper match on the floor. His flat face looked calm and freshly scrubbed, as if the chase and gunfire had brightened his day.

"They did find this." He held up a folded sheet of thin white paper. "Rocket Delivery Company receipt. One package not exceeding five pounds. Picked up 2:15 Saturday afternoon. For Immediate Delivery." He held the paper up over his shoulder without looking at it, and Frederic Kingsley reached for it, refolded it, and put it in his jacket pocket. Kingsley was wearing a baggy tweed suit, perfect for the Scottish moors, and looked hot even in the air conditioning. Brazil, on the other hand, still looked as if he were heading off for shuffleboard on the promenade deck.

"It doesn't say where you sent it, Haller."

"You could ask Rocket. They never sleep."

"I'd rather ask you. Persuade him a little, Bobby."

Bobby walked around Brazil's chair, taking his time and grinning down at me. Then he set his feet and swung the barrel of the Colt, smooth and level with both hands, like Henry Aaron taking batting practice. He split my cheek open from nose to ear and spun my head around like a chair on a swivel.

"Stop it." Frederic Kingsley looked as if he were going to be sick. "You can't just brutalize the man till he talks."

Brazil didn't bother to look at him.

"The thing about Haller," he said thoughtfully to Bobby, "is that he's in the business. He's kind of a professional tough guy. Look at him. He don't really mind you shagging iron off his skull bone. He thinks that's professional, He thinks that keeps the customers coming in that roachy office of his, as long as they hear he's a tough cookie with zipped-up lips that don't spill no secrets. He keeps his mouth shut and his legs crossed." He dropped ashes on the floor. "We could put lead in your pencil, Haller," he said, pointing the cigarette at my crotch. Kingsley gave a tiny squeak. "The professor's got a collection of little surgeon's knives that could keep us going for hours." He exhaled smoke in my face. "Before you know itl we could have you pissing in all directions like a garden sprinkler."

Kingsley came up beside him, murmuring protests.

"Or Bobby could just hold your lids open and I could use your eyeballs for an ashtray. Lot of guys worry more about their eyes than their equipment,"

"I sent it to Hand," I said.

Brazil smiled widely. "Did you now? Tape, pictures, the lot?" I nodded. The smile stayed in place. "Good," he said. "So now the professor and me don't have to worry that the Rocket dropped them off at some handy precinct house or a TV station or something. That's swell, Haller."

"Now you don't," I said. Blood from my cheek was trickling over my chin and down my neck. I pushed my tongue against an incisor that Bobby seemed to have loosened.

"Get the door, Bobby.

Bobby stuck the Colt barrel first into his belt and swaggered across the room to a plywood door. Kingsley stepped back behind Brazil's chair, blotchy skin the color of dried paste, and wrung his hands. We were in a fairsized, windowless room just off the hall-way of the little building in the barn. It was used for storage and as a makeshift office apparently, and jammed with the usual things you find in a room like that: a wooden desk, an olive-green filing cabinet, dusty cardboard boxes stacked and tilted against the thin plasterboard walls, a portable typewriter, an old black telephone on the desk, a wastebasket on the floor. A hostage in the spare chair. The telephone puzzled me a little. No telephone lineman would have failed to notice the structure of the barn or the un-usual fact of having a phone in a barn at all. On the other hand, anybody reasonably mechanical like Bobby Sullivan could prob-ably figure out how to loop a wire into an existing phone cable and get free service. Anybody at all could. The Berkeley phone office spent half its time unwrapping illegal student cords from their overhead wires.

I shifted my weight a little in the chair, pleased to have solved a mystery. The door opened again and Carlton Hand walked in.

"Hail, hail, the gang's all here," Brazil said. Nobody looked very jolly. Hand walked behind him without glancing in my direc-tion, wearing the skulking expression of a puppy who's missed the paper. He had on his usual brown seersucker suit, a button-down white shirt, and a green tie flopping loose on his chest. He didn't have on handcuffs. Nobody held a gun on him. Fells came in next, fists jammed in the pockets of his white lab jacket, impassive mask back in place. Bobby closed the door.

"Hello, Carl," I said softly. I rattled my bracelets. "You got here too late for the party favors."

"I'm sorry, Mike," he said. He started to say more, opened and shut his mouth, sat down on the desk top. His big moon face looked sad and wrinkled from this angle, like a balloon slowly leaking air. His shoulders were hunched up against his neck, as if he were caught in a draught.

"You knew all along, didn't you, Carl?" Anger thickened my voice into something fierce, unfamiliar. "That story conference you had with Webber on the 19th—he told you then, he told you everything he knew."

He shook his head gently, an inch each way. "He only told me he was going after Brazil again. He didn't tell me about Foreman. Or Fells. He was going to spring it all at once." Hand's big voice was bleached, a whisper. "He didn't know what was back of it."

"Or who." I leaned forward as far as the cuffs would let me. "Mrs. Browning," I said. "Still Mrs. Browning all the way, right, Carl? You've got in bed with a praying mantis this time, pal,"

"She's a wonderful woman," Kingsley blurted. "You don't understand, none of you do."

"Shut up, Kingsley," Brazil growled through his cigarette.

"No, really she is," Kingsley told me, flushing. "She has a vision. She's thinking of what this country could only be, if it were purified of violence. Even after what happened to her son and daughter, she still has a vision of peace, of the peaceable kingdom she calls it. She wants to leave a legacy."

He looked hungrily around the room. Behind the granny glasses, his eyes looked like bugs crawling in a bowl. Fells was staring at his feet. Brazil and Bobby Sullivan were watching the space over my head. Hand was watching Kingsley.

"Carlton is the same way," Kingsley said, pointing at him. "She hired him as editor, long ago, because of his crusades against corruption. He shares her vision. He told her so."

"A vision requires a blind spot, Kingsley." My mind was somewhere else, going bitterly over old ground. He had tossed me out front like a pawn, where he could see which way the shots were coming. "That Colt Bobby's holding is called the Peacemaker."

"She's never seen this," Kingsley said with a kind of apologetic groan, splaying his arms stiffly outward in the heavy tweed. "I never saw it until today. She doesn't know what it's like. We set it up two years ago, as a memorial, after my wife was killed. Professor Fells approached a foundation for money for his research—Mother is on the board—and when the foundation turned him down, she did it on her own, secretly. She saw the potential, with her vision. She pays for this through a real estate corporation in Auburn. She pays twice what she has to in taxes, just so the work can go on."

"A patriot."

"Exactly." Kingsley was deaf to irony. And he was given to desperate talking jags when excited, working his mouth faster and faster, spraying little bubbles of saliva as he moved his head constantly from one to another of his audience. "Fells is on the verge of a scientific breakthrough. If nobody else in this country is going to stop violence, if the government isn't going to take away guns and stop assassinations, then we're justified in taking our own steps, in any means of pacifying a violent population so the guns won't be used, in going to the most violent groups—lowering their temperature, she calls it."

"You want to start with Bobby over there?" I said wearily, cutting him off. Tranquility for some was going to work out about as well as equality for some. Kingsley's mouth kept moving in a strange, rubbery way, but no sound came out. He looked at Bobby's gun as if it had suddenly materialized in the room, looked back at me.

"The tapes didn't go to Hand, did they, Haller?" Brazil blew smoke down his nostrils and resumed his button-unbutton routine. "Hand would of told us if they had." He tapped ashes onto the linoleum. "Of course, you have to figure that Hand is still trying to make up his mind. I understand that. Kingsley brought him out here. Kingsley thinks that Hand is going to play ball with us. Kingsley says that Hand don't want to blow a bright political future by turning around on the old lady who's going to bankroll him all the way to the White House. Kingsley thinks we get Hand in deep enough, he's not going to make waves for anybody." He paused to take another deep, slow drag of smoke. "In fact," he said, exhaling with a hiss, "I'm still kinda making up my mind too, about Hand. Maybe he don't want to kill the goose that lays the golden eggs, maybe he does. But either way, I'd already know if he got the tapes."

"I guess it was somebody else," I said at last.

"Yeah." Brazil finished the cigarette and threw it on the floor, where Bobby Sullivan ground it out with the toe of his workboot. Gene Kelly and Fred Astaire. "I'm not going to ream out your prick to make you talk," he said coarsely.

"I didn't think you were."

"I'm not even going to waste a butt on your baby blues."

"No?"

"You'd try to sit tough and take too long and probably pass out before I got what I wanted. No, I'm going to get the professor here to run a little experiment instead on your old pal Fred." He shook out another cigarette and lit it. I didn't want one anymore. They probably tasted like a deodorant stick. "How long you think he'd hold out in the cage with the pooch?" he said.

I sat very carefully in the chair, not straightening my twisted arms, not moving my head, not reacting at all.

"You really are such a sadist, Brazil," Fells said. That was about the extent of his objection.

"Sort of like the dogfights on Eddy Street, right, Haller? Except maybe I'd leave a pair of cuffs on old Fred, and maybe he'd still be too dopey to put up much of a fight. What do you think? Would the mutt go for the face first or the throat? Or maybe the cock." He parted his lips and tasted the last word, letting bright lines of spittle run down his chin. "The cock, probably. Especially if we smear a little hamburger down there. And you'd have a front-row seat, Haller, right by the cage, watching the teeth go after your buddy, watching the dog tear him to shreds a little bit at a time, pulling off bits of his face, his gut, shaking his gut right out of his body like a piece of rope. That dog's juiced to the ears, Haller. It could take hours for old Fred to die, bleeding to death in the cage about one foot away from your face. It could take hours for you to kill him that way."

I tasted salty blood with my tongue, swallowed. Kingsley's mouth was hanging open as if a string in his jaw had broken. Bobby Sullivan had stepped back a foot or two, so that he was standing next to Fells's chair. Fells crossed his legs the other way. Except for Hand, everybody was staring at me, waiting.

I sat, like a drop at the end of a faucet.

"You know I would, Haller," Brazil whispered. "You know goddam well I would."

CHAPTER 24

I sent them to Chan-lui," I said.

"Where?"

"At the place off Grant Street." I told him the number.

"Why the goddam Chinaman?"

"He does me favors sometimes." My voice sounded muffled. "I trust him."

Brazil laughed, a sound like a ratchet. "Tell him where you hired your chink goons, Kingsley."

Kingsley muttered something in the direction of the floor and flushed a dark, unhealthy color. I felt my stomach begin to squeeze slowly. "Not from the old man," I said, more quickly than I meant to.

"The sons," Kingsley said thickly. "They do business on their own sometimes, without telling their father. They just started. I heard about them at the paper."

"They got an independent streak," Brazil sneered. "Like Kingsley here. Kingsley's been learning his way around the hit business, trying to do things on his own too. Before you, it was Webber making him nervous. So he got liquored up the way he does, full of Dutch courage, and tried to buy some spade pistol down in the Tenderloin to save the old lady's reputation. But it's against his principles for one thing and behind my back for another, so he got all nervous again and ran away before the spades even saw his money. You were lucky, Haller. Chinks for gunsels are strictly bush." He scraped his chair around to the desk, motioning Hand to the other end, and pulled the telephone close, "Give me that goddam receipt, Kingsley."

Kingsley jerked the piece of paper from his pocket and skipped back. We all watched in silence as Brazil studied the paper and began to dial.

Then I closed my eyes and tried not to think about the cramps in my arms and shoulders, the sting of the cut across my cheek, the speed with which I had told Brazil what he wanted to know. My head throbbed, untranquilized, unlikely ever to be. How do you measure pain? Do the doctors have a scale? One Haller-full. Half a Fred. Do they grade you on it? I thought of the old guy on Green Street who goes down the block each morning, pushing his little aluminum walker a few inches at a time, twisting his scrawny legs like spaghetti. A ten. I thought of the death of Sergeant Ray Alan Booth in those same gritty Texas fields where he had drilled us, thrown free when our training helicopter had crashed, broken into pieces by the impact. I had huddled under half a ton of roasting metal, trapped, feeling the break in the hip but not the shock yet, and he had come crawling slowly toward me over the sand like a smashed bug, scratching his way back to the wreckage. He had died about three feet from my face, watching me with the one brown, one blue eye, half his jaw ripped away by the crash. For almost an hour, we had lain there staring at each other, in our separate cocoons of pain, until Ray Booth's strange wild eyes had suddenly filled with blood and his head had sunk to the ground. Brazil would have taken the full measure from Fred. One Haller-full. One vigilante-full. I opened my eyes and saw Bobby Sullivan watching me curiously. He smiled faintly, cleared his throat with a hawk, and spat on the floor.

"That's right, number 2771," Brazil was saying. "I just want to check you delivered my package yesterday." He listened intently and wrote something down on die receipt. "No, that was fine," he said and hung up,

"Why'd you have them hold delivery till after six, Haller?" He swung his chair around to face me again.

"Insurance, Frankie, that's all. Hand and Kingsley were going to get back to me before six. If they did, I could call the company and stop delivery. If they didn't, I had a little protection." The chair creaked as I shifted my weight. "I didn't like the way Hand went out of the office."

He looked at Hand, who nodded once. He scowled at the receipt. "Why'd you put Yin-jeng for the name of the sender?"

"Just a joke with Chan-lui. His nickname for me. You wouldn't care."

"Won't he play the tapes?" Kingsley asked Brazil. His voice faded in and out like a distant station.

"He might. He won't do a damn thing though until he sees which way the money runs, not the Chinaman. The old lady can just pay out a little more if she has to." He moved his neck a quarter of an inch and gave Kingsley a stare that would wither grass. "For once in this thing, Kingsley, how about you stick to the money and let me run things the way they ought to be run. You got all of us working overtime cleaning up your mistakes when the professor should be back in the lab, I should be in Oakland, you should be home in your goddam bed." He poked the cigarette back in his mouth and turned the stare on me.

"It's two in the morning," Fells announced in his civilized baritone. "I'm not staying any longer. Brazil, I presume you're going to handle this."

Brazil inclined his head once without looking back at him. Fells walked to the plywood door and pulled it open.

"You haven't got it working yet, have you, Fells?" I said. "You can't drop your pills in the Oakland water supply yet and turn off everybody's limbic system."

"Not yet," he said calmly, pausing. "Serotonin is unstable in water, unfortunately. It breaks down almost at once in most normal chemical environments. I expect that the answer will lie in some accelerant enzyme that will cause the serotonin to replicate faster than it breaks down."

"Keep us posted," I said, but he had already closed the door.

"My wife was killed by a handgun," Kingsley said to nobody in particular. "In a ghetto riot in Detroit. A random shot, an utterly senseless act of violence. That's the kind of thing we're trying to stop."

Brazil stood up, his face set in a decision. Bobby shifted the heavy Colt to his left hand, wiped the free hand on his khaki shirt, and then stood with his belly hanging over his Levi's like a fat man's chin over his collar.

"What time can we start, Bobby?"

"Not before noon," Bobby said. "If we start before noon, the Agricultural Board will send somebody out to give us hell." Then he shook his big body slowly with pleasure. "But from noon on, we're OK," he said, grinning wide. "From noon on is a free burn day."

They weren't planning to lower the temperature after all.

With Hand and Kingsley gone, shooed out, Brazil came close, hands on hips, and told me slowly what he had in mind.

"The professor's gonna have to get along without you, Haller. I got too much else to do, with fixing the Chinaman, watching the editor-boy, changing Kingsley's diapers. We're just gonna have to skip the bed part." He leaned over so that I could smell the stale smoke on his breath, watch the little alligator romp across his bright red shirt. Up close, there were streaks of chalky dust worked into the lines of his face, and his skin looked pitted and dry. "We're going to walk you out into that big mound of rice straw you saw in the field," he said, keeping his eyes six inches from mine. "You and the dead Mex. And then we're going to turn on the torch, the way we do with all the bodies, and incinerate you into half a pound of soot. The difference is, Haller"—he thrust his face closer still, so that I could see nothing else in the room except watery pupils, pale forehead, greasy hair—"the difference is, the Mex is going to be dead when it happens. You're going to be sitting there, tied down on your duff, waiting for Bobby to light it up."

Then he left me alone with Bobby, and Bobby sat down in his chair and told me all over again what was going to happen. He liked doing that. He took a long time to describe the size of the rice-straw stack, the speed with which it burned, the temperature it probably reached, and he worked in lots of savory rural anecdotes about crop burnings, the kind of thing you don't run across in *Walden,* stories about accidents he had seen in the field, about farmers who had tried to burn on days when the wind had shifted, about cars and trucks left too close to a stack, whose gas tanks exploded in the heat, about the third-degree burns that could turn human skin into something like bacon rind or melt an eye into jelly.

"Some of the farms by town even call in the fire department to watch when they burn," he said in his Oklahoma twang. A thumb stroked the pink scar on his cheek where it scurried into his sideburn.

"Not you," I said.

"Not us." Too smart for me.

They had killed George Webber, of course. The second time out, Bobby told me. He knew nothing about Connie Larkin, a big-city statistic, meaningless to him. But Webber had come back with a new map of the property and more questions, still posing as Tommy Shoults. And Brazil had left orders for that. They had shown him the barn on a pretext, tricked him inside, and without benefit of cropduster or diazepam gas, simply turned him over to Fells and his gorillas. Then Estes Sullivan had driven Webber's car back to the city and left it in the Tenderloin, assuming it would be stolen, only the meter maid had got there first. Four days later, when Webber died from respiratory failure brought on by the drugs—iatrogenic—they had stacked him in the makeshift air-conditioned morgue behind the animal-cage room and waited for a bum day. A perfect scheme, as Bobby said. No evidence, no witnesses, no catches. At the end of the fire, there was nothing to be seen but a few feet of blackened stubble, itself plowed under as soon as it cooled. Perfect. I would have to take his word for it.

Somewhere around dawn, the guard changed, and Bobby finally broke off his monologue and went away into the barn to light matches and giggle, or whatever he did to prepare. His replacement was Cassidy, the man from the city, still in his black suit. The suit was dirtier now, stained with brown dirt around the cuffs and knees and shiny all over with dried sweat. His tie had been rolled into a ball and stuffed into one coat pocket. He sat down straight in Bobby's chair and let me look him over. There wasn't much to keep your attention, except for the long-barreled .38 he held in a hand as steady as a curbstone. Even so, his knuckles had taken a beating out in the field, I noticed, and fresh, painful-looking scratches snaked up his wrists and into his sleeves. Two more scratches ran across his face, near the right ear and down his neck into his collar. Fells or somebody had painted them with bright orange mercurochrome, like warpaint. Over the mercurochrome, Cassidy's small close-set eyes watched me constantly, wary as a terrier's. A simple, forgettable face of the sort you might find on an aging foot cop, too hardened to be trusting, too slow to be cynical. A journeyman's face. He didn't have any funny stories. He didn't show me his watch and count the hours until noon, and after a while, I may even have dozed, as people will. Whenever I blinked myself awake, the room was the same. The guard's eyes, the bare, dreary green plasterboard walls of the office, the rust-colored stain on the linoleum where my bloody cheek had dripped. Nobody snuck in with a hacksaw. Nobody rode up on a white horse. The meter maid didn't spot me. Nothing happened at all. The minutes tramped past, monotonous and commonplace as a pulse.

Brazil came in at last. Too soon. He had showered someplace and turned in his yachting outfit for a tan-colored business suit, a blue button-down shirt, and a striped tie like Tommy Shoults's. His hair gleamed with pomade or penguin fat or whatever he used. What to wear to an execution.

"Maybe I should just go home and change into something more formal," I said, feeling giddy and sick of myself as I said it. There was a limit to how long wisecracks could help.

Brazil glared at me and snapped his fingers at the guard, who stood up quickly.

My stomach growled loudly and they both looked at me.

"An empty threat," I said. "Pay no mind."

"I'm going to miss you, Haller. You're as funny as the clap." He snapped his fingers again impatiently at the guard and took the pistol from him. "It's noon, smart-ass," he said to me. "Cassidy here is going to unlock the Peerless one wrist at a time and pull the arm through. He's going to be behind you. I'm going to be in front. Move slow, like you thought I had a gun in my mitt and would just as soon shoot off the family jewels as not."

He could have saved his breath. After a day in his homemade stocks, I couldn't have moved fast enough to swat a floor lamp, much less stocky, well-rested Brazil ten long feet away, turning the pistol in tight little circles. Cassidy got me out of the chair none too gently, knelt down, and relocked the cuffs in front. I rotated my shoulders gingerly, wincing at the stiffness, trembling along my upper arms as the strain on the muscles ended and circulation started to flow.

"Get the door, Cassidy, and walk in front of him outside."

I looked at Cassidy in his dirty suit swinging the door open, turned back, and saw Brazil fumbling with a pair of sunglasses while he held the gun. I was the one who was supposed to be nervous.

"What happened to Connie Larkin, Brazil?" I asked suddenly, anxious to delay, anxious for some reason to know.

"Webber's girlfriend? The one you went to see?" The sunglasses had opaque, silvery lenses and more chrome than a Ferrari. "She was a looker, Haller, tits like cantaloupes." His lips split into a momentary, angry leer. "You should have seen them before Kenny got carried away." Then the nervous impatience came back into his face, he shoved me hard with the pistol, and I walked stiff-legged toward Cassidy, like a busted puppet.

At the door, I stopped and leaned on the frame. Cassidy's orange-striped face watched me impassively from the hallway leading out of the barn.. Brazil clicked the hammer of the .38 and told me to hop. I ignored him and took two deep breaths, slowly, concentrating, as if I were about to dive from a tall board. Then I plunged toward the outer door.

It was a pool of light we dove into: the noon sun slammed down on the top of my head with actual physical force, staggering me a little and bringing me to a halt just outside the barn door. My eyes screwed shut to escape the glare.

"Keep going," Brazil snarled behind me. A fist kicked at the back of my neck, and I stumbled across the driveway toward the familiar white van, where Cassidy already waited by the open doors. The sun had bleached everything into the same shimmering whiteness, until even the shadows were indistinct—burning ghosts that swayed and danced in front of me, mocking.

It was too bright to see the rice-straw mound from there. I was in no hurry anyway.

"I don't know why they call him the prince of darkness," I gasped to Brazil, scorching my throat with another gulping breath. "Ask him for me, will you?"

"Get in the fucking truck," Brazil said, and I felt myself hoisted and shoved against the side of the van. From its shelter, I could see a blue sedan parked at the edge of the barn and blowing little pants of exhaust into the dust. In the front sat Kingsley and Hand, their faces like two smears of paste.

Cassidy's black figure stooped into the van and looked in the corners for trap doors, caches of weapons, creature comforts.

"I left an icepick in here last time," I said from where I lay.

"Get in the goddam cab and drive, Cassidy," Brazil said. He squinted at his wrist. "I want this thing over with now."

"I thought I was getting some backup," Cassidy whined.

"I can't spare anybody else for this job." He looked me full in the face, jowls flushed with sun or anger. Rings of sweat were already creeping from his collar and out of the armpits of the tan jacket. "The Chinaman's in my Oakland office with a couple of dozen goddam sons, talking cops. He wants to know where you are, Haller. You pulled something fancy on that tape package, and I should of expected it. But I can handle the Chinaman. I can handle all the slants in San Francisco, with guns or clubs or Mrs. Browning's money, and there's no way I'm going to pass up watching you fry. Come on, Cassidy, move, dammit."

Cassidy slid out the back in a hurry and slammed the twin doors shut. The heat spread out around me. So Chan-lui had understood the message after all, remembered about Yen-jing, applied it to his sons. One step forward, clever detective, take a bow. But he had acted on it in his own inscrutable way, maybe out of caution, probably because I hadn't made the message urgent enough, had tried to be witty and independent as usual and refused to call for help. Two steps backward. Over and out. Oakland was too far to mean anything now anyway. Eighty miles down the freeway, through the coastal mountains, in the cool, wet bowl of San Francisco Bay. He would never reach me in time, even if he wanted to, even if he knew where to look. I heard footsteps on both sides of the van, doors open, the motor start. Then we jolted out toward the white-hot fields.

Five minutes later the jolting stopped. Cassidy killed the motor. The cab doors opened. I squirmed on my back to the rear doors and raised both feet high, heels tucked close to my calves, hands cradling my knees, ready for one last chance. If Cassidy opened the doors carelessly, stood close enough, I might land a surprise kick, a thump to the face that would stun him and let me scramble for the gun. Not much, but something. Impromptu kung-fu. No belt for losing.

He wasn't careless.

The doors jumped open, he stepped back, and my feet punched a hole in nothing. The follow-through pulled me over and down, and I hit the hard earth with a thud, crumpling. Brazil laughed. Cassidy looked around the empty fields and then laughed too. I lay there, letting the heat press me flat.

Cassidy tucked his pistol into his belt and jerked me to my feet. Behind him, as I staggered up, I saw Kingsley's car scratching to a stop in a low cloud of brown dust.

"Get me that shit in front, Cassidy," Brazil said, coat-less now. "Then wait here with the motor running." His silvery sunglasses winked as he craned his head to the burning sky, and sweat ran in a river down his cheeks, as if the greasy hair were melting. "Bobby makes his first run in about five minutes, and I want to be moving then. He can't see what the hell we're doing until he's right on top."

He shoved me with the barrel of the pistol, his own little armpit automatic, and I stumbled forward a step or two. Immediately to our right was a wide irrigation ditch full of hot brown water. Across its low banks were draped dozens of muddy hose lengths, set in regular intervals like gray stripes, draining water into the furrows. Ahead of us, 25 or 30 yards, loomed a huge bulk the size of an ordinary barn, a great loose mound of yellow stubble and green leaves and stalks mixed randomly together like a giant salad. The ground around it had been plowed clear and beaten level as a firebreak, and beyond the firebreak ran interminable spokes of short green tomato plants, toward a horizon that fused into a bright wall of haze and sky. To the west, you could see a few pillars of smoke from fires already started by farmers in a hurry. You couldn't see the mountains. You couldn't see clouds, blue sky, other people, or buildings. Only a burning plain that stretched away in every direction as bleak and empty as the floors of hell.

I raised my cuffed hands to my face to shield my eyes. Brazil took something long and narrow from Cassidy and drove me forward, toward the mound of straw. The doors on Kingsley's car slammed shut.

"Got a match, Haller?" Brazil jibed as he marched me over the bare ground, his voice rasping with anger, exertion. "Want a last cigarette?" He punched me to move faster. Footsteps followed us at a slower pace.

"The Mex is already here," Brazil said to my back. I twisted my ankle and tilted over a broken furrow, and he punched me savagely in the kidney with the gun barrel. My mouth seemed stuffed with burning cotton. I sucked the thick air and stumbled on. "Fells and I put him in this morning," Brazil went on relentlessly behind me. "Just before noon. Now you and him can barbecue together."

We were walking into the shadow of the huge mound, and I

could see a hollowed-out tunnel, a little taller than a man, extending ten or 12 feet inside it. The stench of the straw was overpoweringly sweet, cloying. I coughed and felt my eyes stinging shut. Sweat rolled out like great drops of blood on my forehead.

"You got away with nothing, Haller, nothing," Brazil said, talking in crude, breathless rhythm: talk, shove, talk, shove. "If I can't buy the Chink, I'll burn him too." Shove. And then we were in the tunnel, out of the assault and battery of the sun, and suddenly I could see the olive-brown tones of flesh, the bare legs of the dead Mexican, skinny and stiff as two-by-fours. The rest of him was buried in shadow. A long white bird spread its wings and fluttered in my belly.

"Get in, you son-of-a-bitch," Brazil said, and flung me toward the body. I tripped, fell head first, rubbed my face against skin smooth as wax, inhaled a rancid smell like spoiled milk, and spun away in an instant of panic. Brazil hit me across the back of the neck and I was thrown back over. I sat up slowly, burning and shivering, gasping for breath. From somewhere far off came the drone of an airplane engine.

"Bobby is going to fly over this thing in about three minutes, give or take a little," he said, stooping down beside me, holding the pistol close to my eyes. With his left hand, he drew two things from the back pants pocket of his suit: a short coil of rope and a pointed wooden stake about the length and thickness of a nightstick, topped with a soldered metal ring. "Bobby's going to spray this whole fucking stack with kerosene. That's what all the farmers do to get a quick burn. Like charcoal starter on this straw." He put the stake on the ground and whipped the rope free. "Then he's going to come back again and drop about a six-pound stick of benzene and gel—they used it a lot in 'Nam—it could roast half a jungle full of gooks—and this thing's going up like the fucking Fourth of July."

Kingsley and Hand came into the tunnel, both of them coat-less and drenched in sweat, Hand bending to fit inside, white-faced even in the shadows. Witnesses for the execution, I assumed, ready to accept complete incrimination. No turning back after this. I looked at Hand with a bitterness that must have struck him like a punch. He didn't speak. He turned blank, clear eyes on Brazil, and Kingsley stared at the dead Mexican and swallowed. Brazil looped the rope efficiently twice around the chain of my cuffs with his left hand and pulled the two ends out full length.

"Push that stake in the ground, Hand. It don't have to go far."

"These handcuffs won't burn, Brazil," I said. "You're going to leave evidence."

He looked at me in mild surprise. For a moment, I thought he might unlock the cuffs, give me one more chance to rush for the gun. My heart thumped furiously against my ribs. I strained forward, extending my hands. But he smiled his shark's smile and said softly. "We'll just have to risk it, Haller. We'll just have to hope nobody runs a treasure hunt for handcuffs in the middle of the goddam Central Valley,"

"You told me he was going to be drugged," Kingsley whis-pered, his wet face wrinkling in horror.

"Put the ends through the loop, Hand," Brazil said. He stood up, curving his back against the slope of the hollowed-out tunnel. The barrel of the pistol glinted in the broken shadows. The stench of the straw contorted his face. The airplane droned nearer.

"You said Fells would make him unconscious, he wouldn't feel it." There were tears in Kingsley's eyes, trickling from under the gold-rimmed glasses.

Brazil gestured with the gun toward the entrance. "Shut up, Kingsley, and get out of the goddam way." Kingsley—the little man with the big eyes and the weak chin and the mother-in-law who had purified her life of violence—Kingsley suddenly flung his arms at Brazil's head, shouting her name. Hand swung the stake and somehow hit Brazil's wrist, purposefully or not I couldn't tell, making a sound like a hammer smashing an egg.

Brazil hung on to the gun.

I stood halfway up, then tumbled back across the Mexican as Kingsley and Brazil wrestled down on top of me. Hand swung the stake again and again. My face was smothered in folds of flesh, cloth. Straw started to slip against us, the sides of the tunnel shifted and heaved, Kingsley rolled back and forth over me, clutching Brazil to his chest. Brazil's gun thumped, like a fist against a pillow, Hand shouted. Kingsley's body twisted over me, and the thumping continued, one, two, while I clawed desperately for ground and the whole wall of straw began to slide and bury us.

"Get up—!" Hand yelled, and the rest was lost in the sudden tumultuous roar of Bobby Sullivan's cropduster, washing the smell of kerosene across us in a wave, slicking our bodies with an acrid brown mist.

The plane soared out of its own shadow, climbed and began to turn.

The rope around my cuff chain tightened with a jerk, dragging me out from under Kingsley like a fish on a line. More straw collapsed across me, sticky as plaster, suffocating. I was drowning in straw, flailing through it as the rope yanked taut again and again, a few feet more, hauling me clear. The drone of the plane grew louder. The mound towered, blocking the sky. Hand wrenched me up by the shoulders and we started to run, half-crouching, half-crawling across the firebreak. Brazil shouted my name.

Twenty yards away was the irrigation ditch, straight ahead. Fifteen yards. We left the shadow of the mound. The white van began to honk its horn and roll. Ten. The shadow of the plane leapt over the straw, a dull crump, then an orange-white fireball and a blast of heat like the end of the world, and Hand and I fell head over heels, tossed like pebbles into the water. The cropduster wheeled in the air, yards above us. Bobby Sullivan's crazed face stared down for an instant. Then the whole dead, burning Valley was rent by an endless scream.

From the mud and water, we looked back and saw Brazil staggering toward us, a sheet of flame from head to foot, blazing like a human torch, and behind him the mound crackled and burned like a thing gone mad.

CHAPTER 25

"ARE YOU NEVER GOING TO CLOSE THAT WINDOW?"

I glanced back at Dinah, grinning, and then turned to face the window again. Billows of fog were still rolling across the bay, obscuring the Golden Gate completely, tossing their manes toward the twinkling lights of Marin County.

"Never," I said. I didn't want to see lights or golden bridges. I wanted to see cold, wet fog, wade in it up to my ears.

"You're still mad because I played *The Firebird Suite* when you came in."

She was lying under two blankets on my bed, her red head blazing against a pile of pillows, a bottle of champagne open on the table beside her. She patted the blankets with one hand. She didn't look as if she thought I was mad.

"Freeze, baby, freeze," I said. "

"Are you still thinking about Hand?"

I pulled a cigarette out of the pack in my bathrobe pocket, lit it, and exhaled into the fog. Well, yes, I was still thinking about Hand.

"I never saw anybody look so surprised," Dinah said after

sipping champagne for a moment. "You must have hit him five feet in the air with that one punch."

"You have to put your shoulder into it," I said. "And twist your wrist. And be pissed off as hell."

"What in the world did he say to you? It was so crowded and noisy in there I couldn't hear a word."

"He wasn't worried about you hearing it," I said. "He was making sure that the microphones and television cameras right on top of us heard it." I let my mind go back to the afternoon, to the long private hearing in the judge's chambers in the Hall of Justice, to the two of us finally pushing our way out into the corridor mobbed with reporters of every possible description, waiting to start the story. Hand must have been born with a press release in his chubby little fingers,

I cleared my throat. "He said, very loudly and very solemnly, 'I guess you owe me a vote of thanks, Mike, for what I did for you out there.'"

Dinah giggled.

I puffed smoke and imagined myself punching Hand over again, harder. I would never know, in fact, what he would have done if Kingsley hadn't jumped. He had said afterward, as we had slogged across that boiling tomato field toward Interstate 5, that he was watching for the right time all along, just the exact moment when it would be safe to tackle Brazil. "Hanging fire," Dinah had said. And maybe he was.

"You are an anonymous kind of man," Dinah said from the bed. "Hand isn't."

"He's a user," I snapped. The anger startled me. "A people user. He used me to poke around where he was unwilling to, where he suspected but wasn't sure, where he didn't want to risk offending Mrs. Browning if he was wrong. And he would have thrown me away like a dirty rag."

"He did it because he wanted the story more than anything else," Dinah said in her best psychiatrist's voice. "That's the way he is. He's got the ego and the shrewdness of a four-year-old. You hung on because you hate the idea of any kind of tampering with people, with human nature, because you hate the kind of power that somebody with Mrs. Browning's money tries to wield. Because you're a Puritan vigilante."

"*Cupiditas*," I said quietly. In the reflection of the plastic lampshade, I could see her frown in puzzlement, then smile. I wondered in passing if anybody would ever pay me for finding Webber. "I hung in there," I told her, "because they had Fred. And because they wanted to use me as a barbecue cut. Don't over-analyze, sweetheart." I did my Bogart imitation that people say sounds like Donald Duck.

"Has he been sacked from the paper yet?"

"Technically, no. Mrs. Browning is surrounded by a mobile field unit of doctors. She communicates with nobody about nothing. If she ever gets free on bail, though, I'd say Hand is out on his ass, yes."

"Even if he wins a Pulitzer Prize?"

"Even if he wins an Academy Award."

I watched the black shape of a freighter plow into the fog, lights vanishing, sounding its melancholy horn.

"You never told me who Yen-jing was," Dinah said over the rim of her glass.

"The Fourth Son of the Emperor Kan-hsi," I said. "Chan-lui is supposed to be descended from him. The Fourth Son rebelled against the old man and tried to take over the kingdom. The old man threw him in the biggest jail in China and wrote a famous edict about not trusting your sons. Chan-lui is more civilized than that, but he got the analogy right away. He just took his own sweet time doing anything about it. And he went after Brazil instead of me."

"He got all of Brazil's files apparently and gave them to the police. The radio said he took everything but the wallpaper out of that office in Oakland."

"Most Chinese were not fond of Brazil," I said. Not to mention Chicanos, blacks, Filipinos, anybody at all with a sense of indignity. Or a sense of reality."

"The radio also said they had caught Fells back East."

I nodded and finally started to work on my own glass of champagne. The wind pushed the curtains to one side, showing me the honky-tonk lights on Union Street. The FBI had located Fells in the Hotel Madison in Washington, D.C., a few blocks from the White House. After Cassidy had disappeared and Bobby's plane had simply vanished into the haze, Fells had somehow made it to Reno, to the airport, then to Washington. The judge had told us that he was making interminable speeches to the FBI and the press about nonviolence through chemistry, the dangers of dopamine, the promise of science for domestic tranquility. No doubt the book offers were already rolling in. The Sullivans, on the other hand, father and son, had got no farther than the Yuba County jail, where they were being watched over by half the Chicano field workers in California. I had to go there tomorrow to testify at another hearing. With Hand. Then to a banquet awarding a posthumous medal to George Webber and presenting his widow with a scholarship fund for the two daughters. I had never finally met Webber, never really found him, though he was as clear to me in one way as the picture I still had in my notebook and the columns I was going to keep bound on the bookshelf. It was a little as if I had been chasing a ghost. A ghost who cast a shadow. A burning ghost. I rubbed out the cigarette in my tin ashtray from Modesto's. He would be a hero for another week or two, until the story died. I finished my champagne, and looked gloomily out at the city and the bay. My fingers strayed to the table and the new porkpie hat

I had managed to buy before the hearing. It was still in its plastic wrapping.

"He's going to be all right," Dinah said softly. "They've got the best people in the hospital on him. Heroin withdrawal is actually the easiest drug withdrawal there is, if you really want to go off it. And that man-with-the-golden-arm stuff is scare tactics for the kids. He'll be shooting pool in a week."

I chuckled, and she asked what was funny.

"He's better already," I said. "He had to fill out an expanded hospital admissions form today."

"We have a new director," Dinah said. "Those forms are dumb."

"Under 'Sexual Preference' he put Raquel Welch."

She laughed that low, unmelancholy laugh of hers, and stretched voluptuously.

"Did you have to fill out one, too?"

"I'm an outpatient," I said, closing the window at last.

"For you then," she said, throwing the blankets aside, "there is an entirely different form."

And there was.

ABOUT THE AUTHOR

Max Byrd is the award-winning author of 14 other books, including four bestselling historical novels and *California Thriller*, for which he received the Shamus Award. He was educated at Harvard and King's College Cambridge, England, and has taught at Yale, Stanford, and the University of California. Byrd is a Contributing Editor of *The Wilson Quarterly* and writes regularly for the *New York Times Book Review*. He lives in California.

Coming in October 2012

THE PARIS DEADLINE

A NOVEL

MAX BYRD

One

THE EIGHTH WINTER AFTER THE WAR, I was living in a one-room garret, a fourth-floor walk-up not much wider than a coat hanger, on the disreputable rue du Dragon.

And no, to get the question out of the way at once, I didn't know Hemingway, though it was Paris and the year was 1926 and every other expatriate American in the city seemed to trip over his feet or lend him money as a daily occurrence. (Years later I did stand behind him in the mail line at American Express and listen to him denounce Woodrow Wilson in very loud and Hemingwayesque French, which had the slow, clear, menacing cadence of a bull's hoof pawing the ground.)

The only literary person I actually did know, besides Gertrude Stein's landlord, was the journalist who sat on the other side of the desk we shared at the *Chicago Tribune* offices on the rue Lamartine.

He was a slender, amiable young man named Waverley Root. He was twenty-six that year, the same as the century, five years younger than I was, not quite old enough to have been in the army. Root was a remarkable person who wrote English like a puckish angel and spoke French as if he had a mouthful of cheese, and a decade or so later he was to find his true calling as a celebrated food critic for the *New York Herald*. The last time I saw him he wore nothing but yellow shirts and had gotten so fat he appeared to have inflated himself in one push of a button, like a rubber raft on a ship.

But in those days celebrity was far over the horizon, and Waverley Root was simply another vagabond reporter who had washed up on the cobblestoned shores of the Right Bank in search of a job. He had gone to Tufts. I had gone to Harvard. He had worked for the *New York World*. I had worked for the *Boston Globe*. He drank anisette and I drank Scotch, and this small divergence in personal character accounted for the fact that on the chilly, rainy Monday morning of December 7, he was leaning against my chair, nursing a French hangover (as he nicely put it), rigid, classical, and comprehensive.

"Toby," he said, "I will never drink alcohol again."

"I know it."

"An owl slept in my mouth last night. My teeth turned green. My poor eyes look like two bags of blood."

"They look like two bags of ink." I typed "30"— newspaperese for "The End"—on a sheet of yellow paper and swiveled to hand it through a hole in the wall—literally.

The Paris edition of the *Tribune* occupied the top three floors of a rambling nineteenth-century structure that had not been designed with modern journalism in mind. Apart from the Managing Editor's sanctum behind a frosted glass door, our editorial offices consisted of one long city room, which held a collection of sprung leather chairs, a long oval table covered with typewriters and ashtrays, and a string of smaller rewrite desks like ours, crammed off to the sides and in the corners. All practically deserted, of course, at this time of the morning. Bedlam arrived later, with the regular reporters, at the civilized hour of noon.

The composing rooms were downstairs (we lowered copy by force of gravity, through a chute in the middle of the floor) and the printing presses were in the basement. Our copyeditors had been banished to an interior room mysteriously inaccessible to us except by going down two flights of stairs and up again three, hence the hole in the wall. More than one visitor, seeing a disembodied hand waving vaguely through a slot in the plaster, had been put in mind of the House of Usher.

"And there is no health in me," Root said and sat down heavily on his side of the desk.

"It's nine thirty-one," I said. "She told us to be there at ten."

Our urchinish French copy boy plopped a thick stack of rubber composing mats on my blotter, murmured "Mon cher Papa," as he did every morning, and sidled away, smoking a torpedo-sized Gitane, to the dark little basement cubby he inhabited down among the rolls of newsprint. He called me "Old Dad," because even at thirty-one, my hair was mostly silver-gray, almost white, like a policeman's helmet. Many people, especially women, assumed sympathetically that something had turned it that way in the war, and if they were young and attractive, I had been known not to correct them. In fact, it had simply happened overnight when I was nineteen, and for some obscure reason, possibly modesty, probably vanity, I had never tried to dye it.

"Goddam 'The Gumps,'" Root said and picked up one of the composing mats.

I sighed and took it back. "The Gumps" had nothing to do with his hangover. They were the Paris edition's most popular comic strip (followed closely by "The Katzenjammer Kids" and "Gasoline Alley"). On Colonel McCormick's personal instructions, the comic strip mats were mailed to us from Chicago twice a month, filed in a cupboard behind the City Editor's desk, and delivered to me every Monday to be arranged in chronological order and chuted down to the printing room.

"She asked for both of us," I reminded him. "Tous les deux. Root and Keats, Keats and Root."

Root closed his eyes in anisette-induced meditation.

I sighed again like the Lady of Shalot and got to my feet. "Suite twenty-five, Hôtel Ritz, if you change your mind."

"Suites to the suite," Root said, with eyes still closed. And as I reached the door he added, sotto voce, "Lambs to the slaughter."

Outside on the rue Lamartine it was raining softly in the slow, sad Parisian winter way and the street was almost deserted: a few soggy shoppers, a gendarme in his cape, a pair of disheartened workmen on ladders stringing waterlogged loops of Christmas tinsel between the lampposts. Another crew was silently studying an enormous and inexplicable pit in the pavement, part of the endless cycle of street repair and excavations in post-war Paris.

I took thirty seconds to gulp a thimbleful of black coffee from the stall in front of our door, and another thirty seconds to frown at the cold gray sky and disapprove of our climate. Then I made my way around the pit and started out, an obedient lamb, for the Ritz.

The *Chicago Tribune* and its Paris subsidiary were owned at that time by Colonel Robert Rutherford McCormick, who had won the Medal of Honor at Cantigny (a battle I'd also attended, in a minor role), and who ran his newspaper along much the same military principles of fear and feudalism that he had evidently employed in the Army.

Fortunately for us, he managed the paper at a distance, coming to Paris only once or twice a year for what he jocularly called "little friendly look-sees," but which had the grim, white-gloved, pursed lips air of a regimental inspection. Like other monarchs he was invariably referred to by his title—in three years at the *Tribune* I had never heard him called anything except "the Colonel"—and like other monarchs as well, he was seriously burdened by family.

In his case, the burden was the Queen Mother, Mrs. Katherine Van Etta Medill McCormick, a grande dame about a hundred and fifty years old, daughter of the famous Civil War reporter Joseph Medill, eccentric even for a newspaper family, and much too fond (in the opinion of the *Tribune* staff) of visiting Paris. She called the Colonel "Bertie," which he hated, and had previously called him, against all evidence, "Katrina," until at the age of nine he rebelled.

Mrs. McCormick liked Root, as everybody did, and the Colonel liked me, because he thought I was a project in need of completing. When Mrs. McCormick had errands to be done in Paris, she summoned us both and reported the results, good or bad, directly back to Bertie.

I stopped at the corner of the rue de Provence and

watched a girl herding five or six goats down the street, still not an unusual sight in Paris in the twenties. An old man leaned out of a third-floor window and shouted to her, and while I crossed to the rue Rossini I could hear the goats' hoofs clattering as they went up the stairs to be milked.

I was a long way from Boston, I thought, or even Cantigny, and turned my gaze to the smallish blonde woman on the opposite sidewalk.

She was studying a tray of croissants in a bakery window, she had no herd of goats, and she was well worth looking at. She wore a nicely tailored green waterproof coat, which was beaded with rain and showed off her waist and her calves and her sensible brown brogues. Her hat was a blue trilby of a style I had never seen before and which, if I were not five thousand miles from home, I would have called foreign. And she had a brilliant red feather in the hatband, like a Christmas tree bulb.

In the buttery reflection of the shop window it was hard to see her face. She seemed to be counting coins in her palm. And despite the relative emptiness of the street, she also seemed completely unaware that she was being followed.

The follower in question was half a block down the sidewalk, a squat, broad-shouldered, gypsy-featured man about my age. He wore a dirty gray quilted jacket and a scowl, and carried a leather-covered billy in one hand, like a swagger stick, and moment by moment he was inching closer to her.

Up to no good. Obviously a pickpocket, I thought, and I took a step off the curb with the idea of making some sort of warning gesture to my fellow foreigner. The swarthy man transferred his scowl to me and then, to my utter astonishment, bared his teeth in a wolfish snarl.

At which precise moment the skies over Paris broke apart in a stupendous clap of thunder and a squall of freezing hard rain swept across the cobblestones with the rattling sound of coal going down a slide.

I don't mind rain. I grew up in New Mexico, where rain is so important that the Navajos have dozens of different names for it, the way Eskimos have for snow. But thunder and lightning are another story, another story for a soldier— ask Colonel McCormick about it. As the first boom rolled overhead I closed my eyes and clenched my fists as I always do, and counted silently till the last vibration had died away.

When I opened my eyes again both Red Feather and Dirty Jacket had vanished like a dream.